DAFFODIL DANCING

Daffodil Dancing

Jean Jardine Miller

JM PUBLISHING

Library and Archives Canada Cataloguing in Publication

Jardine Miller, Jean, 1945-
Daffodil Dancing / Jean Jardine Miller.

ISBN 0-9731376-4-9

1. Social phobia—Fiction. I. Title.

PS8619.A735D34 2006   C813'.6   C2006-901393-4

Cover and text design: Design and Copy Consultation Services.

Jardine Miller
- publishing what is significant to today
Limehouse, ON L0P 1H0

PRINTED IN CANADA

To the memory of my father, William Jardine,
who introduced me to the magic of
storytelling at an early age.

1987

Chapter One

"It's almost as if she's snubbing me," Terri said, turning away from the phone. "I just don't understand it. We've known each other just about all our lives. Why should she suddenly act like this?"

"Maybe something came up." Mark shrugged. "Something too complicated to explain on the phone. You know how it is sometimes..."

"No, it's not anything like that," she said, taking the glass of wine he was holding out to her. She moved away from the kitchen phone and through the archway into the high-ceiling-airy-lightness of the living-room. What they'd skimped in the kitchen space, the designers had more than made up for in the spacious living-dining area of the apartment. She walked over to the floor to ceiling windows.

Mark followed. "Hey," he said, as she started to raise the glass absent-mindedly to her lips, "we have to make a toast to our new home. That's what we bought this ultra expensive wine for..."

Terri turned, raising her glass higher. "I'm sorry," she said. "I wasn't paying attention. To our new life in Toronto – well, Mississauga, anyway..."

"To you and me, my love."

Mark raised his glass to hers and they both sipped their wine.

"It wasn't a case of something coming up," Terri continued. "There was no excuse at all. It was more like what I just said... I was snubbed by my oldest friend. I feel really – well... shocked, best describes it. I was so looking forward to seeing her again."

"P'raps you misunderstood..."

Terri knew that she hadn't misunderstood. Alison just did not want to see her again. That wasn't exactly what she'd said, but it had to be what she meant. How else could you interpret the comment about the four years Terri had spent in England being too long a time to make up? Things change. They were different people now, she had said. Well, she'd certainly changed! Terri felt angry. Why wait until now, when the food was practically on the table to tell her that things change? Well, actually, they'd planned for Mark to go and get a takeaway because they'd only just moved in and were missing too many basics to cook a meal. But if things had changed so much, Alison should have said so when Terri called her from Anna's house, to let her know they'd bought and borrowed enough furniture to be able to move into the apartment today and would like her to be their first guest.

"Cheer up, love," Mark said, finishing his glass of wine. "I don't like to interrupt all those indignant thoughts chasing each other around your mind, but it isn't the end of the world." He moved towards the kitchen. "No sense in my going out to get Chinese food now – or do you still fancy it?"

Terri shook her head.

"Then, since we're limited to eggs, cheese, salt and pepper, I'll make an *omelette gourmet à la maison* – no, make that *à l'appartement*... something like that."

Terri smiled. She loved Mark.

Terri and Alison had grown up on adjacent, leafy suburban Islington streets. They had not actually met until the first day of kindergarten. Terri's parents had brought her home, from the obstetrics department at Queensway Hospital, to the house where they and their three older children had already lived for seven years. Alison's family had moved into the neighbourhood when she was three. While Terri went to the cooperative nursery school in the nearby United Church basement and to Sunday School in the same church, Alison went all-day to the Bo-Peep Nursery School which was, despite its name, a day-care centre. Day care was not the huge business, in the late sixties, that it became later – at least, not in their area where mothers mostly stayed home with their young children. Alison's family did not go to the United Church or any other church. Her parents needed Sundays for relaxation time, she told Terri when the subject of Sunday School came up within the first few weeks of their acquaintanceship. Terri wasn't quite sure what this meant, but she found a lot of things Alison said a little strange. She assured her new friend that one day, when they were older, Alison could come and sleep over and go to Sunday School with them the next morning. Terri's older sister and brothers sometimes had their friends stay over and they'd have to go to church with Terri's family on Sunday morning. Alison found this information quite fascinating and wondered when they'd be old enough. Terri figured probably not until they were about seven or eight.

As it happened, they did not have to wait that long, after all. Their mothers, as often happens when children are young, soon became known to each other through the girls' attendance at birthday parties and Saturday morning ballet lessons. The next summer, when they were six, Alison's mother landed in hospital with an ectopic pregnancy and Alison came to stay with Terri for a whole week, including Sunday. Sunday School, however, was closed for the summer and Alison had gone with Terri and her brothers to Grandma Johnston's cottage, near Beaverton, instead.

By this time, the little girls were considered old enough to be allowed to walk around the corner and along the street to each other's homes and, when Alison's mother went back to work, arrangements were made for Alison to come home with Terri after school, instead of getting on the shuttle-bus to be taken to the Bo-Peep Nursery School's after-school program. They each found the home of the other intriguing. Terri was fascinated by the fairy tale murals Alison's father had painted on his daughter's bedroom walls and the attic workroom he had made, with a special corner for Alison, where they could paint and make things and never worry about making a mess. Unused to having other children around, Alison loved being at Terri's house where Terri's older sister and brothers and their friends were forever coming and going.

The two girls were inseparable throughout their public school years and remained close friends, despite different academic courses, in high school. Destined for university, Alison remained in school for grade thirteen when they were eighteen and Terri went to England to spend a year working in the flagship natural body care products store, *Envirodermics*, which her father's sister, after franchising several stores in Britain was beginning to franchise in North America, starting with Canada. The strategy was already in place for Terri's older brother, Scott, a recent MBA graduate, and his wife, Emily, to launch this North American arm of the business and Terri's interest in environmental concerns and lack of desire for further education led them to include her in their plans.

Mark Havers, a nephew of her aunt's husband, was in his third year at the London School of Economics when Terri met him at his cousin's wedding halfway through her first year in England. Neither of them knew many of the other guests, Mark having grown up on his father's Cumbrian farm which, from the south of England perspective of the rest of his family, might have been just as far removed from their orbit as Terri's native Canada, and found a consequent empathy in each other, not to mention unexpected attraction. Terri's nominal year in England extended into four years while Mark obtained his MBA and they both learned the natural health products business. The plan now was for Mark to work with Scott, who he had come to know quite well during Scott's frequent business trips to London, to eventually take over Canadian operations so that Scott could concentrate on marketing *Envirodermics* franchises in the U.S. Terri did not regret the four years away from home – in fact, she could easily end up making the UK her home – but she was beginning to feel badly about what it appeared to have done to her relationship with Alison. She had phoned Alison, from London, as soon as they'd booked their flights, and told her how they were coming home and would be working indefinitely in the Mississauga head office. She explained that they'd be staying with her parents at the lakefront condominium, which they had bought after the children had all left home, for the first night, then moving into an apartment they were subletting from a friend of a friend, nobody Alison knew, the next day, assuming they could scrounge enough furniture from family members to make it liveable. Terri went on to tell Alison about her plans for a Christmas wedding, just to make their parents happy really, because marriage was becoming quite irrelevant today, wasn't it? Alison would be her maid of honour, wouldn't she?

The problem was, Terri realized, that she had been so excited and happy that she had chattered on nonstop and, now, couldn't remember Alison saying very much at all. She must have sounded like an overbearing idiot... And she'd been just about as bad last night when she called to ask Alison to dinner because she'd been so happy at the thought of their seeing each other again. The last time she had been home, in the summer two years ago, Alison had been working with poor families in Guatemala on a student program sponsored by, Terri couldn't remember which, humanitarian aid organization. They had seen each other briefly when Alison and her father had made a stopover in London on their way to Paris the Easter before and, further back, Alison had flown over to spend Terri's first Christmas in England with her, at her aunt's house. By the time the next Christmas came around, Terri had met Mark and Alison was immersed in university life with new friends and new interests. They'd written intermittently, both busy with their own lives, and Terri had to admit that Alison was right – things change, they were different people now. It still didn't explain Alison's rudeness...

* * * * *

"Hello, Terri?"

"Yes?"

The voice was familiar, but Terri couldn't quite place it. The ringing of the phone had awakened her and she felt disoriented waking so late – a glance at the clock telling her it was nine forty-five – in the new apartment and alone in the unfamiliar bedroom, although the sounds of Mark in the shower did eventually register in her befuddled mind which was probably still a bit jet-lagged, anyway.

"It's Moira. Moira Fraser, Alison's mother..."

"Oh... Moira! Hi. How are you?"

"I'm fine, thanks. Look, Terri, I-I... I think some explanations are owed to you. Are you free for lunch, today?"

"Yes, I think so..."

"Do you have transportation?"

"Mark – my fiancé – Mark's meeting my brother and some other people for a business lunch," Terri replied, "but, I imagine I can have the car if I drive him over to the office first."

Scott had provided them with a company leased car. Terri, who had not long had her driver's licence when she left Canada, was a little nervous about driving on North American roads again. She hoped Moira would suggest somewhere not too hard to reach and which didn't require turning corners into too many city streets – that's where she would have the worst time remembering which side of the road she was supposed to be on.

"Where's that? I'm sorry, I expect you've told Alison, but she hasn't told me..."

"That's all right. I'd hardly expect it to be the hot topic of conversation," laughed Terri. "I haven't been there myself, yet. It's near Square One somewhere, although I have a feeling that the whole area around there is going to look a little different from the last time I saw it!"

"You're right there. So, in that case, you remember the little Italian place out on Dundas where we used to go for special occasions when you and Alison were in high school?"

Terri tried to visualize the best way to get to the restaurant from the direction opposite to the way they would go from Islington. She thought she knew the simplest – albeit, slowest way – from Square One...

"Yes. I'd best go down Hurontario and along Dundas from there, right?"

"I would imagine... Will you be all right? I hadn't thought about you having to get used to driving here again..."

"It's okay, Moira. I'm sure I'll be okay. I shan't be able to get there until close to one, though. Is that all right?"

"That'll be fine," Moira replied. "I'll see you then... and thank you, dear."

"See you. Bye, Moira"

Terri hung up the phone and lay back on the pillows. Mark came out of the bathroom rubbing his still wet hair.

"Who were you talking to?" he asked.

"Alison's mother. She asked me to meet her for lunch. I said I imagined I could have the car if we got you over to the office first, okay?"

"Okay by me. I told Scott I'd be there some time after twelve. I suppose I should learn to say noon... or is it noon hour?" Mark was pulling on clothes as he spoke.

"Noon. Noon hour's more American, although people do say it here, too."

"She just rang to ask you to lunch, then?" Mark asked.

"She said she wanted to explain something. I s'pose I'll find out when I get there."

"Well, that's that for now. You going to get up today?"

"Very funny. How often do I sleep in?"

"Okay, bad joke. I'll put the coffee on. Want some toast or

cereal? No point in eating more than that if we're both going out for lunch..."

"I'll just have coffee."

* * * * *

Terri spotted Moira getting out of her car just as she pulled into the restaurant parking lot. She touched the horn and waved as Moira looked round, then continued driving between the rows of cars until she found an empty space.

Moira appeared to have changed little in the four years since Terri had last seen her. She remembered how, when they were children, she had envied Alison having such young, attractive parents – envied her and felt disloyal to her own parents at the same time. Having been Alison's best friend throughout their childhood, she had spent a lot of time at her parents' house and had known them both quite well. Moira was now the publisher of a women's magazine. When they were children, she had been a sales representative and, while Terri had not understood exactly what that was for many years, it had seemed to be a very glamorous kind of occupation for a woman. Later, she had discovered that very few women were magazine sales representatives in those days and rather hero-worshipped Moira, for a while, considering her to be something of a crusader. Alison always said – not within Moira's hearing, of course – that she would have preferred a mother like Terri's who stayed home and had lots of children.

Terri parked the car and ran over to catch up with Moira who was walking slowly towards the restaurant entrance.

"It's so nice to see you again, Terri," Moira smiled, giving her a one-armed hug. "You look so – well, so grown up..."

She let go of Terri and opened the door to the restaurant. "No problem with the driving?"

"No," Terri laughed. "I'm okay as long as there's other traffic. It's only when there's just me that I tend to get a mental block about which side of the road I should be on."

The maitre d' approached them.

"Good afternoon, ladies."

"Hello," said Moira. "Fraser – table for two for one o'clock. We're a few minutes early..."

"That's all right, madam. Your table's ready. This way, please."

"You're okay around here at this time of the day, then," Moira said, when they were seated. "Driving, I mean. There's a lot of traffic."

"Yes," replied Terri. She looked around the restaurant. "It looks just the same. Do you still come here much?"

"No," said Moira. "No, not really. I just thought it would be convenient for you. With your being in Mississauga, I mean." The waiter was approaching. "Would you like a drink while we decide what to have?"

"Just a glass of white wine. The house wine's fine."

"We may as well get a half litre, then," Moira said, turning to the waiter. "We'll have a half litre of the house white and a few minutes to look at the menu, please."

They both studied the menu while they waited for their wine.

"D'you think the lasagne's still as good as it used to be?" asked Terri. "Sometimes things don't live up to the way you remember them, right?"

"Yes, often. But I think the lasagne will. How are your parents?"

"Oh, fine. It still seems a bit weird, their being in the apartment there, instead of our old house. Do you know the people in our old house?"

"Not really. There's a family with two or three children, but I've never actually met them. You know how it is. You only ever seem to meet your neighbours when you have something else in common. It must be nice living there, overlooking the lake – your parents..."

"Oh yes. They like it. It's really handy for downtown – theatres and everything. And they have the cottage that was my grandmother's for the summer. So, they're really quite happy although Mom, especially, missed the house for a long time."

The waiter brought their wine and they ordered their meals.

"Well," said Moira, raising her glass, "here's to a happy homecoming."

"Thanks," Terri replied.

"How does your fiancé like it so far?"

"Well... it's early days, but he hasn't had any complaints so far. Although he probably wouldn't admit to having them anyway. He prides himself on being adaptable."

"Oh. The strong, silent type?"

"Sort of. Perhaps you can meet him some time."

"I'd love to. I've been shopping at the *Envirodermics* store downtown in the Eaton Centre – near my office. The concept really seems to be taking off. I like the products. Tim does, too."

"How is Tim? I should have asked before."

"Oh, same as ever," Moira grinned. "Staying youthful-looking like the rest of us with the help of those *Envirodermics'* products."

They both laughed.

"Seriously," Moira continued, "he was quite sold on the whole concept after you showed him the flagship store in London. You must be a good salesperson..."

Terri laughed. "Not really. I was working in the shop – store, that is – at that time, but retail sales isn't really my forté, not that the other sales assistants take you very seriously when you're the owner's niece. And, in terms of franchise selling which, I imagine, is what you mean really, I'm a bit too young to be taken seriously. You kind of need an MBA like Mark and my brother to be perceived as believable. I just look after money."

"Accounting, you mean?"

"Ah-ha." The waiter brought their salads. Terri took a bread roll, broke and buttered it, then continued. "I've been taking a diploma course at evening classes. There I go again – at *night school* and... well, I seem to be quite good at it. I should be able to transfer into a management accounting program here."

"You sound surprised."

"I am. Sort of. I was always so awful at math – at school, I mean – I never expected to do more than things like looking after stock, checking orders when I started working for my aunt, then I met Mark and somehow my I.Q. increased."

"I think that's wonderful," said Moira. "I don't mean I think it wonderful that your I.Q. *increased*. Obviously, you just didn't strike the right chords before. It had nothing to do with your IQ. Anyway, I think it's wonderful that you've found your niche."

"Thanks. Here comes our lunch."

They were silent for a few minutes while they ate their lunch. Terri decided that, surprisingly, the lasagne *was* as good as she remembered it being. Moira and Tim had often brought her and Alison to this restaurant for birthdays, graduations and other special occasions. The first time had been when Alison had won the Best Actress Award at the drama camp they'd attended the summer they were ten. She remembered how grown up they had felt sitting at the candlelit table drinking *Shirley Temples*. The drama camp program had included a trip to Stratford where they had experienced Shakespeare for the first time. The Mediterranean décor of the restaurant seemed to them to be much like the set for *Much Ado About Nothing* and Alison immediately decided that she was Beatrice and Terri was Hero. Terri remembered arguing that she should be Beatrice because Alison's father was here and it was like she was disowning him. Tim had laughed and said he didn't mind and that Terri could be his daughter any time her own father could spare her. Terri remembered being surprised because she had always suspected that Tim found her a rather boring child. Alison said none of that had anything to do with anything because this was a play and they could be whoever they wanted. Moira said they were making 'much ado about nothing', which made them all laugh, and strategically drew their attention to the menu. The chief topic of conversation turned to whether it was okay to cut up spaghetti in a restaurant or risk have it slide into your lap. Both girls had avoided the situation and ordered lasagne.

Eating her lasagne now, Terri reflected that she'd been rather fortunate being the best friend of an only child throughout her childhood. Most people don't get the kind of in-depth exposure to family life, other than their own, that results from being consistently invited along as company for an only child. Of course it had worked the other way on, too. With Terri, herself, being the youngest in the family, her parents had been in the same position as Alison's parents once their older children had begun to follow their own directions, and had included Alison in many of their plans. For the two girls, it had really been like having two families.

"How's the lasagne?" asked Moira, breaking through these thoughts.

"Great," Terri replied, "just as I remembered it. I'll have to bring Mark here. He would never believe me when I told him that there's a place in Canada where they make lasagne as good as they do at a little trattoria we go to in London. How's yours?"

"Terrific. Let's finish the wine." Moira poured the remains of the wine into their glasses. "I'll order some coffee, then try to explain about Alison..."

Chapter Two

"So you're going to get it then?" Ian Shaw's father, Ralph, asked from behind his copy of *The Toronto Star*.

Ian wondered how his father knew who had come into the room, that anyone had come into the room, for that matter, and why he had the television on so loudly when he was reading the newspaper, anyway. He sat down on the opposite end of the couch from his father and the newspaper and replied, "Yes, I decided to take the plunge into debt again."

"I'm surprised they gave you the money with your student loan still to be paid..."

"I explained to you, Dad, before. The repayment plan for student loans is fixed. It doesn't impact on applying for a car loan. Well, not unless you don't have the cash flow to cover both. Don't worry about it. You brought me up to be financially responsible and... I am." His father only grunted, so he continued. "I'm not about to run off anywhere and leave you responsible for my debts. I didn't even need a co-signer for the car. They trust me."

"Take no notice of your father, Ian," said Janet Shaw, coming into the room. "He's still living in 1957."

Ian grinned. It was true. His father's old-fashioned values made discussion of his own plans almost impossible. Every year when he came home from university, it was as if he was expected to go back to being a twelve-year-old again and a 1950's twelve-year-old at that! Now that he had graduated, and his part time job had become a full time position, and he no longer had to save most of his earnings for the next school year, he was in a position to get a place of his own. But his father would be mortally offended if he did. According to his older sisters, the only escape route was through marriage.

"It's okay, Mom. Dad's just annoyed that the banks weren't so free with their money back when he was salivating over that gas-guzzling monster with all the chrome and the tail fins and everything he wanted when he was a twenty-something." His father lowered the paper and glared at him. "Just kidding, Dad. Listen, I'm not getting the car for the sake of having a car. I really do need it. All the while I was working summers and co-op, they had me working on city clients' systems. Now I could be sent just about anywhere in the GTA and beyond and it's not feasible without a car."

"You can't expect him to go to – say, Pickering, every day on public transit, Ralph," said Janet, adjusting the television volume and sitting down. While she understood her husband's caution, she also appreciated the fact that her son was embarking on his career in a far more risk-oriented environment then his parents had had to deal with. There would always be an element of risk in signing any financial agreement for her son because there was little likelihood of the kind of job security, today, that his father's generation had expected and acquired before going to the bank for a car loan. She caught Ian's eye and frowned.

Ian picked up the hint. "Look, Dad, I'd like your opinion on this car before I sign on the dotted line. Think you can meet me after work tomorrow and take a look at it?"

The last thing he really wanted was to run the risk of his father putting down his selection, but his mother had assured him that since the two-year-old coupe was not imported and not a sports car, it was within his father's range of sensible choices and getting him involved would win his approval of the project, making life more comfortable for all of them.

"Tomorrow?" Ralph asked after a long pause.

"Yes, Dad."

"At the dealer's?"

"Yes. I can hold off going down there until it's convenient for you."

"I may as well come home and pick you up, first, then."

Janet smiled and made a thumbs up sign. Ian grinned at her.

"Great, Dad," he said. "Thanks." She was right. His father had only been against him getting a car because he hadn't involved him. "So, I'll be ready at quarter to six then?"

"Have you checked with your mother about making us late for supper?" Ralph lowered the paper at last and looked in Janet's direction.

"Yes, he talked to me about it, dear," she said. "Now, are you watching this or can we put something more interesting on?"

"It's up to you. I'm reading the paper."

Ralph turned a page and became engrossed in the newspaper again. Janet smiled at Ian. "Have you talked to Alison lately?" she asked.

Ian's faced clouded. "No," he said. He had met Alison Fraser, nearly two years ago, at a party thrown by a fellow Waterloo student for his girlfriend and a group of fellow U of T students who had just returned from spending most of the summer in Guatemala on a World Vision project. They had spent the evening – most of the night, really – talking, almost exclusively, to each other and then seen each other almost every day until school started. During the school year, she had driven over to Waterloo several times to spend the weekend with him, this being easier than him travelling home to Toronto because both her parents had cars and were quite happy to let her have one of them. They had spent time together at Christmas and Easter. He had known she had some problems with depression and was on medication, but he had not been prepared for her sudden decision, a year ago, that they stop seeing each other because she felt it was not fair of her to subject him to her problems.

At first he had nursed his hurt and made no attempt to get in touch with her then, on discovering that she was no longer seeing any of her U of T friends either, he had attempted to call her. Each time, there was either no answer or one or other of her parents would explain that she was not available at the moment and agree to have her call him. She never called back. Other people were experiencing the same thing. He had only ever met her mother a couple of times, but the next time she answered he explained – because he didn't like to claim that he was her boyfriend or ex-boyfriend, under the circumstances – that he was the friend that Alison used to visit in Waterloo and, instead of just leaving his number, asked if she was all right.

The first time, Moira Fraser had just said that Alison was fine and she'd tell her he'd called. The next time she had apologized for not being completely honest with him before, but the truth of the matter was that her daughter was clinically depressed and, unfortunately, becoming very reclusive. She had not explained the situation to him, or her other friends, before because she had been hoping that Alison would snap out of it and did not want to risk jeopardizing the chances of her patching up the deteriorating friendships by doing so. While she did not actually say so, he realized that she had also been attempting to protect Alison from the stigma associated with having a mental health problem as opposed to a physical one. She had then suggested that he drop over one evening.

After supper, a couple of days later, he had borrowed his father's car, which was always a dicey proposition, because it was a bit like pulling teeth to get him to lend it to him in the first place and not getting it back before he retired for the night resulted in even more of a problem negotiating terms the next time, and drove over to Alison's house. The Frasers had just finished supper on the patio behind the house and Moira invited him to join them for coffee. Alison didn't exactly fall over herself in welcoming him, but did talk to him and introduced him to her father, Tim, who he hadn't met before. He found both Alison's parents very friendly and easy to talk to, but Alison followed her mother into the kitchen when Moira went in to look after the dishes and when she did not reappear, he told Tim he should be on his way. Tim accompanied him to the car and urged him the drop by again.

After that, taking Tim up on his invitation the drop by, he called several times when he was home from school, although it was not often that he actually talked to Alison alone. She would stay around, maybe even join in the conversation with her mother and father, but find some excuse to go upstairs to her room if she sensed that she was going to be left alone with him. His own mother missed seeing her because she had enjoyed Alison's company on the occasions when Ian had brought her home for supper. In fact, even his father had liked Alison. He had brought her to meet them quite early in the relationship and, because of that, they had assumed that this was *'it'*. He'd tried to explain the situation to his mother and, for some reason, she had concluded that *he* had upset Alison in some way. At least, that's the way it seemed.

"Look, Mom," he said now, "I think you should understand that Alison and I aren't going to get back together again."

"Don't look on the black side, son," Janet said. "You never know how things'll turn out."

* * * * *

Moira swore softly to herself as she drove up the York Street ramp onto the Gardiner Expressway and joined the late rush hour traffic that was still backed up there. She had hoped that things might have cleared a bit by now, but no such luck...

"Oh well," she murmured, turning the radio volume up a little as signature music heralded the six o'clock news, "turn the downtime into relax time. There's not much else you can do about it."

The day's news failed to engage her attention for very long and her mind wandered back to the earlier part of the afternoon. Terri had grown up to be such a lovely girl. She'd been such a mousy little thing as a child – always a part of Alison's life, but never really making an impression as an individual. The combination of working in England and meeting this boyfriend seemed to have completely turned her around and created a personable young lady to replace the ineffectual, though rather bossy little girl. Her parents must be proud of her though maybe not so keen on this living together bit, but that seemed to be the trend now. Of course, all their children seemed to have done quite well. Scott had apparently become quite a business tycoon with the franchising and the younger boy was a high school teacher now. Anna was teaching at the elementary level, although only as a supply teacher since the birth of her third child a year or so ago. Moira thought back and tried to remember when she had last seen any of them. She had remained in touch with Stella and Paul, attending, along with other neighbours, the house-warming party which Anna had arranged when her parents had sold their house and moved into the condominium apartment on the lakefront. Later, she had met Stella for lunch now and again. It was Stella, of course, who kept her up to date on what her children were doing. The lunches, to Moira's relief, had become less frequent over the last year as Stella came to know her neighbours and began to develop a new circle of friends. Nothing against Stella, of course, but it was just darned difficult to spend a whole lunch listening to somebody singing the praises of her children when your own child's life was going just about nowhere.

Moira glanced over at the tennis courts of the adjacent Boulevard Club, as the Expressway traffic came to a standstill, and thought of the days when she was Alison's age and she and Tim had played tennis there. They had met, when he had come for an interview at the advertising agency where she had a job as receptionist. He had been considered too young and inexperienced for the art director position for which he was applying, but had contrived to run into her, a few days later, at the old Honeydew restaurant on Bloor where she often went for a cheap lunch. How the conversation had turned to tennis she couldn't remember, it wasn't as if it was a popular sport in Toronto in the early sixties, but they had discovered they both played and he'd invited her to the expensive club on the lake shore. It hadn't been called the Boulevard Club then and he had used a friend's membership because, he confided later, he didn't know where else there was to play outside of Upper Canada College where he had gone to school, and they could hardly go there, and the private courts of a couple of family friends. Moira usually played with her roommate on the public court, where you took your own net, in the park near her basement apartment and hadn't realized before this confession that she was dating somebody from an 'Establishment' family. She still wondered what had attracted him to the skinny kid from the sticks.

Her reverie ended when the driver behind her hooted and, startled, she realized that the traffic was, once again, moving. She hurriedly accelerated out of the world of twenty-five years ago and caught up with the car ahead of her. Back in the slow but steady stream of traffic, she thought about her conversation with Terri and hoped the girl wouldn't mention it to her mother too soon. The last thing she needed was Stella wondering why she hadn't confided the problem to her. How did you explain that Alison's problem was not something you told everybody about because you wouldn't want to jeopardize her being able to build on whatever little remained in terms of her social relationships if she ever did come out of it. She hoped Stella wouldn't take it as an insult. Surely she would understand that it was necessary for Terri to know...

It was not something she was going to worry about, Moira decided, as the highway sign for Islington Avenue finally came into sight. More to the point was: would Terri be able to stir Alison out of her deep depression? Or, would Alison see through the carefully contrived plan for her unannounced visit? It was so hard to know what to do.

If Alison gets upset, she's just going to have to understand that I could hardly leave Terri out in the cold after the way she behaved to her last night. Surely she must see that? If I'd known she was going to do that, she thought, I'd have phoned myself and made some excuse about her being sick or something... Maybe she did it in response to me all but forcing her to call Terri... Oh God, why did this happen to us? I wish I knew what to do.

Moira made a concerted effort to get out of the downward spiral of negative thinking as she pulled off the highway and onto Islington Avenue. Nearly home...

*   *   *   *   *

"How was your lunch?" Mark asked, following Scott Lydford's Audi out of the office parking lot. He had been instructed to keep Scott's car in sight because he hadn't the faintest idea where he lived and they were on their way to have dinner at his home in Oakville. Terri was sure Scott would be watching in the rear-view mirror to make sure he didn't lose them in the traffic, though.

"It was lovely seeing Moira again," she said, "and we'll have to go there, Mark – the restaurant, I mean. You'll like it, I know. Emily tells me you were just across the street yourself at *La Castile*."

After lunch with Moira, Terri had driven back to the *Envirodermics* office to meet her sister-in-law, Emily, to be shown around and introduced to the people she'd be working with next week. She found that Emily tended to make people feel insecure and she rather hoped that dinner at her house might just be a little less than absolutely perfect, but imagined that she'd turn out to be just as super-efficient around the house as she was around the office.

Terri had been fourteen when Scott and Emily were married and, at fourteen, she had hardly been their first choice for company. Her sister, Anna, was closer in age to Emily, but had never come to know her well, either. Indeed, Anna had actually voiced some reservation about the viability of Terri working with Emily, but Terri had laughed and told her that their aunt had ensured that she learn to work with all kinds of people, and she was sure she could manage however much of a battle-axe Emily turned out to be. It would still be nice to find a chink in Emily's armour...

"You're not going to tell me about it?"

Terri started at Mark's question. "Sorry," she said. "I was woolgathering, wondering if there's any chance of Emily not being quite so perfect at being a cook or mother or, even, as a homemaker as she is at being a business executive. I know that's mean but she acts as if the last four years never happened and I'm still her little high school kid sister-in-law."

"She seemed all right at lunch."

"Well, you were already a graduate student when she first met you and you knew as much, if not more than she did, about *Envirodermics*. I was a gangly twelve-year-old the first time Scott brought her to our house and that puts you at a disadvantage when you reach the stage of interacting as adults."

"I'm sure you'll straighten her out..."

"If she doesn't fall down on something this evening, I'm going be a nervous wreck when we return their hospitality."

"Well, I suppose we'll just have to pray that she burns the potatoes."

"I doubt that she stoops to anything as mundane as potatoes when she entertains," Terri said, grumpily. "To change the subject, have you ever known anybody with phobias? I don't just mean people who act out and make a big deal about spiders or mice or something, I mean a phobia as a – as a disability?"

"You mean like Howard Hughes or something?"

"Well... that sort of thing, I suppose."

"At least, I think it was a sort of phobia. He was afraid of germs or something... Oops, Scott seems to be turning right –" Mark hurriedly changed lanes to follow the Audi around a corner. "Is that what you mean?"

Terri sighed. "I don't know... I suppose so." They were driving along residential streets now. "I think we must be nearly there. We'll talk about it later."

"Okay," Mark nodded. "I think you're right. He seems to be about to turn into his drive." He followed the Audi. "So this is your brother's new house."

They both inspected what they could see of the front of the property as they pulled into the driveway and parked the car.

"Looks a little ostentatious..." muttered Terri.

"Well, glad you said it. He's your brother – I wouldn't have mentioned it myself..."

"The soul of diplomacy, aren't you, my love?" Terri teased him. "Better get moving. Here he comes."

Scott, having parked his own car next to the one used by his wife in the double garage, was walking back towards them. Terri and Mark simultaneously got out of their car.

"Nice place," said Mark to Scott.

"Well... we're getting there," Scott replied. "We only moved in two months ago, so most of the paint and wallpaper is the way it was. We decorated the kids' rooms – well, even the guest room was pink and, while he maybe only two-and-a half, Adam knows that pink is a girl's colour – but we haven't got around to anything else yet. Come on in."

They followed Scott through the open garage to a door at the back that led into a mud room off the kitchen.

"We're here, honey," he shouted. "She must be upstairs with the boys," he said to Terri and Mark when there was no response. "She can't leave them if they're in the bathtub and probably can't hear us over the noise. Come through to the living room."

They followed him through the kitchen and into the living room from which an archway led into the foyer where they could see a curved oak staircase. Childish shrieks and splashing water would be heard from upstairs.

"Sit down," Scott said, waving vaguely in the direction of the couch. "What would you like to drink? I'll hold off showing you around the house until Emily comes down. I'll just go and get some ice from the kitchen. Would you prefer a beer, Mark?"

"Well, I suppose I'd better get used to Canadian beer. Sure, I'll have one."

Scott went back to the kitchen and reappeared, a moment later, with an ice bucket and two cans of *Export*.

"What are you having, Terri?" he asked, opening and pouring the beer into glasses at the drinks cabinet which was part of an intricate wall unit filling one wall in of the room.

"Just a small gin and tonic, please. Here, I'll come and get it and you won't have to make two journeys."

"Trips," Scott corrected.

"What?"

"You used to say 'trips' before you went over there."

"Sor-ree. Here, I'll take Mark's."

"So, how's it feel being home again, anyway?" Scott asked, carrying his beer over to a chair adjacent to the couch. "Apart from getting pissed off over people correcting everything you say?"

"I wasn't getting pissed off..." Terry said, passing Mark his drink and sitting down beside him with her own. "When you survive growing up with two older brothers teasing you all the time, you learn not to let such things bother you. When will Derek be back? Mom said you'd know."

Their brother, Derek, was on a canoeing trip with a school party. Derek had been about to start his first high school teaching position at the time of Terri's last visit home. While he was four years her senior, he was the next youngest in the family to Terri and the closest to her and she was looking forward to seeing him again and introducing him to Mark. He was the only member of the family Mark had not yet met and she knew the two of them were going to be great friends.

"As far as I know, they'll be getting back next Tuesday or Wednesday – I'm not sure which. Karen'll know. D'you want her number?"

"I don't even know her."

"So call and introduce yourself."

"Okay. Give me the number then."

"Remind me before you leave," Scott said going towards the archway through which his small son, Adam, could be seen coming down the stairs.

"Hi, Daddy," Terri heard the little boy say as she rose from the couch and moved towards them.

"Hallo, son. Come and meet your Aunt Terri." Scott led the little boy into the living room with Emily following, their younger son, broadly smiling one-year-old William in her arms.

"You should have come up, Terri," said Emily, "and joined in all the fun of bath-time."

"You won't remember Auntie Terri, Adam," Scott continued. "You were just a tiny baby, smaller even than William, the last time you saw her."

Terri smiled in acknowledgment of Emily's statement and held her arms open to Adam. "Hello, Adam," she said. "You said hello to me on the phone to Grandma's the other night. Do you remember that?"

Adam nodded solemnly, without speaking, and hid behind his father's legs.

"And this is William," Emily said, holding her younger son towards Terri. "If you'd like to take him, I'll go and get the *hors d'oeuvres* my charming husband was supposed to put out."

"Me?" asked Scott. "Oh. Sorry, I guess I wasn't listening."

"Hello, William," said Terri, taking William and sitting down. "You're a big boy, aren't you? Can you walk yet?"

"He can walk," said Adam, coming out from behind Scott's legs. "You can walk – eh, William?" He moved forward and put his arms around his brother, rubbing his cheek against William's. William chuckled. "Wanna see?" Without waiting for Terri to answer, he helped William climb down from Terri's lap and, once William was standing, stepped back a few paces. "Come on, William. Come to Adam."

Still chuckling, William lurched towards his brother.

"There!" cried Adam, catching the baby's hands and pulling him to the floor.

"Adam, what are you doing?" said Emily, coming back into the room with two platters of appetizers. "Don't get him excited now. Neither of you will be able to go to sleep."

"I'll take them up," said Scott, bending down to pick William up.

"I ride!" Adam said, throwing his arms around his father's neck from the back.

"Hold tight, then. I don't want to drop you."

Scott grasped William under one arm and crooked his other arm behind him to provide support for Adam.

"Looks like a manoeuvre you're pretty familiar with," said Mark, laughing.

"You bet," replied Scott. "Say good night, boys."

"G'night!" called Adam. "Giddy-up, Daddy."

"Good night, Adam. Good night, William," said Terri.

"Good night," called Mark. "Is he always like that?" he asked Emily. "William? So happy?"

"Oh yes. He's always been a contented baby. Help yourselves to something to nibble on. I'll just go and check things."

"Do you need some help?" asked Terri.

"No thanks. Everything's under control. The baby-sitter stayed while I got things ready, so it's just a matter of making some sauce now." Emily replied, going back to the kitchen.

When they were alone, Mark turned to Terri. "Is that what the problem is?" he asked, "the problem with Alison? A phobia?"

"It's hard to explain. Moira says she's been treated for depression for the last couple of years, but the doctor who's seeing her now says the depression's secondary – caused by something nobody seems to have heard of called social phobia."

Chapter Three

Appetizing smells wafted from the kitchen as Moira let herself into the house at the side door. Since his car wasn't in the garage, Tim definitely was not yet home, Moira thought, so Alison must be cooking dinner. She must be feeling – well, halfway sociable, anyway. Thank goodness.

The two white poodles threw themselves at her, almost falling down the basement stairs in the process. She set down her briefcase. "Good dogs. Now calm down – you'll snag my panty hose. Down now, Charlie. Good girl, Angel." She bent down to pet the dogs. They had been a present for Alison's twelfth birthday and had been named, by Alison and Terri, in honour of their favourite television program at the time. Moira picked up her briefcase and, followed by the dogs, went on into the kitchen.

"I've made a fricassée with the leftover chicken, Mom," Alison said from the kitchen sink, where she was washing some baking trays, "and I've baked cookies and brownies. Should I put the rice on? Or won't Dad be in yet?"

"He didn't say anything about being late, so he should be home any minute." Moira moved towards her daughter. "It's really nice not having to cook. Thank you, dear." She kissed Alison's cheek. "I'll just go up and change. You go ahead with the rice. Here's Daddy now. I just heard him pull in. There goes the garage door." As if to back up her claim, the two dogs ran to the side door and began to paw the doormat in anticipation of Tim's arrival.

She was almost dressed when Tim came into the bedroom, preceded by the two dogs. "Hi, honey," she said, emerging from the sweatshirt she was pulling on.

"How did it go?" Tim asked, kissing her lightly on the forehead.

"With Terri?"

"Ah-ha."

"Well... she was about as mystified as anyone else I've attempted to explain it to, but she's eager to help. She's coming over tomorrow evening."

"Let's hope it does some good. Here, you're really tense." He put his arms around her. "Relax..."

"I got stuck in traffic and you know how totally powerless it makes you feel... then you start thinking – brooding, really, about how *more* totally powerless you really are..."

"Yes, I know. But it's not a question of being powerless –"

"On the Gardiner?"

"You know that's not what I mean, but I'm glad your sense of humour's coming back." He stepped back and held her at arms-length. "Things will work out with Alison, you'll see. Now, off you go and let me get changed. Out of my way." He walked her to the door. "Alison," he yelled over the bannister, "give your mother some work to do down there. She's in my way up here."

Moira was grinning as she went downstairs and into the kitchen.

"What did you do?" asked Alison.

"Oh, he's just fooling around – cheering me up after the slow trek home on the Gardiner. I'll lay the table..."

"Already done, Mom," said Alison. "It was only the rice I was holding off on. Look, I'm sorry I was such a jerk last night. I just couldn't..."

"I know. Perhaps –" she paused and took a deep breath. "Maybe it would help if we invited Terri over here one evening..."

"I don't know..."

"Well," said Moira, brightly, "we don't have to talk about it now. I'll put the bread on the table."

She picked up the basket of crusty bread, which Alison had sliced, and took it into the dining room. She'd planted the idea of Alison meeting Terri again on home ground. Summoning up her courage to make the arrangements would get Alison used to the idea and, hopefully, help her to feel more receptive to it by the time Terri arrived 'unexpectedly' tomorrow evening.

After placing the basket on the dining room table, Moira went through to the living room, turned on the radio and crossed to the open patio door. Sliding open the screen, she stepped out onto the patio, Charlie and Angel, suddenly appearing out of nowhere, to accompany her. She and Tim had cleaned and set out the patio furniture two weeks ago but the weather had not yet cooperated in producing warm, summer evenings. Nevertheless, she sat down on one of the chairs. Charlie immediately ran to fetch a ball and brought it to her. She obliged, throwing it onto the lawn for the two dogs to run after. Angel reached it first and raced back to Moira with Charlie in hot pursuit.

Moira continued throwing the ball for the dogs until she heard Tim calling from the living room.

"Are you out there, Moira?"

"Yes," she called, rising.

He opened the screen door. "Here we are working our fingers to the bone and you can't even be at the table on time."

Moira stepped into the living room. "I don't remember seeing you do anything," she said.

"I carried the crock pot in," Tim replied, with dignity. "I think we'll close this – it's getting chilly. Are you guys coming in or staying out?"

The two dogs came in and he closed the door.

Moira went through to the powder room beside the front door and washed her hands. By the time she arrived back in the dining room, Tim and Alison were serving themselves salad and the dogs were in their customary place under the table waiting for somebody to drop something. She shivered as she sat down.

"You're right," she said to Tim, "it *is* getting chilly out there."

"It was nice this afternoon," said Alison.

"Did you sit out there?"

"Well, I didn't exactly sit out there, but I was out playing with the dogs for quite a while. The weather's definitely taking its time warming up this year, though..."

"It'll probably get hot very suddenly, any day now, and we'll all be wondering what we were complaining about," said Tim. "Or rather, we'll all be complaining about it being too hot, and wondering what we were complaining about when we were having this deliciously cool weather."

"I'm not so sure I would call it *deliciously cool*. More like *bloody miserable*, I'd say," Moira said, "Can you pass the bread, Alison?"

"This is the bread I made," Alison told her, passing the basket.

"It is? I'm sorry, dear, I didn't notice. It looks so professional. I had no idea. Look at it, Tim. It certainly doesn't look home-made, does it?"

"You made it?" Tim asked Alison, taking a slice and buttering it.

"Yes, I made it," Alison replied. "I was feeling quite proud of it, but aren't you both overdoing it a bit?"

"No, you really did a good job." Tim bit into his slice. "Tastes delicious."

"It really is good, Alison" said Moira. "what made you go all out with the cooking?"

"Actually," Alison said, "it was because I got so chilly, out there in the garden, that I thought how nice and cosy the kitchen would be if I did some baking. I expect a psychiatrist would interpret that as a desire to get back into the womb or something..."

"Let's not worry about what a psychiatrist would think," Tim said, firmly.

"Sorry, Dad," Alison murmured. "I know I shouldn't be cynical."

But it was difficult not to be cynical about the mental health profession, Moira thought, after the experiences of the last year. It was hard to believe that in the mid-eighties – after the sexual revolution of the sixties and inroads, made in the seventies by feminism, into changing attitudes towards gender roles – that health professionals were still muttering Freudian platitudes in the face of a psychological problem. At least, this latest one seemed to be a little more progressive. He had looked beyond the depression, anyway, and diagnosed the primary problem. It was one step in the right direction, but hardly encouraging given that the diagnosed condition had yet to be recognized by whatever health organizations were supposed to recognize disorders and there was no specific treatment, other than taking the same tricyclic medication already prescribed for the depression and group therapy when a place could be found. The worst part was that imipramine supposedly had been found to be effective in treating anxiety-related conditions but it wasn't known how or why this was, which did wonders for one's confidence in the medical profession! Oh well, it was, she supposed, a more intelligent line to take than the first psychiatrist they had approached, with his ominous theories of childhood trauma arising out of penis envy and similar nonsense.

"I can't believe that you made leftover chicken taste so good," Tim was saying to Alison. "Finish your salad and try some, Moira."

"Yes, Mom, come on," Alison added. "What are you so deep in thought about? You haven't heard a word we've been saying, have you?"

"Sorry. I have to admit I haven't been paying attention to either the meal or the conversation. But I've had enough salad, so I'll try the fricassée." She hastily helped herself to the chicken and sampled some. "Very nice," she grinned. "What did I miss conversation-wise?"

"Oh nothing spectacular. Dad was just talking about the new computers which are going to put him out of a job."

Startled, Moira looked from Alison to Tim who both laughed.

"We have your attention now," Tim said.

"It's okay, Mom," smiled Alison, "He just has to adapt. I think he's bright enough to re-learn his profession, don't you?"

"What are you talking about?"

"I was telling Alison about how the Apple Macintosh computers are going to completely change the way print production is done."

"How does that put you out of a job? It's only typesetters that are affected..."

"Yes, at the moment, but you should have been at this symposium Magnus and I attended today."

"A peek at the future? What did you see?"

"A whole new world."

"Come on – it's not that bad surely..."

"Bad enough for Dad to have to buy a new computer," put in Alison.

"I was telling Alison that this Macintosh I've ordered can be packed into a bag and carted around," Tim explained, "so I'll be bringing it home and we can all take a look. Graphics software is in its infancy right now, of course, but in a few years time, the mouse and the computer will replace the marker and layout pad as the tools of the art director."

"You use the mouse, you see, Mom, like a pen or pencil," said Alison. "How did it get to be called a mouse?"

"I don't know," replied her father. "Mousing around as in a cat hunting? You tell me. Anyhow, what about you mousing on out to the kitchen and bringing in some of those brownies for dessert?"

"Sure." Alison stood up and collected the dirty plates. "D'you want tea or coffee, Mom?"

"Tea, I think. How about you, Tim?"

"I'm easy."

"You want tea, Alison?"

"Sure. I'll put the kettle on, but I'll let you make it." Alison said, on her way to the kitchen. "You never like it when I make it."

Moira looked at Tim. "Into cooking and computers on the same day," she said softly. "I thought she'd be hiding in her room for a week after last night."

"I think it's probably a relief reaction," Tim said, "now that she no longer has the challenge of seeing Terri and meeting her boyfriend to be afraid of... Here come the brownies."

"I used a different recipe," Alison explained, putting the plate of brownies on the table and sitting down again, "so I hope we all like them. Have you used that recipe in the *Chatelaine* book before, Mom?"

"Oh yes. It's a more moist one. I like it better, I think. I didn't think we had any walnuts, though."

"They were at the back of the cupboard. I don't know how long they were there, but they didn't seem to be rancid, so I used them."

"I'll go and make the tea," Moira said, getting up from the table to go to the kitchen. "Thank you for the lovely supper, dear." She patted her daughter's head, as she passed her chair.

* * * * *

"So, how was she?" Moira asked Tim when he came into their bedroom later in the evening.

"No problem."

Tim and Alison had taken the dogs for a walk after supper while Moira looked after the dishes and then relaxed in the bath. Aroma therapeutic bath oil and silky-soft, frothy water had smoothed the worry away and she felt a lot better. Sitting at her dressing table, she rubbed her wet hair with the towel she'd brought from the bathroom.

"Where did you go?"

"Oh, just over to the park," Tim replied, taking the towel from her and gently rubbing her hair. "It was getting too dark to let them run, though. Alison gave them their supper and they're both down in the rec room with her watching television. Well, Alison's doing the television watching. The dogs are asleep. So, tell me what you planned with Terri."

"She's coming over after supper tomorrow by herself. I explained that the prospect of meeting the boyfriend probably caused a large part of Alison's panic – more so than seeing Terri, herself, again. I'm not sure if that's a hundred percent true, but I thought it might make Terri uncomfortable to know that Alison finds seeing *her* intimidating, too."

"What was Terri's reaction to Alison's behaviour in the first place?" Tim interrupted, sitting down on the bed, still holding the towel. "Last night, I mean."

"Well... I think she was more upset than she let on, but she *did* feel she was being snubbed. She thought Alison just didn't want to know her any longer." Moira ran a comb through her damp hair. "I told her what had been happening during the last eighteen months and the difficulties in getting psychiatric help until we chanced on the clinic at Sunnybrook and the social phobia diagnosis, which I explained as a severe kind of shyness. That was not really the right way to explain it to her though, because, as she said, Alison was never shy. So, I said that I was using the condition of shyness to explain the effect rather than the cause. That, naturally, led her to wonder about the cause, so..."

"You had to say that was something none of us had figured out and did the usual spiel on fears and phobias and biochemistry that sounds as if we're just making excuses..."

"Precisely," said Moira, sadly. "Her reaction was of the usual *something must have happened to cause it* variety." She shook her head, helplessly. "I said that the fact that it had just happened rather than been caused was what made it so very difficult to explain and, more importantly, to make people understand. Of course, she was totally confused by the time we parted, but she wants to help if she can. She says she wishes she'd kept in touch more, but I told her, that with the two of them being involved in different things and on opposite sides of the Atlantic, nobody could expect them to be as close as when they were children."

"It's only natural to feel that you didn't do enough when you find out that things have gone so wrong for somebody you were very close too." Tim said. "Those two were closer than most sisters are."

"Well," Moira stood up as she spoke. "Let's hope they can be friends again and that Alison doesn't just cut her right off as she did her university friends."

"They were more recent friends who wouldn't have the same level of interest as Terri in maintaining a long-standing bond."

"Let's keep thinking positive, then. D'you want a cup of tea before we go to bed?"

"Sure, if you're going down to make it. I just need to find that strategy I was re-reading in bed last night and forgot to put back in my briefcase... I'll be right down."

Chapter Four

After Ian, with his father's blessing, picked up his car, his mother suggested he take it over to show Alison. He thought he had made the decision to put his relationship with Alison behind him at Easter, after spending yet another evening talking mostly to her father. He still cared about her and wanted to help, but his visits to her home were making no difference and... well, he had his own life to live. He *thought* that was what he had determined to do but, as soon as his mother put into words the very thoughts he had been subconsciously toying with himself, he decided to drive over to Islington after supper.

As he drove along Dundas, he wondered if, perhaps, he should have given the Frasers a call first. They might have company on a Friday night. He was nearly there now so if there were visitors, he could always just drive by. Both Tim and Moira had encouraged the idea of dropping by unexpectedly because that way Alison was caught off-guard and forced to respond. He'd have to get hold of some books on depression and neuroses since he'd have more time to read up on the subject now that the school year was over. When he was last there at Easter, Moira had given him the name of some Australian doctor who, she said, had written books that explained something of Alison's problems. He'd have to ask her for the name again and he'd go to the library. Wait a minute, he'd already decided to put it all behind him. It was obvious that she didn't want him around. Well, she was polite enough when she wasn't making herself scarce and leaving him to talk to her parents. Maybe she even resented him hanging around, after all she'd told him she wanted the relationship to be over a year ago, hadn't she? And he had to get on with his own life. What was he driving along her street for, anyway?

The driveway was empty. He drove in and parked in front of the side of the double garage where he knew Moira's car was kept. There was a car parked at the curb, but it could be somebody visiting the house next door since the space in front of the house was all occupied. Maybe they were having a party there.

Moira answered the door.

"Ian! How nice. Did you just get home? Come on in."

"I came home a couple of days ago," he said, stepping past her to receive the enthusiastic welcome of Alison's two white poodles. "Hallo, you guys, still falling over each other? You're not busy, are you Moira?"

"No, of course not," Moira turned towards him, as she closed the door and walked towards the basement stairs. The dogs followed. "As I keep telling you, you're welcome any time. We're downstairs in the rec room. Terri's here – Alison's friend who's been living in England."

"Oh, well, don't let me interrupt."

"No, no. You'll be a great help. So far, the going's been – well, a little uneasy all round. I'm sure you understand. Alison's spoken of Terri, hasn't she?"

"Oh yes. I've heard all about her. When did she get back?"

"Just this week. Come on down. Tim's working late. He should be home soon, though..."

She led the way to the basement stairs.

"Look who's here, Alison..." Moira called as they went down.

Alison looked up as Ian reached the bottom of the stairs which led straight into the open style recreation room. The two girls were in the seating area around the fireplace which, while not in use, was decorated with a dried flower arrangement.

"Hi, Ian," Alison said. "Ian, this is my friend, Terri. Terri Lydford – Ian Shaw."

"Hallo, Terri. I'm glad to meet you. I've heard a lot about you."

"Hi. Nice to meet you." Terri stood up as he reached her and, smiling, held out her hand.

Ian shook the proffered hand. He had the feeling that she had heard little, if anything, about him. "So, you just got back from England?"

"Yes, on Monday. Sit down. And you guys sit down, too," she added, addressing the two dogs.

Terri sat back down and indicated that he sit on the couch beside her. Angel flopped down at Alison's feet beside the tub chair she was sitting in. Charlie continued to stand, wagging his tail.

"We're drinking wine, Ian," Moira said, crossing to the corner bar. "But there's some beer, if you'd prefer it."

"Please."

He stopped halfway to sitting down.

"It's okay, sit down. And, Charlie, you sit down and stop bothering him. There's *Canadian* or *Blue*."

"*Canadian*, please."

Ian sat down. "So, how does it feel to be home again?" he asked Terri.

"A bit like when I first went to England, actually," she laughed. "Like being somewhere entirely new. Coming here tonight is more like things were four years ago."

"What she means," Moira said, giving Ian a glass and a can of beer as she sat down next to him on the couch, "is that her parents sold the house around the corner where she grew up, so she had to come here to come home."

"Exactly," Terri agreed. "Right, Alison?"

Alison smiled. "Terri and I hopped from one house to the other all the time we were growing up..."

"...so, coming here is more like coming home than going to my mother's," Terri finished and both girls laughed remembering their childhood.

"They also finished each other's sentences all the time," remarked Moira.

"That was the toughest thing to begin with, in England, nobody to finish my sentences for me," giggled Terri. "Or –"

"– start them either!" laughed Alison.

Ian began to laugh, too. It was good to see Alison as she used to be. They continued chatting for an hour or more until they were interrupted when Tim Fraser came home.

"Is there some kind of party nobody told me about going on down here?" he asked, coming down the stairs.

"Sort of. Not one, but two surprise visitors, Dad," said Alison.

"Terri! How are you?" cried Tim, striding over to them. Terri jumped up and they hugged each other.

"Now I really feel like I'm home," she laughed. "How are you, Tim? Moira's been telling us how overworked you are."

"Oh, just a few deadlines that happened all at once right after a symposium that couldn't be passed up on," Tim said and turned to Ian. "And how are you, Ian? Finished for good?"

"Yes, finished and into the work force for ever on Monday," Ian smiled, shaking the hand Tim held out to him.

"How did you do?"

"Oh, not exactly brilliant or anything, but I didn't expect to. I'll have my piece of paper next month and the company's taken me on permanently, so I can't grumble..."

"He came over to show us his new car," Moira said, "and we've all been so busy catching up that we still haven't been out to see it."

"Well," said Tim, "it's still just about light enough, although it won't be for long. So, let's go." He headed to the stairs. "The one in the driveway or is that Terri's?"

"No, mine's in the road," Terri said, "and, believe me, it's nothing worth looking at. My brother hasn't realized yet that when you're marketing environmentally correct products, it doesn't do to lease a fleet of gas guzzlers."

"You'll have to straighten him out on that one," Tim laughed, halfway up the stairs. "You girls coming to see Ian's car?"

"Sure," said Terri, "come on Alison."

"It's in the driveway?" Alison asked, looking uncertain.

"Ah-ha," Ian replied, standing aside to let them pass. "I'd like your approval, Alison."

Alison appeared to make up her mind and grinned. "Are you going to take it back if you don't get it?"

"Of course."

"Right..."

"Right!"

"Let's hope I like it then," said Alison, starting up the stairs. Ian followed her after looking back towards Moira, who was holding the two little dogs, not wanting them to join the exodus to the driveway. He silently shaped his finger and thumb into an okay sign.

They went outside and inspected the car. Ian considered asking Alison to come for a trial run, but decided it might be pushing things. Despite the flippancy of their exchange on the stairs, she was obviously ill at ease and seemed relieved to get back into the house again. They all returned to the recreation room and continued talking together until, at about quarter to eleven, Terri announced that it had been a lovely evening, but it was time for her to love them and leave them or Mark would be wondering where she was.

Tim and Moira both pressed her to bring Mark over to meet them next time she came and to say hello to her parents when she saw them. Terri suggested that Alison bring Ian over to supper at her apartment one day next week. Ian said that it sounded like a good idea and, while Alison didn't exactly commit herself, she didn't actually refuse, either. Terri said she'd call her on Monday.

Moira and Alison went up with Terri to see her out.

"I guess I should be on my way, too," Ian said to Tim.

"You haven't finished your beer," Tim pointed out.

"I mean when I have finished it..."

"Nice kid, Terri. She invited Alison over to see her apartment and meet her boyfriend the other night, right after they had moved in and Alison, unfortunately, reneged... Poor Terri was pretty upset apparently – had no idea about Alison's problem, of course."

It occurred to Ian that perhaps the Frasers referred to whatever it was that was wrong with Alison as *"Alison's problem"* because they didn't really know *what* the problem was.

"So, what happened?" he asked.

"Moira met her for lunch yesterday and filled her in," Tim replied. "They also set the scene for tonight with Terri dropping in so that there'd be no time for Alison to get cold feet. The way we fixed things up with you... and we've really appreciated your help, by the way, Ian. I don't think either of us has actually remembered to thank you..."

"You don't have to thank me. I just wish I understood."

Chapter Five

Alison pulled the bedclothes over her head in a futile attempt to drown out the sound of the telephone ringing. When it reached the ninth ring, she'd know it was her mother. Anybody else would have rung off by then. On the eighth ring, she could stand it no longer and reached out, picked up the instrument and put it down again. The sound of the connection and disconnection would be enough to satisfy her mother that she was still alive.

She lay looking up at the ceiling without really seeing it, then turned over, curled herself into a foetal position and closed her eyes. The two dogs, making themselves comfortable again after being disturbed by Alison stretching out to pick up the phone, buried themselves into the comforter alongside her.

If only she could go back... ten years back to when she'd first had Charlie and Angel, to the summer days she and Terri had spent training the puppies, playing at being grown-up, trying to get their hair to look like Farrah Fawcett's and imagining exotic lives for themselves in the years ahead. Now she scarcely had a life, let alone an exotic one! Perhaps it was her charmed childhood that had caused her problem. She had never learned to handle fear. That didn't explain why she had suddenly become afraid, of course, but it could be the reason that the fear was completely destroying her. No, it wasn't the fear that was destroying her. It was the embarrassment that was doing the destroying or... maybe, the energy it took to keep mending the bridges created by the fear and embarrassment, the energy she had given up trying to find and maintain now. She'd worked so hard, during her second year at university, at fighting the fear that threatened to keep her out of lecture halls, forcing herself to interact with fellow students and professors and battling the constant overpowering self-consciousness that accompanied every movement. She'd tried – tried so hard until it had finally beaten her into submission.

God! She was wallowing in it.

"This won't do, Angel," she said to the dog nearest to the head end of her bed. Angel wriggled closer and licked her cheek. "No, we have to get up. Do something to get the endorphins moving..." The dogs jumped to the floor as she quite violently forced herself to get out of bed.

She went downstairs to the basement exercise room thinking that five miles on the stationary bicycle would help her break through the depression that had engulfed her since – yes; it was a week ago – since the evening when Terri and Ian had visited her.

She sat on the bicycle, adjusted the tension and began to pedal.

She had enjoyed the evening. It had been quite wonderful, really to have her childhood friend back and to have her boyfriend – sort of boyfriend, anyway, around. What did you call someone who had been your boyfriend and seemed to want to remain your friend even when you never actually went anywhere with him? Anyway, it had felt good talking to Terri again and then having Ian drop by to be introduced to Terri and to have sat chatting with them both like a regular person...

Come on, endorphins, do your stuff...

Yes, she had felt – well, not at ease exactly... but, pretty close. Terri had done most of the talking, telling them about the huge success of her aunt's chain of stores in the UK and how phenomenal the move to natural products was likely to be over the next few years. Not just the skin-care products manufactured and sold by *Envirodermics*, but food and cleaning products, clothes – everything. Natural products stores would be springing up all over the place once North American consumers caught on to the trend. In Britain, she said, the idea of buying only products derived from natural sources was no longer equated primarily with hippies and environmentalists. It was fast becoming a mainstream thing. Of course, many stores like *Envirodermics* had been born out of sixties' hippie counterculture and seventies' New Age ideology. Terri's aunt was the first to admit that her youthful passions, of twenty years before, for living off the land and demonstrating against vivisection, pollution and the agricultural use of insecticides were what had fuelled her interest in developing natural products, but the general population was far more environmentally aware now and was creating a demand for purity in processing.

Alison wondered about some of the things Terri had talked about. What exactly *was* New Age? She supposed, being in university, she should know more about trends than someone who wasn't, although it sounded more like a Boomer thing than a youth trend from what Terri was saying. It was said that students in the eighties were more serious about their studies than their predecessors. Maybe that was why she hadn't come across it. Of course, she knew about theosophy, transcendental meditation and the Age of Aquarius idea. She just hadn't realized that so many people were into transcendence, self-realization, yoga, meditation and things like that... well, not to the extent that it was creating a whole new retail arena, anyway. Terri sounded as if she was very much influenced by her aunt which, of course, was hardly surprising considering she had lived with her for most of four years – until she had moved in with Mark, anyway.

She remembered Terri's aunt from that first and only Christmas she had spent away from home...

It had been her last year in high school. Terri had gone to England in the summer and Alison had felt rather lost without her. They'd been in different courses all through high school but had remained best friends and it had felt strange to be going to school by herself instead of with Terri, breaking the pattern of twelve years... Terri must have been feeling just as lost because she had almost begged Alison to come to England for Christmas. They'd had a lot of fun. In fact, it was one of her best-loved Christmases, although that might have been because Christmas becomes a bit of a bore during the teenage years and this had been an opportunity to do something different. Alison had been surprised by Terri's aunt, however. Having known her brother, Terri's father, for most of her life, relating him to his younger sister had been a major challenge. Just the very fact that she had always addressed Terri's parents as Mr. and Mrs. Lydford, while Terri called *her* parents by their first names, spoke volumes. Terri had introduced the aunt by her first name and Alison would never have connected the – well, almost *hippie* – lady with the solid, dependable Mr. Lydford. She remembered her staying at Terri's house once, years before, when they were still in public school, but had not known her well. Apparently it was soon after she had returned to England that she had been married in a very non-traditional ceremony in a farmer's field somewhere and she and her husband had started what was then a soap-making operation in a deserted factory in the East End of London. Opening as strategically located boutiques at first, *Envirodermics* had soon become a franchise operation.

For the two eighteen-year-olds, away from home for their first Christmas, it had been almost a coming-of-age. Terri had been given the two weeks off and they had explored London and the museums and taken train trips to the coast in the daytime and gone to the theatre on a couple of occasions and out with a group of kids Terri had come to know on some of the other evenings. Terri's aunt had had a New Year's party and they had, *en masse*, taken the Underground to Trafalgar Square to see in the New Year.

Alison kept pumping the pedals through six miles and on to seven as she recalled the fun of that Christmas. She and Terri had grown apart after that. A few months later Terri had met Mark and decided to stay in England and Alison's own life had become focused on getting accepted at U of T and then on adjusting to university life. It had all been part of growing up, of course, but she had somehow lost confidence in herself along the way or something like that...

She turned back the tension dial and got off the bike. She had been peddling fast at quite a high tension and was feeling a bit wiped. Dizzy, too. Probably need something to eat, she thought, as she stumbled to the stairs. Well, things were looking up – she was actually quite pleasurably anticipating making herself a boiled egg and toast after she'd had a shower...

* * * * *

Terri found the slip of paper, with Ian's phone number on it, at the back of the telephone index. She wished Mark wasn't such a neat freak. She'd left the number where it would remind her to call this evening. He must have cleaned up the telephone end of the kitchen counter this morning while she was in the shower and he was getting breakfast. Well, at least he hadn't thrown it out...

She dialled the number and asked Ian's mother – at least, she assumed it was Ian's mother – if Ian was home. He came to the phone almost immediately.

"Hello?"

"Hi Ian. This is Terri Lydford. We met at the Frasers' house last week?"

"Of course, Terri. How are you?"

"Great, thanks. Moira gave me your number. I haven't had any luck in persuading Alison to come over here for dinner. Remember we talked about the two of you coming over...?"

"Ah-ha."

"Well, Moira said you'd understand, but I wanted to apologize anyway for not getting back to you."

"That's okay. I did – understand, that is."

"I was wondering if we could get together some time to discuss this – this problem. I – well, I've known Alison nearly all my life and this whole thing is really confusing for me and, since you've known about it longer than me... You see, I had no idea until Moira told me about it... Mark, that's my fiancé, and I were over there the evening before last and Alison wouldn't even come out of her room..."

"I don't know a heck of a lot about it, myself," said Ian. "Moira gave me the names of some books, but I really didn't have the time to look for them during the school year – I just finished a four year computer sciences degree and – well, it was pretty heavy. Anyway, I did find one of the books in the library last weekend, but I've only skimmed it so far."

"Would you be into discussing it? I thought, perhaps, you could, maybe, come over to supper sometime... Mark doesn't really know Alison, of course, but he's upset about it because I'm upset, so we'd both really appreciate it if you could give us the benefit of your experience. Moira says you've stayed in touch the last few months despite Alison breaking up with you, so – like, you must still care about her. Right?"

"I guess so. I don't know if what you're calling my 'experience' warrants a whole supper..."

Terry laughed. "Look at it this way – if this – this thing hadn't happened to Alison, and you and she were still going together, we'd all be friends by now, right? So what's a supper between friends? I should warn you, though; I'm not exactly the world's best cook..."

"Okay, Terry, I'd love to come over," Ian said. "When do you want me?"

"Thanks. I don't want to mess up your weekend, so how about Monday?"

"Sounds fine. About seven?"

"Sure," said Terri. "I really appreciate it." She gave him their address and explained where it was. "See you on Monday, then."

"Okay. See you. 'Bye."

"'Bye, Ian."

Terri put the phone down. He seemed like a nice guy, she thought. And he must really like Alison or he would hardly have stuck around this long.

She cleared off the kitchen table and washed her supper dishes which didn't take long. Mark had gone out to dinner with Scott and one of the larger *Envirodermics* suppliers, so she'd had soup and a sandwich by herself.

The week had flown by. She'd managed to adapt to the accounting systems in place at the office and was remembering, most of the time, to use Canadian accounting terms and not the British ones with which she was more familiar. She was learning, too, not to react to Emily when her sister-in-law appeared to forget that she was no longer just Scott's little sister, but a woman with four years of training in the hands of the company's founder. Of course, she had a distinct feeling that Emily saw Maggie as a flaky lady who'd basically got lucky, in which case the four years probably didn't count for much...

I will not let what Emily thinks bother me, she said to herself, I have to make things work for Mark's sake. She half wished they were back in England where she hadn't had the problem of Emily to deal with or the whole situation with Alison.

The buzzing of the intercom broke her reverie and she hurriedly answered.

"Hallo?"

"Terri? It's me... Alison."

"Alison!" Terri was so surprised she couldn't think what to say.

"Terri?"

"I'm sorry, I... Oh, Alison, I'm so glad – come on up." She finally found the presence of mind to press the button to open the lobby door.

By the time she heard Alison's rather tentative tap on the door, she had finished putting the dishes away, poured water into the coffee maker and was measuring coffee into the basket.

"Alison, I'm so glad you came!" she cried, opening the door. "Where did you come from... I mean, how did you get here? God, I sound like a perfect nitwit. Come in." She closed the door and guided Alison into the living room. "Come on through here. I was just putting some coffee on..."

"Terri, it's great to be made so welcome, but please... do shut up!"

They both burst out laughing. How many times had Terri been the one, exasperated by Alison's babbling excitement over something, who begged *her* to shut up?

Terri took Alison's hands in hers and said quietly. "Well, I really am glad you came. Sit down and I'll go and plug in the coffee maker." She pushed Alison onto the couch and went into the kitchen. "Where *did* you come from?"

Alison laughed. "My mom dropped me off. I set out to borrow her car and come by myself, but thought I might chicken out and got her to drop me off and drive away. She waited till she saw you let me in so she could go without worrying that I might still be dithering in the lobby." She rose and walked over to the window. "Quite a view you have here. Where's Mark?"

Realizing that it must have taken quite some effort for Alison to psyche herself up to meet a perfect stranger on unfamiliar territory, Terri almost wished Mark was home. "He's out to dinner with Scott – a business thing..." she said, joining Alison at the window and pretending not to notice the other girl almost visibly relaxing. "It *is* rather different being able to see so far. I've never lived off the ground before and it's taking a bit of getting used to. I mean, in *my* head, front doors are supposed to open to front steps and a garden path – not a corridor."

"That's how I'd feel, too. Guess we've led sheltered lives..." They both grinned. "Can't be helped. We'll just have to make the best of it. Do you remember how my Dad used to kid us about making the best of the dreadful misfortune of having to endure a privileged childhood whenever we thought we weren't getting a fair deal?"

"He was great with kids, wasn't he? Remember that Hallow-een contest he ran when we were in Brownies?"

Alison smiled. "Oh, yes. Remember how miffed you were when Tracy Robinson won and –"

"I know, I told my mother that he didn't pick me because I was his daughter's best friend so it would have looked like fa-vouritism. It was only because she had worked so hard on my costume and I didn't want her to be disappointed. I was too young to realize how patronizing it would make your father look and, of course, I didn't know Tracy Robinson was listening..." Terri turned to go back to the kitchen. "Well, it was a good lesson for a kid, anyway, having just about everybody involved mad at me. I have never made a devious claim about anything since! I'll get the coffee. You can turn the radio off if you like – it was just on for company while I was eating my supper."

"It doesn't bother me. I do that myself. DJs become good friends when you're alone." Alison sat down as Terri brought in a tray with mugs of coffee and the coffee carafe itself on a tea-light warmer.

"I don't know if this thing works," she said. "The entertain-er's coffee set. Anna gave it to me. She's had it for years and never used it. I seem to have just about everything the various members of my family have had for years and never used. Even my brother Derek got into the act and brought us his microwave. He says they're indispensable in the modern kitchen and both he and Karen had one when they moved in together so they don't need both. Neither Mark nor I had ever used one. I suppose we're not very modern..."

"Funny, I would have thought Derek the last person to use a microwave..."

"Me, too. Karen must have domesticated him."

"What's she like?"

"Seems nice enough. I only met her for the first time last night. Derek and Mark really hit it off, which I expected. I hope he doesn't drag Mark off to the wilderness too quickly. There was mention of the four of us camping on the Victoria Day weekend but I don't exactly relish fighting off the black flies. I didn't want to look like a wimp though, so I didn't say anything. He just came back – Derek, I mean – from taking a school party canoeing around Timiskaming somewhere which I would have thought terribly dangerous at this time of the year. I mean, there's still ice melting up there, isn't there? It's supposed to be character-forming but, if I was the mother of a teenager, I wouldn't want my kid going. Scott got it wrong and told me he was in the Yukon or, maybe, that was just Scott's way of saying the back of beyond, or something like that. I thought it seemed a bit odd. I mean, has the ice melted up there at all? Anyway, the microwave is jolly useful."

"We've had one for a while now. It's good for warming things up – stuff like that, but it hardly fits Derek's persona. Shows how we all make trade-offs for convenience, I guess. Look, Terri, I really came to apologize and we seem to be discussing just about everything else so, before we go any further, I need to say I'm sorry about Tuesday night. I don't know why it happens but, over the last couple of years I've developed what my parents call *"Alison's Problem"*. It's really called social phobia, according to the psychiatrist I'm seeing now, anyway. I just can't handle social interaction sometimes. Well, most of the time, really..."

"Look, Alison," Terri said, "you don't need to try to explain. It's okay and it's okay with Mark, too. Don't worry. We've been friends too long to get put out by misunderstandings. I'm really glad you came over and pretty chuffed really that you made such a great effort to get yourself here. I'm not going to pretend that I understand because I don't, and I do appreciate the apology, but the important thing is that we're friends and we always looked out for each other and we're not going to stop now."

"Thanks, Terri," Alison smiled sadly as she went on, "you're the first person I've really tried to explain it to. The first non-health professional I mean." She laughed, a little wistfully. "You sound so English..."

"*You* sound so dismal. Is sounding English such a terrible thing?"

"No, of course not. If I sounded dismal, it's because you and everybody else is moving forward and I'm sort of stuck. It's envy, not disapproval."

"But you're going to beat it and move on, too..."

"I seem to end up taking three steps backward every time I move a step or two forward – anyway, let's not talk about it. How are you getting on with your job?"

"To be honest about it, just before you arrived, I was wishing we were back in England where everything was familiar and I didn't have to deal with my sister-in-law on a daily basis." Terri said, pouring herself some more coffee. "This seems to work okay, if you want a refill, by the way."

Alison shook her head and sipped the coffee which she had barely touched.

"I know that sounds awfully selfish," Terri continued, "and you're the only person I'd ever dream of saying it to, but I really don't feel comfortable there at all."

"Maybe it's just a matter of getting used to new surroundings..."

"No, it's not. There really isn't a job."

Terri stopped, surprised at herself. That was it. *That* was the problem. It wasn't her own failing. There was no job. She turned to Alison. "You won't believe this but I only just this moment realized it. I've been so down on myself thinking that I'm not capable, that I'm only there on sufferance, that people think I'm only taking up a desk because I'm family which, of course, is true, but I'm not taking a *job* because I'm family. The truth is that a job has been made for me and it isn't really there. That is *such* a relief..."

"How d'you mean? I would have thought..."

"Yeah, I know it doesn't solve the problem or anything, but I was feeling so stupid, so useless around Emily, you see. Not that I mind being stupid and useless around Emily – I've felt like that all the time I've known her. It was feeling stupid and useless, in terms of doing the job, that was getting to me. I mean, in England, I never had any doubts about my job performance but, each day this week, I've lost a bit more confidence. Now I can put a stop to that and –" she grimaced "– decide what to do..."

Alison poured some coffee into her mug and, this time started to drink it while it was still hot. She was silent, knowing that Terri needed time to collect her thoughts.

"You know," Terri said, at last, "there's no reason why I shouldn't get a job somewhere else. The natural products industry's starting to really boom and I've worked in it for four years, so it shouldn't be difficult. Maybe even a part-time job so that I can finish the CGA course faster..."

"Sounds like a good idea," Alison agreed. "You'll need to make an impression anyway to begin with. I don't know about the CGA course, specifically, but people who transfer credits from other countries generally tend to get viewed with suspicion at first in most programs."

"I haven't even investigated yet, but I have my transcripts and was told there shouldn't be any problem. Anyway, now that I've figured out where I stand, I can go forward. I'll get it sorted with Mark and tell Emily I won't be in on Monday. I don't think I need to give notice for a made-up job, do I?"

"I shouldn't think so. How will Mark take it? I thought he was to take over Canadian operations. Won't he think you're not being supportive?"

"I don't see why he should. He'll probably be relieved, actually. I mean, it must be uncomfortable for him with me being given a made-up job so that Scott can have somebody in the family take over from him. It's not as if I'm not prepared to be a corporate wife or anything – that's all way down the road, anyway. This whole marketing strategy for the U.S. is long term and still in the research stage and I'm not Mark's wife yet anyway, let alone a corporate wife..."

"So, Scott's not actually going to relocate to the U.S. or anything?" Alison asked.

"No, no... not for the foreseeable future. It might end up that way depending on the way things go with the franchising. It's more the need for him to reduce his workload that resulted in the idea of handing off Canadian operations to Mark, and Scott concentrating on the U.S. It's a great opportunity for Mark. I mean, he's an operations type rather than a marketing person, whereas Scott has really grown the Canadian business to the point where he needs new challenges. So, with Mark and me getting engaged, it was sort of a natural progression that he move into Scott's job..."

"But you would have preferred to stay in England really?"

Terri looked a little startled, then grimaced. "Yes, you're right. I knew what I was doing and I was comfortable with it. Oh well, there we are – time to move on. Anyway, that's enough about me..."

"Well, I'm hardly interesting, so let's not talk about me."

"But, Alison, don't you see? I just got myself sorted by using you as a sounding board –"

"And you think we can do the same for me?"

"Why not? It's worth a try."

"Because I've spent the last eighteen months in some form of therapy or another and know that it doesn't do any good. I know that sounds defeatist, but it's true. And I'm basically okay one-on-one so it's easy enough to formulate strategies. Putting them into practice is the problem. I've already decided, anyway, to finish my degree in a distance program. It won't carry the weight of a U of T degree, but it's the best I can do at the moment. I can't let everything go down the drain, can I? And, let's face it, options for agoraphobics are a bit limited anyway, so it's hardly going to affect my job prospects."

Terri didn't know quite what to say and, to avoid sounding patronizing, remained silent. Annoyed at her own thoughtlessness, she desperately tried to think what to do to salvage the situation, but it was Alison who broke the silence.

"I'm sorry," she said. "I didn't mean to sound like such an ingrate. I appreciate the thought but, really Terri, it doesn't help. In fact, putting a glorious plan together, then not being able to go through with it, makes everything worse."

"I hadn't thought of that," Terri said. "But I can see how it would. It would be like me making all my plans to find another job then, for one reason or another, ending up back with Emily and losing all confidence in myself."

"Sort of... But that's not going to happen to you. You have lots of job experience and applying for positions isn't going to present more than a normal amount of anxiety. My anxiety – panic, really – is anxiety which shouldn't be there –" she laughed "– unearned anxiety, you could say... Changing the subject," she continued, slowly, "how much does an *Envirodermics* franchise cost?"

"Well... there's the franchise fee, of course, but it's the location costs – the lease and stuff – and setting up the store that's the expensive part. I mean, all the up front costs of starting any kind of business. Why?"

Alison didn't answer. Instead, she asked, "I suppose there are restrictions on the kind of location? Like it needs to be in a major mall, for example?"

"Yes. It has to meet certain specifications. There's a set list," Terri answered. "Why are you interested in that, Alison?"

"So... say, in this area – Etobicoke and Mississauga – we're talking Sherway Gardens, Square One, the big shopping malls?"

"Actually Southern Ontario's pretty well developed. You'd be looking at one of the newer malls, even one still on the drawing board, or one that's being upgraded, not that I really know a lot about..."

"That's what Mark will be working on?"

"Yes. He probably already knows where every existing store in Canada is. So why...?"

"I was thinking about how you said how much more comfortable you were in England which made me remember how you said you loved working in the store in London that first Christmas. Then, when Dad and I met you at the one where you were the assistant manager – remember that Easter?" She didn't wait for a reply. "I mean, you sold my dad on the products for life! You were really happy there. So, what about us, you and me, becoming franchisees?"

"Sounds brilliant, but what do we do for money? My family might own the company, but they're hardly likely to be giving away franchises!"

"They'd be bound to give you some kind of break on the franchise fee, but the other start up costs would need to be raised just the same way as any two women going into business – what we have and what we can borrow."

"Which is hardly going to be enough. We have no collateral..."

"Terri, your aunt would be ashamed of you! There'd be no *Envirodermics* at all if she'd had such a defeatist attitude!"

Terri immediately felt ashamed. Here was Alison, the old Alison – enthusiastic, eyes shining, ready to take on the world, and she was being a wet blanket. Why shouldn't they be able to do it? They were young. There was lots of time to work off the debts they'd accumulate. Their parents would probably be willing to guarantee bank loans. Well, let's face it; Alison's parents would do anything if it meant there was a chance of it helping their daughter to regain her mental health. On the other hand, what about *'Alison's problem'?* Where did somebody who was afraid of people fit into a retail store? The new doubt must have shown on her face.

"You're wondering why a person, who dropped out of school because she couldn't handle people, wants to work in a store?" Alison said.

"Well..."

"It's okay, don't apologize. Obviously you have to consider it. All I can say is that I think I can handle it. I mean the idea of people coming to me for advice and information doesn't bother me. That's not to say I won't have a panic attack if somebody argues with me. What I mean is that this whole natural health products thing is new to people and we're the experts – well, you are, but I will be – " she grinned " – so it's not like some cheap dime store with people criticizing the goods, the service and everything. You know what I mean..."

"I think I see. Your panic problems happen when there's hostility..."

"At the risk of sounding paranoid, *perceived* hostility, discomfort, whatever. Seriously, Terri, what do you think? I have the money my grandmother left me to start us off. That's not to say we won't need a bank loan and some kind of deferring arrangement with the franchise fee..."

"You really want to do it?"

"Yes. I'm putting my money where my mouth is, aren't I? Offering to, anyway."

"It'll take a long time to get it back. The money, I mean."

"You're the accountant. I believe you. It's okay, we're only young once. Look, it's something you'd rather be doing for a living than working directly for your brother and it's something I can do, and my options are pretty limited..."

Terri knew that it was Alison who was taking the bigger risk, quite apart from putting up the money. She, herself, knew the business, had experienced managing a store – well, assistant managership, anyway – and, even if, Alison wasn't able to meet her expectations of herself down the road, well, they'd have employees to do the job. It wasn't like in England. The stores here had to stay open to nine every weekday, so they'd need to have a roster of part-time, even full-time help. And, in a disaster, she had her family to fall back on. But, for Alison, with her precarious self-esteem, failure would be devastating. And Alison wanted to take the risk...

She held out her hand.

"Let's do it," she said.

Alison clasped the proffered hand and shook it with mock ostentatiousness. "Let's have something a little stronger than coffee to seal the deal."

"Right. There's the bottle of Asti that was meant for when you came for dinner... I'll go and open it."

1990

Chapter Six

Mark picked up the tongs and pulled the foil-wrapped baked potatoes from the embers of the campfire as Derek Lydford squeezed a little more lemon juice from a plastic lemon over the fillets of brown trout, flipped them and divided them between the three tin plates. He picked up the other pan which had been keeping warm at the edge of the grill and added a heap of fried onion, mushroom and tomato to each plate and handed one each to Derek and Ian. Mark dropped a potato on each of their plates which they cut in half and smeared with the remains of the rather melted butter, which was getting a bit rancid on their second day out but not too badly so, and all three hungrily settled to eating, although Ian stopped long enough to place a pot of water on the grill to heat up ready for the cleanup duty he'd drawn for tonight.

"You guys ready for more coffee?" he asked picking up the coffee pot and topping up his own mug.

"Sure, mine could do with a warm up," Derek said while Mark shook his head and indicated his full mug. Ian filled Derek's mug, set the battered pot on the edge of the grill to keep warm and returned to his meal.

They had driven up to South River the previous day and come

into the park, via Lake Kawawaymog, and portaged to North Tea Lake where they had set up camp on an island site and Mark had cooked the steaks they'd brought in with them for the first night's meal, while Ian made a salad. This evening, having had the luck to catch trout, after making camp at a site on the north side of Manitou Lake, they were not reduced to using their dehydrated food supplies, except for the vegetable slices. All three were now pleasantly tired and looking forward to relaxing around the camp-fire after supper before crawling into the tent to sleep. An early start was needed tomorrow to get them back to the car for the minimum five hour drive home in holiday traffic.

In the three years since they'd know each other Mark and Derek had, as Terri had foreseen, become good friends. Ian, while teased for being a computer geek, was usually invited along on the guys-only camping and canoeing weekends they liked to take periodically. He had demurred the first few times that they'd asked him, not being wildly adept at transporting himself in a canoe, but had eventually caved into pressure and put himself in Derek's hands to learn the outdoorsman skills which Derek, having developed expertise in imparting them to his high school students, taught extremely well. The first time they had come here to the north end of Algonquin, he had been afraid of being a drag on the other two, both of whom had grown up around boats and water – Derek under his grand-father's tutelage during summers on Lake Simcoe and Mark on the brooding Cumbrian lakes of northwest England where he had grown up. Things had worked out, however, and he was now well able to hold his own whether partnering some-body else or paddling alone. He and Mark had borrowed Derek's equipment on a number of occasions and taken excursions with Terri and Alison, although the girls preferred that one of them be available to the staff at the store in case there was a problem, despite the fact that the employees were fully experienced and reliable and that there was always somebody from one of their families willing to be an emergency contact person. Now that the store was flourishing they weren't so bad, he was pleased to see. It was normal to feel indispensable during the start up of a business, he supposed, and neither of them had felt justified in relaxing their vigilance until their cash flow jmerited the bank's dropping the need for Alison's parents to guarantee their bank loan. Tim and Moira, of course, had been only too happy to do so. The bank loan, Tim had told him at the time, was actually less than the cost of the treatment program in Colorado that they had been trying to talk Alison into taking and, since she was actually motivated in the case of opening the store, it could prove – and, in retrospect, had proved – to be better therapy, anyway.

The store or the desire for the store to be successful had, indeed, proved therapeutic for Alison. There had been relapses but none bad enough to send her back to the almost agoraphobic existence of the year before Terri came back to Canada. She had received her degree this summer after obtaining her senior course credits by doing distance education programs. It had taken a while, course work often having to take a back seat to work at the store and simply learning how to run a store, particularly in the early days before sales justified employing more than just part-time students after school and on Saturdays. More recently, they had been able to afford to employ a daytime sales assistant and free up more time for themselves.

"Ian? Hey, Ian..."

Ian was suddenly aware of Mark's hand waving close to his face and pulled himself away from his thoughts with a start.

"So where've you been?" Derek asked. "Here we are having a scintillating discussion on the credibility versus the *in*credibility of tree-huggers and find you've just about fallen off the radar screen."

"Tree-huggers?"

"We were talking about Clayoquot Sound. Old growth forests? Clear cutting? Environmentalism?"

"Sorry, guys, I guess I was miles away... The place on Vancouver Island?"

"Right. Never mind – you had to be there..."

"Were you? I didn't hear..."

"Not there. Here – participating..."

"You lost me..."

"Never mind him," said Mark. "He was just getting up on his environmental issues soapbox again. You want this water for the dishes? It's boiling away here."

Ian got up and carefully wrapped a cloth around the handle of the pot and moved it off the grill. Derek collected the dishes for him and then picked up a shovel to go and bury the detritus from their meal in the bush away from the camp while Ian added cold water and biodegradable detergent to the pot and washed the plates and utensils. He left the mugs which they'd need for the fresh pot of coffee Mark was putting on.

Darkness was approaching and, by the time, the chores were competed and they were all three sitting back around the campfire, night had fallen completely. They heard the first loon's cry of the evening, out on the lake, immediately followed by the croak of a bull frog somewhere in the bush behind them. Ian's experience of the great outdoors had been limited to boy scout camping and two weeks at camp when he was thirteen and his best friend's mother talked his own parents into sending the two boys together. Family vacations tended to be taken at family lodges and, when they travelled, their nights were spent in motels rather than in campgrounds. He still felt a bit clumsy around a campground but, nevertheless, enjoyed being out of doors and away from the city.

"So, how's it feel – fatherhood just around the corner, Mark?" asked Derek.

"To be honest, I haven't had a lot of time to think about it. I finally did find time to paint the baby's room walls last weekend so that Terri can get on with organizing it..."

"I heard she threatened to do it herself if you didn't," Ian put in.

"Yeah, well... it was a threat that worked. God knows what the Lydfords would have done to me had I let her up on the stepladder at seven months..."

"Oh, we'd have done a bit of hanging and quartering for sure," said Derek. "Actually, I think it's the stretching that's supposed to be avoided rather than climbing ladders. I seem to remember Colin making a big deal about that back the first time Anna was pregnant."

"Colin probably made a big deal about everything. I wonder Anna was even allowed out of bed in the morning."

"He is a bit of autocrat, isn't he? Karen and I wanted to bring Jon, the eldest one, along on a camping trip we took up on Manitoulin last month, with Karen's sister and her husband and kids, but Colin said it was too early, at ten, for the kid to start having vacations outside of the family. He's right in a way, I suppose, the immediate family unit doesn't last long if you look at from a parents' perspective, but the poor kid gets fed up with having to do everything with his younger sisters."

"Terri holds Colin up as the kind of father I'd better not turn out to be," said Mark. "We shouldn't criticize, though, when we don't know how we're going to do at it ourselves, after all."

"My father was like that. Still is, I suppose," Ian laughed sardonically. "He hasn't stopped feeling insulted that I should have wanted a place of my own and that was only two years ago. That's how long it took me to escape. My mother was good at coming up with strategies for making him think that what I wanted – or, what she wanted for me – was his idea, but he was still insisting on family vacations when I was well into my teens when the last thing you want is to be seen with your parents!"

"Colin's father was like it, too, so you'd better watch you don't turn out that way yourself. Could be upbringing that causes it," Derek told him.

"At the moment, I can't get Alison to even consider marriage, let alone parenthood, so I hardly need to worry."

"I was just kidding. I don't think you need to worry. Anna's as much the problem as Colin is. It's probably the big sister thing – being my big sister, then Terri's, too. She was probably so used to following Mom's instructions that she just carried right on doing whatever Colin said when she had her own children."

"Well," said Matt, "the baby's room walls are painted and very nice they look, too, even if I do say so myself, and your mum's all set to make curtains and things and my mum keeps sending so many things she's knitted that there's no way the baby's ever going to get to wear them all, so let's get on to more serious things. You got the cards, Ian?"

* * * * *

Terri hung the length of fabric over the back of the yet unpainted, but stripped rocking chair and stood back to look at it.

"Sorry, Mom, it's a bit of a mess in here and the trim's still not painted," she said, turning to her mother who came into the baby's room, looking around her.

"Pretty colour," Stella nodded approval. "I had my doubts when you said tangerine, but it's really nice..."

The freshly painted walls were a very pale tangerine with which Terri had fallen in love while looking for alternatives to shades of yellow or green, deciding that it wasn't too feminine for a boy, while working well for a girl, too.

"Mark did it last weekend and I'm going to do the trim this afternoon," Terri explained. "It's a dull ochre which is why I told you predominantly yellows for the curtains and I'd say you've managed to get just the right tones."

"Serendipity," laughed her mother. "Although maybe it's something genetic making us tune into the same colours..."

Definitely a remark she'd have hated a few years ago, Terri thought, but now it made her feel very warm towards her mother. Probably something to do with being seven months pregnant. Well, pregnancy certainly did make you feel closer to your mother...

"Are you going to do the rocking chair the same colour?" asked Stella, her gaze settling on the rocking chair itself after appraising the fabric and the wall behind it.

"Yes, but I think I'm going to leave that for Mark. He said I could go ahead but I'm afraid of messing up. He spent so much time stripping of the different coats of paint and stain, then sanding, I'd feel terrible if I ended up clogging the carving with paint or having it run on the spindle bits."

"I was just asking because I bought enough fabric to make cushions for the rocker as well, so there'll be curtains, crib coverlet and cushions."

"It'll really look nice, Mom," said Terri, warmly. She and Mark had spotted the rocker in a garage sale and her mother had only heard about and not seen it when she offered to make the curtains. She rolled the fabric back up and handed it Stella.

"Let's go and drink our coffee outside," she said, leading the way back downstairs. She was glad that her mother's choice of fabric had turned out to be such a good match. In fact, she'd been worrying about it since Stella's call of the previous evening to tell her of her find. She'd expected her mother to come over and see the colour scheme they had selected before actually buying material to make the curtains and coverlet as she had proposed. It was a relief because, while she certainly didn't want her mother running the show, she did want her involved in her newest grandchild's entry into the world.

This would be the first baby in the family since William's birth four years ago when Terri was still in England. She knew that Emily, as a daughter-in-law rather than a daughter had not really given Stella much opportunity to participate in preparations for William's birth, nor Adam's the year before. Terri also remembered how upset her mother had been at her sister, Anna's, polite, but definite, refusals of help both before and after the births of her children. *Their* children, she should say, Anna and Colin being one of those couples who made a point of always using plural pronouns when talking about their children. Terri thought this affected – by all means *'our* 'when you were together, but saying *'our'* like that when you were alone seemed to her almost like declaiming your superiority over people who used the traditional *'my'* when talking of their children. Anyway, Mark wasn't like Colin, busy running mother-in-law interference when there really wasn't any, thank goodness, and she felt really happy not only to have her mother involved, but also for her to be able to feel like a grandmother.

In the kitchen, Terri poured the coffee and carried the mugs on a tray, with some bran muffins she'd put ready earlier, through to the sunny patio at the back of the house.

"I'm so glad the fabric's right," Stella said, "I can get going this afternoon, now."

"There's no big hurry, Mom. It's a holiday weekend..."

"*Life's* a holiday when you're retired, Terri. We're only home for a few days. Your father wants to get back up to the cottage on Thursday. Anna and Colin and the children will be going home then. So I'd like to get the sewing done before that. He'll just make a big fuss if I want to take the sewing machine up with me. The idea to be home for the week was just... well, to go to this wedding anniversary party tonight and let Anna and Colin have the cottage to themselves for a bit. But, you know your father; he doesn't like staying in the city any longer than he has to in the summer..."

"Well, don't go making Dad late for his best friend's party."

"If I don't have a chance, when I've finished, to get them to you, I'll leave them for you to pick up when you go over to water the plants."

As the child living closest to her parents' apartment, it had become Terri's job to look after the place when they weren't there. "Don't worry about it, Mom. The baby's not due for nearly two months..."

"Yes, but you'll want to get the curtains up and have everything ship-shape once you've got the painting finished, see if you don't. I know I would. I had the nursery ready six months before Scott was due. In fact it was the first room in the house to get decorated. We'd only just bought it when I found myself pregnant. It was planned, of course, but we hadn't really expected it to happen that fast. You and Mark have got yourselves far better organized than we were. You've got your own business so you don't even have to give up your job – although, I hope you're not intending to be in that store to any extent the first few months."

"No, Mom, of course not. I'm taking a proper maternity leave. Alison is going to be at the store everyday and on call any time she's not actually there. She doesn't claim to be a brilliant book-keeper but she can do what's necessary and I can organize taxes and paying the bills and stuff for her and go over it all when I do go in."

"Well... as long as my grandchild is your first priority. The room is really going to look pretty... Of course you've done a wonderful job on the whole house. When I think about the mess it was in when you bought it..."

Terri and Mark had bought the house, which had been badly in need of renovation, the year before. It was not far from the area where she'd grown up and they had not really expected to be able to afford anything there when they had decided to purchase a home rather than sign a new lease for their apartment. They'd come across it when taking a different route home after dropping Alison and Ian off at the Frasers' house one day when they'd all gone out somewhere in one car. It had been lived in for most of a lifetime by an old couple who had died within months of each other, leaving the proceeds from the sale of the house to be divided between several grandchildren, some of whom were in need of the cash. Most prospective buyers were deterred by the need, at the very least, for complete redecorating, including plaster and floor repairs, throughout and, consequently, offers had been few. As first time buyers, Terri and Mark did not need to make their offer conditional upon selling a property and the money-needy grandchildren persuaded their siblings to accept it despite its having been less than what they wanted.

"There's still a lot that needs doing," Terri said, "but, at least, it's presentable now."

"You'll get there," Stella told her. "That's part of building a life together. You're the youngest so you don't remember our old house before we put the extension on it. It was just a little two bedroom one-and-a-half storey with Scott and Anna in the tiny bedrooms which we'd had one of the rooms divided into and your father and I in the other, so when we found Derek on the way, we started looking for a larger home, but then decided to enlarge the house instead. There was nothing in our bracket available in the neighbourhood and Scott was happy at the school and Anna had just started kindergarten there, so it was the perfect solution – sort of... I ended up much like you have, pregnant amidst a chaos of building rubble and plaster dust, but with two kids to run after! The important thing was the feeling of accomplishment when it was finished – Scott and Anna with their own bedrooms and the sparkling nursery all ready for Derek and a big ground floor family room. Took years to pay for, of course."

"Then I came along and you had to start reconstructing all over again."

"Oh, that was just minor – partitioning off the sitting area of the master bedroom to make a new nursery. Anna thought her bedroom was big enough for two – it would have been for a few years, then we'd have all the problems of a teenager and a preschooler in one room..."

"Did you know I was a girl, then?"

"No, the mandatory ultrascan for older mothers was still some years away, then. No, Anna had just decided you were a girl – she was nine, just the right age to be a big sister. "

"You mean I should wait nine years before getting pregnant again?"

"No, of course not. I just meant that when she was five, Derek's birth was more of an inconvenience than something to participate in while, with you, she was old enough to be a little mother. Sometimes that's helpful, sometimes not. I think, personally, that three-and-a-half to five years is the ideal. You have time, what they now call quality time, with both children because the older one is at nursery school, kindergarten, whatever and the baby has you to himself and you can spend time one-on-one with the older child when the baby's sleeping. Scott and Anna got sort of lumped together too much, as children, because of being close in age. It didn't do them any harm long term, but I sometimes feel that they still resent each other a little."

"That could just be their different personalities... Anyhow, neither of them has taken your advice, or didn't you give it?"

Stella laughed. "I wasn't advising, dear – just telling you what I think. Maybe three kids in five years works for Anna, and Emily's a law unto herself..."

"I won't comment on that," said Terri. "It's funny, though, isn't it? How Scott and Anna both married more dominant personalities, while Derek and I have more give-and-take relationships. Maybe your theory about having the so-called quality time with the children on an individual level is at the root of it?"

"I wouldn't go that far. I'm no psychologist and I was really speaking more from my own perspective than from the children's, anyway..."

"But, it's something to think about, isn't it?"

"Maybe," Stella finished her coffee. "Moving on from playing at Dr. Spock, we should thin out the peonies up at the cottage and you could plant some around the patio here. It would look really nice and they're not like irises and lilies and things like that which look awful once they've bloomed and died off. Peonies give you nice foliage for the rest of the summer. See what Mark thinks... I wouldn't want to get on the wrong side of the son of an English gardener!"

Stella and Paul had visited Mark's parents the spring before last, during a holiday in England. Stella had heard about the Havers' brilliant perennial garden, which rippled down the fell, causing drivers to stop on the narrow road to gaze up at it and back up the traffic on the single lane Cumbrian road, but hearing about it hadn't prepared her for how beautiful it really was. Mark's mother had won so many awards that she had stopped entering the local flower shows in order to let other people have a chance. Her garden was, however, a feature of several Lake District scenic drive route pamphlets despite the many more eminent gardens which bring tourists to the area.

"Oh, Mom, Mark's not like that. He's hardly his mother's son, anyway, when it comes to the garden. The only reason he cut the grass the last couple of times was because he felt guilty about me doing it while I was so noticeably pregnant. Otherwise, the garden's pretty well up to me. And, yes, I'd like the peonies, but don't cut them down yet. Wait till the end of the summer – only you may have to plant them because I doubt if I'll be bending down much by then!"

* * * * *

"Looks like we've caught up with the traffic," said Tim. "Or, the traffic's caught up with us, I'm not quite sure which, but it's definitely going to be slow from here on in."

They had reached the 400 highway on their drive home from the weekend cottage get-together, near Pointe au Baril, with a one-time publishing colleague of Moira's who was now retired and living there year-round.

"Well, we've done pretty well so far, for holiday Monday traffic, I mean, so we shouldn't complain..." Moira shrugged. "Why don't we take a break and stop for dinner at that little place in Cookstown. It's six-fifteen, so it'll be close to seven when we get there, given the rate of the traffic, I mean."

"I don't know – twenty-seven highway'll be even worse than this the rest of the way."

"It couldn't be any worse. It's up to you, you're driving. I just thought you'd like the break..."

"Okay, be it on your head though, if things get worse."

"Barring a complete stop, I don't think it can be worse than this," said Moira, as they actually did come to a full stop. "So it's worth risking my head."

They, in fact, reached the Cookstown restaurant some time after seven but, after a short wait, since many other people had had the same idea, were given a table in a quiet corner where they could relax over a meal and a glass of wine for an hour, hoping that the traffic would be better by the time they were underway again.

"It's much better doing it this way, then we can just fall into bed when we get home instead of having to cook supper and everything," Moira pointed out. "Besides, I like this place."

"Okay, no more justification. I like it, too. So what did you think of Arthur's new pride and joy?"

"The boat? Well, I'm not exactly a boat person. It's nice for the amount of time we spent on it, but I don't think I could handle being on it days at a time without going hairy..."

"They seem to enjoy it – days, at a time, I mean. I'm with you, though. I think I'd find it a bit claustrophobic. So, I guess, we don't go that route when we retire."

"Retire!" exclaimed Moira. "We have a good few years to go yet but, no – not the boat life, thanks. I don't think their winter life's for me, either. Remember all that snow-shoeing the last time we spent the weekend with them?"

"They always were very active – could always wipe the court

with us at tennis in the old days... and they were the first people I knew to buy mountain bikes."

"*Old days* – you're making us sound positively ancient."

"Well, with Alison finally moving out of the house and the dogs moving on to doggy heaven, we're into the next phase of life, aren't we? Empty nesters – or whatever else it is that your demographers call us..."

Moira looked at Tim, sharply thinking, perhaps, that Alison's move to Ian's apartment the month before had sparked a bit of an identity crisis in him. He had tended to seem a bit lost the last couple of weeks now that she came to think about it.

"...it'll be no time at all before I'm jiggling grandchildren on my knee," Tim continued, disregarding Moira's surprise. "Then there'll be the fights with Ian's parents over spoiling them with too many gifts at Christmas and..."

"Tim, they're not even married yet –"

"You don't have to be now. You just move in together nowadays, to hell with benefit of clergy, etc."

"Alison's not flouting convention. She just wants to make sure that Ian can stand living with her indefinitely. She's just afraid for *him*, that's all. It's nothing to do with her own feelings. She doesn't want him feeling that he's tied to a *neurotic*, as she puts it. She explained it all to you and you agreed that it was probably the best route to take..."

"I know," Tim reached across the table and took her hand. "I'm just worried about it, that's all. I think I'm just seeing the future the way I want it to be, but – well, being afraid it won't be, I guess."

"There's no point in worrying. I think experience has taught us that, hasn't it? I do rather wish that she'd either done it before now or waited until after Terri's baby – the stress of too many adjustments at one time... well, you know..."

"She's been okay with the store before when Terri's been away..."

"Yeah, but she hadn't just started living in a different environment at the same time."

"Moira, this started with you trying to quash my anxiety, now you're the one finding things to worry about."

"I am, aren't I? Well, like I said, there's not much point in worrying. Whatever happens will happen, whether we worry or not. Let's have some cappuccino and then get on our way."

Chapter Seven

Terri manoeuvred herself from the car, closed the door and walked across the parking lot to the back entrance of the store. The shopping mall had opened less than three years ago, but the area it served was growing fast and its market area had expanded even more quickly as people from further afield found its large array of stores and services both attractive and convenient. The *Envirodermics* concept had also continued to attract, not only the environmentally-aware, but shoppers who simply liked the products and their presentation, so that their own franchise had already become one of the most successful in the country and was consistently shown as a model to potential franchisees. Mark and Gordon Innes, the VP Franchisee Relations, were, in fact, bringing somebody over later this morning and, although it was really Alison's morning to open, they'd switched because Alison's fear of scrutiny was particularly hard to control under conditions of genuine scrutiny.

Amanda Hawkins, their daytime part-timer, caught up to Terri just before she reached the door beside the receiving bay. If Amanda knew about Alison's anxiety problem, she didn't mention it.

"Hi Terri," she said, "How's it going? Alison not coming in this morning?"

"Hello Amanda. All's going fine, I think. Alison's working on the new ads, back-to-school stuff for the flyers."

"Guess it's easier to concentrate on that at home."

Terri wondered if Amanda was fishing but decided to ignore it. She unlocked the door, opened it and turned off the alarm system.

"Ah-ha," she nodded, then continued. "We need to get all the *EnviroAroma* products on shelf," she continued, pointing at the shipment which had arrived late the previous afternoon, "and the promotion stuff cleaned away before we do anything else. We've got visitors this morning."

"I thought we were going to wait for them to sell out before we put out the new ones..."

"We were," said Terri, "but half empty shelves in that section aren't exactly as impressive to potential franchisees as they are to shoppers who think they'll miss out on a good deal unless they act immediately. Anyway, they're almost all gone. We'll put the rest in the clearance bin."

"I'll put the coffee on first, okay?"

"Sure. Bad morning?"

Amanda always seemed to arrive at the store gasping for a cup of coffee, something which Terri found a little difficult to understand since she lived within walking distance of the mall and didn't start work until 9:30 – three quarters of an hour after her children had to be at school.

"Oh, just the usual problems getting them up, dressed and fed... You'll find out how it is in a few years," Amanda replied, filling the coffee carafe at the washroom sink.

Terri went through to the small office between the storage area and the store and turned on the computer. She was actually getting a little tired of the patronizing remarks which most first-time pregnant women endure and had decided that the best thing to do was to ignore them. She picked up the waybill for the goods she wanted to get out on the shelves this morning before Mark arrived with the potential franchisees, and studied it far more intently than it deserved to prevent further discussion on the difficulties of getting children to school on time. It worked and Amanda passed the doorway and went into the store, where she turned on the lights and began the dusting and general tidying up that was her first duty for the day. Terri made a quick call to head office to check on the status of a back ordered *EnviroAroma* product then opened the safe and took the cash float into the store.

"The chamomile and lily-of-the-valley is back ordered," she told Amanda. "Are there any left from the sale?"

"Mmm... yes. Enough to make a facing, I think. Anyway I was just going to get a coffee – it should be ready by now, then I'll get right on to checking the *EnviroAroma* shipment. Shall I get yours while I'm at it?"

"Please."

Terri went back into the office and started sorting yesterday's cheques and credit card slips. Amanda brought in the coffee, put Terri's on the desk and, deciding that Terri wasn't feeling like a chat while they drank it, picked up the waybill and took her own coffee back out to the storage area. By the time Amanda wheeled some boxes of product on the dolly into the store, Terri had finished making up the deposit and followed her in, picking up a box slitter on the way.

"We'd better both work on it and I'll look after the reconciliation afterwards," she said. "We're going to have to open in a few minutes, too." She slit one of the boxes. "The design really freshens it up, doesn't it?" she said, holding up a bottle for Amanda to see. "We aren't going to get away with putting the old chamomile and lily-of-the-valley with them though. Oh well, if any one wants it, they'll get it cheaper anyway at the clearance price and we'll have to hope the visitors don't know enough about the line to notice that it's missing."

"Wow, I like the lavender and passion flower," exclaimed Amanda, holding one up for Terri to see.

"They're all definitely an improvement. They should have got on with it before... I think there were too many of the glass containers in stock for it to be economical or something. I'm glad Scott's doing so well in the States. It's made him realize, at last, that the company has to get more professional with the packaging. They'd already moved package design out to an agency in England while I was still over there. I mean they'd recognized that you eventually grow too big for the home-made look to work any more and that was more than three years ago."

"I like the old look, but this is, as you say, more professional," said Amanda, "but it's not slick, either. I mean, you wouldn't mistake it for a Unilever product or anything because it seems to retain the sort of folksy, down-home look, too."

"That's what professional package design does. The creative director is able to look at it objectively which can't be done by somebody on the inside," Terri told her, then decided she sounded a little patronizing. "Actually, that's not an original thought," she said. "I got it from Tim Fraser, Alison's father. He's in advertising. He put Mark onto these people, actually."

"I remember him. He came in one day. He'd been at a meeting or something near here and was taking Alison to lunch. He was really nice and friendly, not like... I expected."

Terri had a feeling she was going to say "not like Alison" but had diplomatically changed her mind at the last minute. While Alison had little problem being gracious in handling customers, she was not completely comfortable with Amanda, or with the students who worked evenings and Saturdays until they'd been around a while. Terri knew it was her social phobia but the girls tended to interpret it as arrogance.

"Alison's actually very like her father," she said, forgetting that Amanda had not actually said what she was going to say. "She just finds it difficult to relax around people until she really knows them well." Then, to prevent Amanda from observing that she'd been working for them for nearly a year now, she changed the subject. "I think we'd better open. Can you do the door?"

Amanda went into the office for the keys and out to the front of the store to unlock and pull back the barriers, opening up the store to the mall traffic while Terri opened the third box of aromatherapy oils.

"Look," she said when Amanda came back to work on shelving them. "I'll finish filling the shelves, while you stack the rest underneath. I really don't think I can manage bending and reaching into the cupboard."

"Don't you dare try," laughed Amanda, the previous topic of conversation obviously forgotten. "The last thing we need is a pregnant woman getting into problems when there's the top brass and potential franchisees arriving any minute, 'specially when the top brass happens to be the father-to-be... Your husband is bringing them, isn't he?"

"Ah-ha. He and Gord – you've met Gord Innes before, haven't you?"

"He came in the last time – at least, the last time I was here. Dark hair with a moustache?"

"That's right. I think that must have been the couple they sold back in May, wasn't it?"

"Probably. The time flies. It doesn't seem that long..."

"It was a husband and wife team. They're opening somewhere in the Ottawa area, I believe. I told Alison we should lobby for a rebate on our franchise fees since they use our store as a display model so often and so successfully.

"Well, that's just about it, I think," she went on, stepping back to survey her work. "I'll take the cartons out back if you'd like to just take those last two bottles... Great. Can you ticket the clearance ones now? Leave them at the sale price, but replace the sticker with a clearance one. I'll get on with my reconciliation."

"I'll take the cartons," said Amanda, getting up and closing the doors to the cupboard. "I need to warm up my coffee if you don't mind waiting in here for a minute?"

"No, go ahead," Terri replied, turning towards the opposite side of the store where she'd been aware of a shopper in the men's products area, where a little assistance was generally appreciated. "I'll see if this lady needs any help."

* * * * *

It was later in the day when Janet Shaw spotted Terri walking, through the mall, back to the store from the bank.

"There's Ian's fiancée's partner," she told her visiting sister-in-law who was seeing the mall for the first time. Janet still felt uncomfortable, though not as uncomfortable as her husband,

Ralph, with the fact that Alison had moved into Ian's apartment, the existence of which, in itself, had been a contentious issue with his father for some time after Ian had made the move. She knew that Ian really did want to marry Alison, so she found the term *fiancée* the best way to describe the relationship.

"Terri!" she called now, waving and making her way around the tropical plants down the centre of the aisle, "Terri!"

Terri turned and caught sight of the two women and started to walk back towards them.

"Hello, Janet. How *are* you? And what are you doing way over here?"

"I brought my sister-in-law over to show her the store. Terri, this is Pat. Pat, Terri."

"Hello, Pat."

Pat smiled and nodded.

"Pat's visiting from Halifax," Janet continued, "so I got Ralph to let me have the car for the day and we've been sightseeing this end of the city. Well, not sightseeing exactly. We saw the new Mississauga city hall, not that it's so new any more, and it *does* look like a penitentiary, doesn't it? And we went down to Oakville and took a walk along the lake, then had lunch at a patio restaurant. And now we're here at the newest shopping mall..."

"Alison isn't here at the moment," Terri said, when Janet, at last, slowed down. "She should be in shortly, though. Why don't you come down to the store, anyway? Do you know the *Envirodermics* stores, Pat? There is one in Halifax – two, or three now, I think, and one in Dartmouth, too."

"We're a bit of a way out and don't really go into the city much but Janet's been telling me all about how your aunt started the idea in England and your brother got it going here in Canada and is now opening stores in the States. It all sounds so exciting."

They had arrived at the store by this time and Janet immediately started to show Pat the products. Terri went through to the office to put the deposit book away, indicating that all was under control in response to Amanda's questioning look.

"Alison called and said she'd be a bit late," Amanda told her as she came back into the store. "D'you want me to stay until Donna comes in?"

"No, you go ahead. One or other of them will be here soon and it's not as if it's madly busy."

"You wait – as soon as you're on your own, they'll be in droves. It's always the way."

"Well, I don't know about droves, but I know what you mean. Come and meet Janet and Pat first, though. Janet and Pat, this is Amanda, our indispensable assistant. Janet is Ian's mother, Amanda."

"How d'you do?"

"Having a great time," laughed Janet. "Pat's my sister-in-law from Halifax and she hasn't been to Toronto since – well, this area was all still country the last time she was here – right, Pat?"

"Oh, it's changed tremendously," said Amanda, "even since I've lived here. We watched this mall being built. The big thrill for my son, at that time, was the fact that there'd soon be a movie theatre. I must admit, though, that it's handy. They're both old enough to go on their own now, not that he likes having to take his sister."

Pat smiled. "Well, I remember what is now Mississauga as a group of little towns and villages," she said, "where you went for a drive in the country. We were almost all the way to Oakville today before there was any country. The Halifax area's the same, though. I suppose that's progress for you."

"Yes, that's the way things go. Still, I do like my house and neighbourhood. It's been nice meeting you both. I'd better be on my way – the kids'll be home from day camp soon and I have some grocery shopping to do, first. There's a lady coming back for this, Terri," Amanda moved over to the counter and indicated a gift-wrapped package. "She was in a bit of a hurry and had to run over to *Hallmark* to get a card. Oh, here she is now..."

Amanda handed over the package to the customer, who thanked her profusely before hurrying off again. With a little wave to Terri and a mouthed goodbye, she picked her purse up from under the counter and left herself. Terri approached a young man who had just come into the store and was hovering a little awkwardly around the soaps and bath products, obviously needing some assistance. Janet resumed looking at facial moisturizing creams with Pat.

"That's the one I was telling you about, with the carrot seed oil. Alison gave it to me in a gift pack last Christmas and I've been using it ever since. I should get some while I'm here since the one I have is almost finished now."

"Do they make the gift packs up with whatever you want?" asked Pat. "I think I might take some home with me as little gifts for the girls."

"Oh yes, they'll love this kind of thing. We'll get Alison to help us when she comes in. She'll know what they'll like best. There's lots of men's stuff, too, if you want something for Roger and Jason."

"Jason, maybe. I can't really see Roger going for it, though."

"That's what I thought about Ralph at first, but he's using the soaps and deodorants, and the aftershave, too –"

"Hello, can I be of any assistance?"

They hadn't noticed the arrival of Amanda's replacement, a pretty blonde teenager, and Terri was still busy with the young man buying bath products.

"Oh, no thank you," Janet said. "We're actually just waiting for Alison. I'm Ian's mother – her fiancé?"

"Oh yes. I'm pretty new here, but I met him last week when he and Alison went to Goldie's for supper."

"Ah. And how are you liking it?"

"Terri and Alison are great to work for. I'm so glad to get the job and to get used to things before school starts. I'll be going to Sheridan and you don't need a new school and have a new job to get used to at the same time so when I saw the ad, it seemed like a good idea to apply even though I'm still lifeguarding for Parks and Rec at the outdoor pool." She followed Janet's glance toward the cash desk where a customer was standing. "Oops, I'd better go..."

"We could have had her do the gift packs while we're waiting," remarked Pat. "Maybe I should ask her when she's finished with that lady."

Janet knew that Alison would be more comfortable, at what was really their intrusion into her world, if she were able to maintain her store owner persona. She did not fully understand Alison's odd disorder, but did know that new people and situations caused problems for her and that being in her own environment made it easier for her to deal with them. This was partly the reason for bringing Pat here to meet her. Pat, like the rest of Ralph's family tended to take offence easily and, if she didn't meet Ian's fiancée while she was visiting them, would interpret it negatively. On the other hand, inviting Alison over had already resulted in delaying tactics which would have the same result if Janet didn't do something drastic. Ian had pretended that Alison had unexpectedly had to work when he came alone to dinner on Friday, but she had guessed that the real reason was Alison's anxiety.

Fortunately, before she had fully formulated her reply, Terri came back over to them, having dispatched the young man and his purchase to the girl who, Janet suddenly realized, hadn't told them her name, at the cash desk.

"I think I just heard the back door go," she said. "It'll be Alison, unless Amanda forgot something, but she'd hardly use the back door during store hours. I have to clear some things up before I go so I'm going through to the office and I'll tell her you're here. It's been nice seeing you again." She smiled and turned to go, continuing over her shoulder. "I'll tell Alison that Donna's busy on cash so can she look after Pat."

"Thanks, Terri." Janet smiled ruefully. So Terri had been aware of her dilemma all along. Well, of course – she probably understood the situation even better than Ian did.

Chapter Eight

Moira closed her eyes as the plane climbed high over Lake Superior and wondered if she'd be lucky enough to sleep during the flight. Hardly likely, she supposed. Once they were cruising and she could put the seat back, they'd start serving drinks, then lunch or a snack, whatever and she'd have to put it back up again. May as well forget it, but it would be nice to sleep.

She'd not had a proper night's sleep for the whole week and a half she'd been in Thunder Bay. Until her sister, Pauline, had arrived, she'd spent almost twenty-four hours a day at the hospital, napping in the large armchair which she supposed they supplied for the purpose in the terminal illness ward. She and Pauline had spelled each other for a couple of days and John and Hal had not arrived until after their mother had taken her final gasping breath. At least John had taken over at that point and relieved her of the job of making the funeral arrangements which she had fully been expecting to have to do when neither of her brothers could be pinned down on when they were arriving if, indeed, they were coming at all. Hal kept saying that it was another false alarm and he couldn't keep coming up with the money to fly from Vancouver to Thunder Bay every time it looked like the cancer was finally winning the battle their mother had been fighting for a year. She could understand his feelings. After all, flights back and forth to Thunder Bay had put a pretty large hole in her own savings over the last more than three years beginning with her father's stroke just after Christmas 1987 and his death three months later, but one look at her mother's emaciated body told her that there was no doubt, this time, that she had only days to live. John's problems were more business-oriented and Pauline, full of good intentions, seemed to have difficulty doing anything without her husband, Vince, who had, in the end, agreed to leave their small town real estate agency, just west of Sudbury, in the hands of their son while they drove to Thunder Bay.

John and Hal had both left the day after the funeral leaving herself and Pauline to sort out their mother's effects and ready the house, which they had put into the hands of a local real estate agent who Vince knew by reputation and who Hal remembered from high school. She had seen Pauline and Vince off yesterday and spent last night alone in the house where they had all grown up.

Tim had offered to fly up after he got back from the corporate video shoot in Montreal, which had prevented him from accompanying her in the first place. He would not have been in time for the funeral, and she knew Pauline's and Vince's company for two days would be more than he could take, so she'd said she was okay and not to worry about it. Alison had phoned the afternoon of her grandmother's death to say that Terri had gone into labour at the store and she'd taken her home because, although it was too early to go to the hospital, she didn't think it was a good idea for her to drive herself. Her mother was coming over so that Alison could get back to the store where Amanda, who had hurriedly called her neighbour to look out for her kids, was waiting to go home. Moira decided not to tell her about her grandmother until later and was thankful she'd been too concerned about Terri to remember to ask about her. The next morning she had called again to announce the safe arrival of a seven pound, two ounce boy and mother and son were fine and that Mark, who had just called her with the news, was going home to sleep after being at the hospital all night and that she and Ian would be going over to the hospital for a quick visit, in the evening, after she'd closed the store. This time, Alison did remember to ask about her grandmother and Moira told her that she had died the previous day, without mentioning when, and told her that she was not to worry about not being able to attend the funeral because she obviously couldn't leave the store and none of her cousins had been able to come up anyway.

That was not strictly true, as it turned out, since Pauline's younger daughter, Marie, who had just started attending Laurentian University, had cut classes and travelled to Thunder Bay by Greyhound bus after deciding that, since she was her grandmother's namesake, she was obligated to be there. Moira wondered if, perhaps, it was as much difficulty in settling into university life as the obligation to be there that had prompted her unexpected reaction to the death of the grandmother she'd scarcely seen in recent years and not very frequently even before. There had been some debate over the possibility of Marie driving back with her parents but she had bought a return ticket to avoid having to wait for them and left immediately after the funeral.

Moira thought about Marie's unexpected action now, as she dozed on the plane, and felt sad that her parents had scarcely known their grandchildren. Marie and her older brother and sister had spent time, on occasion, during the summer at their grandparents' house, either being taken by their parents or, as they grew older travelling by Greyhound bus, until summer jobs had taken precedence. Marie, as the youngest, had been the most recent to have done so. Neither Alison nor John's son, Jackie, had ever visited them without their parents and Hal, their youngest child, had married late and had only recently become a father for the first time, and lived way out in Vancouver, anyhow. She was suddenly overcome by an almost desolate sadness for her mother's lonely life and felt the tears spring to her eyes. She turned to look out of the window – thank heaven for the window seat – blinking them away and hoping nobody would notice. The plane was not full and there was nobody in the seat next to her. Her mother had never harboured any ill feeling about both Moira's and John's decisions to see as little as possible of their home after leaving to get jobs in the city as soon as they were old enough and despite the fact that their father had mellowed considerably in the years since he had treated them so cruelly that the Children's Aid had interceded. Pauline had been too young to remember and Hal had not been born until later when their father had stopped drinking and they were all back together again. Moira and John had been wary around their father even as grownups and John had never been able to forgive his mother for never attempting to defend either herself or her children from their father's drunken rages. Moira had come to know her mother better in the past couple of years, since her father's death, having visited her several times, once with Tim and with Alison on one occasion when they'd had driven the distance, breaking the journey and staying overnight at Pauline's as they did when the children were all younger. She could understand something of her mother's own fear of her husband and was able to see that it was a lot more difficult for women to leave their husbands and bring up their children alone in those days than it was now, and no longer felt the contempt she had as an adolescent. As a man, John had little comprehension of a mother's difficulties today, let alone then, and would never get over his unhappy childhood, she supposed. She suspected that he had only shown up for the funeral to evaluate his potential share of the estate as fodder for the ever hungry quick print business he had been trying, less than successfully, to get off the ground for the last five years. Not that the sale of the little house was likely to yield very much split four ways and there was no life insurance. When John said he'd make the arrangements, Moira, suspecting that he would not prove a good credit risk, had volunteered to have the funeral expenses billed to her on the strength of knowing that she was named as executor in the will their mother had made when her cancer had first been diagnosed. She remembered the many times John, as a young boy, had shielded her from the vicious blows of their father's belt and taken the worst of the beatings himself and knew that, under the circumstances, she could hardly blame her brother for his mercenary attitude to their mother's death.

While she had never discussed it with her, Moira was of the opinion that much of the reason for their mother's failure to make any attempt to protect them from their father was due to psychological problems of her own. When Alison's social anxiety had begun in the second year of university and they had persuaded her to undergo psychological evaluation, both she and Tim had been asked about their family background. At the time, since it was something she had conditioned herself not to think about for years, she had not mentioned the domestic trauma of her childhood and admitted only that her father was a recovered alcoholic and not even thought to mention her mother's passivity. Later, after the social phobia diagnosis and becoming aware that it had genetic implications, she had begun to wonder if, perhaps, her mother's avoidance of social contact predated the violence of her marriage as opposed to resulting from it. Most likely that had been the case and it would, obviously, have made her vulnerable to the unexpected attention paid to her by a good looking young man. It was because she realized that her parents' marriage had quite possibly resulted from the attraction of a domineering, bullying personality to a submissive, fearful one and/or vice versa that she had encouraged Ian's visits to their house when Alison was refusing to see him. She hadn't really liked coming on like some kind of old-fashioned matchmaking mother, but fortunately Ian hadn't seen it that way, and he'd turned out to be only too eager to help, thank goodness.

The clinking of the drinks trolley in the aisle near her brought Moira back to the present and, once again, she thought how nice it would be to just go to sleep.

* * * * *

Alison's biggest fear, when she was working in the store, was that of having to deal with an irate customer. It was not something that had a high likelihood of taking place and, in fact, it had never happened to her. *Envirodermics* products were of good value and unlikely to give cause for complaint. They selected part-time help carefully and did not hire until they had found applicants who had both a positive attitude towards customers, products and employers and a capacity for taking direction, thus minimizing any possibility of customer dissatisfaction with service. However, just the anticipatory fear of not being in control would cause her find some reason for needing to be in the office, when a not entirely happy-looking customer came into the store, and hoping that he or she would not demand to see the manager. Usually the perceived hostility was just that and the customer's visit would turn out to be entirely without incident, but the fear was always there. She wished she wasn't so sensitive to peoples' demeanour. There were a thousand reasons for someone to feel disgruntled with none of them involving personal criticism of her.

Today, she was feeling particularly vulnerable. She knew it was largely due to fatigue. She had worked too many ten and twelve hour days during the last few weeks trying to discourage Terri from coming in so much as the baby's due date loomed closer. Upon reflection, she could have left the training of the new daytime part-timer to Terri since she insisted on coming in anyway and was a much better teacher. Now that the baby had arrived and, while she would be coming into the office to go over things, Terri would definitely not be working in the store for the next few months. Accordingly, Alison was drawing up a timetable which, barring illness on anybody's part, they were going to firmly adhere to.

They had prevailed upon Amanda to become an Acting Manager while Terri was away, opening the store each weekday morning and working the morning hours with the new part-timer. She, herself, would come in after lunch, look after the banking and administrative details while the daytime staff was still here, and work with the student part-timer – two of them, on Thursdays and Fridays – until closing. This would be the last morning she worked for the next few weeks. Either she or Terri always worked in the evening, since whoever closed up was also responsible for putting the cash in the night deposit at the bank and everything else in their own safe, a responsibility which they both agreed was an unfair burden on a student part-timer. On the rare occasions when this had not been possible, Amanda or a family member had come in to do it but they didn't really like imposing on anybody unless it was really necessary.

Their Saturday staff was comprised solely of students which meant she had to open and close but the mall itself closed at six making it a shorter working day. In any case, they had decided, some months ago, to promote one of the girls, Natalie, who had worked for them both as a high school and university student and was now in her second year at the nearby U of T Erindale campus, to officially supervise the others on Saturdays and to have a key, alarm system password and the code for the safe, enabling her to open up. With one or other of them being on call for her and somebody available to go in to close up, this enabled them to be away from the store, even at the same time now and again at the weekend. While she was not intending to be away on the next few Saturdays, Alison was glad they had Natalie in place so that she wouldn't have the pressure of *having* to come in after already having worked a solid week. She thought about the current lobbying for Sunday shopping and hoped it would never happen, although she supposed it was probably inevitable. Hopefully they'd be able to put the same system in place with a different supervisor for each of the weekend days when it did happen. There was no way she was going to be responsible for one student getting stressed out by too much responsibility.

Inking in her own name, Amanda's, the new part-timer, Christine's, and Natalie's, she found that her long mental conversation with herself had completely calmed her down and she was no longer fearfully anticipating having to deal with complaining customers. The one who had triggered the fear must be long gone by now, whatever her problem – if, indeed, there had been one – having been dealt with by Amanda. She pencilled in the names of the student part-timers for the next month, with instructions to ink in the names as they were or organize any changes needed with somebody else, then pinned the chart up in the coffee area where everybody would see it and confirm their hours. She put on a fresh pot of coffee while she was there, then turned to go back into the office just as Amanda came through from the store.

"Just coming to get a coffee before Christine goes for lunch," she said.

"Bad news," laughed Alison, "you'll have to wait. I just put a fresh pot on. Look, I want to start the new system from Monday, so you'll be opening and I won't be in until after lunch. Are you okay with that?"

"Yes, of course. I expected you to do it this week instead of working twelve hour days. You'll wear yourself out."

"I would have done actually but I wasn't completely satisfied that Christine would be a help rather than a hindrance. No reflection on her. I just don't think I'm a terribly good teacher. We should have started training her earlier but, that's hindsight for you. Anyway, you're quite confident that she has enough product knowledge to manage okay if you have to come back here to take a shipment or go to lunch, whatever?"

"Oh sure. I've only served when she's been busy with somebody all week, so she must have experienced anything that might crop up by now," Amanda said, rinsing her coffee mug. "And I only ever take my half hour lunch if I have to pick up something in the mall, but I can leave anything like that until later so I'll be right here eating my sandwich if she needs me."

"Well, you'll have a chance to practice working on your own with her today. My mom's coming home from Thunder Bay and my dad called earlier to say he won't be able to get out to the airport in time so I have to go and pick my mother up at one thirty and drive her home."

"How is she?" Amanda asked, aware of Alison's grandmother's death.

"Oh, okay. They're not a close family and her mother did have cancer so it's not really traumatic or anything. I mean, I imagine it's still hard to take but not as bad as if my grandmother were a big part of our lives. I hardly knew her. It sounds as if they were a pretty dysfunctional family. My mom never talks about it but my cousin, Jackie – her brother's son – told me some stuff once that he got from his father. She and my uncle were in foster care for quite a while as kids... So, anyway," Alison shrugged, "it's not as upsetting as it would be otherwise. Coffee's ready."

She hoped Amanda didn't think she was being flippant but she really didn't want to get into a conversation about her mother's family, of which she knew so little anyway. She actually suspected that her mother's grief for the might-have-beens was likely to be as upsetting as actual grief. She felt a bit that way herself, remembering being ten or eleven and envying her cousins who got to stay at their grandparents' house without their parents and wondering why she had not been invited. Her father had discouraged her from questioning her mother and, later, the conversation with Jackie had given her enough insight into the situation to understand why there was tension on the few occasions when they visited her mother's parents in contrast to the warmth that greeted them on visits to her father's parents in the years before their deaths when she was in high school.

"Well," she said, holding up the carafe, after pouring her coffee, to indicate she'd pour Amanda's if she'd put her mug down, "I have work to do. Call me if you need me." She poured Amanda's, put the carafe into the coffee maker and went back into the office to review the inventory records and figure out what she should order for next week, wishing she was as good as Terri at deciding what would move fast at this particular time and which products didn't rate money being tied up in them at present.

Chapter Nine

"They inherited a bunch of PS2s when the head office upgraded," Ian was telling Tim, "and I have to get the entire staff plugged into the new corporate network and get all these people, who are still doing their accounting manually and don't have a clue about computers... Well, get them equipped for the future, I guess. That's how the CEO put it. I tried to get through to him that he'll have to upgrade everything in, probably, in less than two years. In other words, the whole thing's false economy. But, anyway, it'll keep me downtown for a few weeks which'll be nice after having to drive out to Oshawa every day all summer. I can even use the subway and get some exercise walking over to the bus stop."

"I'm always glad to be able to leave the car at home when I can," said Tim, sipping his glass of wine. "How long does that kind of job last?"

"An installation starting from scratch? Oh... including initial exploration and analysis, sometimes two or three months, sometimes five or six. It depends on the organization, what software best does the job and how much work is involved in customizing it and then how well the staff makes the transition. You have to be on call for them, too, for however long it takes. My trips out to Oshawa are by no means over and I had to spend a day over in Guelph last week where I did an installation last year."

"Software glitches or human error?"

"Bit of both. This was human error. It takes some of the older – no offence intended – employees a while to catch on. They've spent their working lives balancing manual ledgers and panic because the old methods of tracking down an error don't apply any more and often the mistake's not even noticed until it's compounded to the extent that there's obviously something wrong somewhere and it has to be the system screwing up, so send for those people who installed it – that sort of thing..."

"But you enjoy it. I mean, you don't regret your choice of career?"

Since Ian had mentioned that he was going to be working in the building where Tim's company was located, Tim had suggested they get together for lunch sometime. They were eating in the steak house, on the building's ground floor, which was convenient and provided a reasonably priced meal. Ian had been glad when he called and found that Tim was available for lunch today because he'd been having a frustrating morning with his client whose heart was obviously not entirely in joining the world of information technology. As if there were a choice! That's what some of the older people, clinging to their ledgers and cheque registers had difficulty understanding. There was no longer any choice. To stay in business in the nineties you had to embrace technology. It was as simple as that.

"Oh no," he replied to Tim's question. "I like being a pioneer. Well, that's romanticizing it a bit. The real pioneers were the guys on the mainframes in the sixties, I suppose. What I mean is getting small and medium-sized businesses networked and set up within environments they can control themselves as opposed to the old coding and keypunching of the seventies and floppy disc world of the eighties. What can be done with personal computers is in its infancy now but this is the decade when business communications are going to change completely."

"You're right. No doubt about it. I meant, in terms of trying to get through to all the people who must almost start their careers all over again in order to keep their jobs or any other job, come to that..."

"You mean don't they all hate me?"

"Something like that," Tim grinned, as their waiter brought their steaks and took away their salad bowls.

"You're right. It's hard feeling resented. People know it's their company's decision, not the systems guy's, but some of them do tend to take out their feelings on you," Ian told him. He drank some water and began to eat his steak. "Some are really eager to get to it, though – the ones who can see the future and invested in Commodore or Atari home computers, learned a bit of Basic programming and enrolled their kids in computer camp during the summer. How do you find people adapting in your industry?"

"Sadly my look into the future sees advertising creative getting turned over to the kids graduating from the new design courses in community colleges and my generation taking early retirement on Salt Spring Island or whatever. Not me, though. As you know, I got myself a Mac as soon as *Pagemaker* was developed and taught myself to use it, but that's not the norm. Most art directors want to hang on to their marker rendering pads and hate the move to improperly trained people setting type. I tend to agree there, in that typesetting is going to become a lost art. Copywriters, generally, are more enthused – not just from the point of view of writing copy to fit space without having to get into counting characters and doing the mental arithmetic – but with being able to better communicate their ideas to art directors, but they're even more incensed about typesetters becoming a dying breed. There's really no doubt about the fact that print medias are not going to look so good for a bit as the conversion to digital production takes place. It'll right itself as time goes on with better applied arts courses and improved and more functional software – *user-friendly* as you guys put it."

"User-friendliness," said Ian. "That's going to be key to everything, but it's coming – the whole future world the way we used to read about it in science fiction." He grinned. "Romanticizing again. It'll be a lot of hard work really for all of us, other than the kids growing up over the past few years playing computer games. They're the ones who'll be best equipped –"

"– for your *brave new world*?"

"That's one way of putting it."

"Are you getting into this new bulletin board thing?"

"You mean the Internet. I've had access since university days, but it'll be getting more user-friendly soon, too, with the new hypertext language. In fact, it'll be completely commercial in a few years."

"I don't know what you're talking about exactly, but I believe you," laughed Tim. "How's your steak?"

"Good," Ian replied. "I won't have to bother cooking something for supper after this. A sandwich will do."

"How are you managing with Alison working every evening?"

"Oh, I wasn't complaining. I'm perfectly competent to cook my own supper. My mother looked into the future and foresaw that women would no longer be relegated to the kitchen and men would need to know how to fend for themselves. It's just that it's not much fun cooking for one so I've gone back to making lunch my main meal which is what I did before she moved in."

"She's okay, though? I mean aside from the long hours."

"She's not really working longer hours than usual," Ian explained. "It's just that she's doing all the afternoon and evening hours instead of alternating mornings and evenings with Terri. They have to learn to delegate though, both of them. There's really no reason for not having an employee close up two or three evenings a week so that they don't run into this problem when one or other of them is away. Granted this is the first time it's happened on a longer term basis and, thankfully, Alison is not working all day, everyday as they've each done in the past when the other has been away. They've got Amanda taking charge in the mornings now and one of the young girls is looking after things on Saturdays, so it's much more organized."

"I think Alison knows her limitations. The last thing she can afford is to get stressed out and lose her confidence when Terri's not available."

"Exactly," said Ian. "Now that they have the store established and the debts paid down, they have to let up a bit and pay someone else to do the job instead of feeling inexpendable and getting pressured."

"Alison was telling her mother that the new woman they've got working with Amanda isn't averse to working evenings so that'll be helpful if it works out. The main reason they insist on one of them being there to close up is because of taking the cash over to the night deposit..."

"They'd rather get mugged themselves than have one of the students get into trouble. I can appreciate that, but a Mississauga shopping mall is hardly New York City."

"I think it's a bit more than that," said Tim. "They don't want a student having the responsibility for the entire process of stashing money for the night, not just getting the bulk of the cash into the night deposit. It would mean the kid having the safe combination and setting the alarm, etc. then being at front and centre if they did get broken into – all that sort of thing..."

"Roll on the day of the computer," laughed Ian. "Bank accounts, credit cards will all get processed immediately and there'll be less and less cash around to worry about."

Tim smiled.

"Coffee and dessert, sir?" asked the waiter, clearing the table.

"Just coffee."

"Same for me, please," added Ian.

* * * * *

Mark pulled into the Frasers' driveway and brought the car to a gentle stop, hoping not to wake the baby who had been lulled to sleep while they were driving.

"I'll get him," he told Terri. "You grab the equipment."

Terri grinned. He was referring to the diaper bag and the reference was still too new to have worn out its amusement value. She got out of the car and picked it up from the floor behind her seat while Mark pushed his own seat back forward and unhooked the infant carrier from the belt in the seat behind.

"Sound asleep," he whispered, straightening up.

"I'll go ahead," said Terri, "and let them know we're here so that they don't wake him up when they open the door."

She walked down the driveway to the kitchen door and knocked gently, putting her finger to her lips as Moira opened the door.

"He was being a bit fussy before we came out and finally fell asleep in the car, so we're hoping he'll stay that way for a bit," she explained.

Moira laughed. "Sure. Take him through to the living room, Mark," she said quietly as Mark came into view with the baby carrier. "How are you, Terri?" she continued, giving Terri a quick hug. "You're looking good. How does being a mother feel? Here, let me take your coat."

Terri put down the diaper bag and shrugged out of her jacket which Moira took through to the hall closet. Terri followed her.

"It seems pretty lazy driving such a short distance but I didn't think so much night air would be good for him on the way back."

"No, you're probably right. You go ahead and loosen up his clothes and we'll leave him in there where it's quiet and we can all have a drink in the dining room. Here comes Tim, now"

"Hello there, Terri," said Tim, coming down the stairs. "How are you? And where have you hidden the offspring? I'm eager to see him at last."

Tim had yet to see the baby. Moira had dropped by with a baby gift, shortly after Terri brought Daniel home from the hospital, and extended the invitation to supper for as soon as Terri felt she could cope.

"He's sleeping," Moira told him. "Mark's taken him into the living room. Here's Mark now."

Mark had come into the hall from the living room while Terri went in to loosen Daniel's clothes without waking him up.

"Can you take Mark's coat, Tim," she continued," and we'll have a drink in the dining room so as not to disturb him before dinner." She went into the kitchen to pick up the diaper bag and take it into Terri, while Tim, after hanging Mark's coat over the bannister led the way through the kitchen to the dining room. The Frasers' dining room was large and had a small sitting area at one end of it. Easier access from the kitchen tended to result in its being used more often than the living room.

"Here," Moira whispered to Terri. She set the bag beside the end of the couch where Mark had placed the baby carrier. "He's so sweet..."

"He wasn't very sweet before we came out," Terri said in a low voice, stepping back from opening up the baby's blanket so that he wouldn't get too hot. "I was ready to call you and cancel. Then Mark suggested that the car ride would likely get him to sleep."

"Probably just gas," said Moira. "Let's go and get that drink. He'll be quite safe there and we should hear him if he wakes up."

"Oh, we'll hear him," rejoined Terri. "He has a powerful set of lungs. Did we get here early or is Alison late?" she asked as she followed Moira into the dining room.

"Oh, they should be here any minute. Are you back to drinking gin and tonic?"

"Mmm, yes. That should hit the spot. It's nice being able to have the odd drink again. Just very weak, though"

"Can you get Terri a weak gin and tonic, Tim? And maybe shove a bit more ice into my drink there beside you, please."

She continued speaking as she indicated for Terri to sit on the couch. "They weren't scaring everybody half to death with threats of birth defects and foetal alcohol syndrome back in the good old days when I was pregnant but I suppose it's better to be safe than sorry. Was it difficult to do? I mean, not that I'm a great boozer or anything, but I find a drink a godsend when I'm really stressed out or feeling down."

Terri grinned.

"Oh, it wasn't that difficult," she said. "I'm not sure about all the scare tactics but, as you say, it's better to be safe than sorry. "

"There you are, Terri," said Tim, handing over her drink. He picked up his own glass and held it up. "Official toast to Daniel," he said.

They all joined him. "To Daniel."

"Mark was just telling me about what an ideal father he's turning out to be..."

"That's not what I said..." protested Mark.

"Actually he is pretty good," laughed Terri. "He's already learned to change a diaper and I know for certain my father never did such a thing. Bet you didn't, either."

"Well, men weren't expected to when your generation were babies..."

"Some excuse!"

"... anyway, I was afraid of sticking a pin in her. I remember doing the disposable ones a couple of times when she was older."

"I don't really think Alison would be too enthusiastic about all this talk of changing her diapers if she were here," remarked Moira.

"Where's she got to?" asked Tim. "I thought she was the one who wanted to eat at seven thirty so that she'd have plenty of time to get home after closing up the store, and seven was rushing it a bit. It's seven thirty now."

"So they've done themselves out of a drink and a lovely conversation about you changing or not changing her diapers. I don't really think she'll mind missing that."

"Sounds like them now," said Mark, "unless somebody's breaking in at the back door."

"Hello. We're here." Alison's voice came from the kitchen doorway. "Sorry we're late."

Tim jumped up and went into the kitchen.

"Ssh. Sleeping baby in the house," they heard him saying as he went.

"I'll go and finish the dinner," said Moira getting up just as Alison came in. "Hello, dear. Was there a problem at the store?"

"No, no. Ian's car was acting up so we decided to be safe and go back and get mine. Terr-ee, how are you?" She hugged Terri who had risen from her seat. "Hi Mark. Where's Daniel?"

"In the living room," Terri told her. "We can go and see him if you don't wake him up."

"Sure. But we can let him wake up before you go, can't we?"

"Of course. I just don't want him disturbing dinner. For my sake as much as for the rest of you."

They both laughed and went into the living room.

"He's so sweet..." Alison whispered.

"That's what Moira said, too, but he's not so sweet when he wakes up feeling gassy–"

"Oh, you put the sleepers I gave you on him. That's the real Winnie the Pooh, not the Disney one..."

"You mean the real original illustration. The real Winnie the Pooh was a real bear..."

"You know what I mean. Anyway, he looks cute in them."

"The dinner's ready, and I think your mom's a bit worried about it getting overcooked, so I think we should go and help her get it on the table."

"Yes, you're right. I'm starving.

" Me, too."

They returned to the dining room and went through to the kitchen and helped Moira, who had already told the men to sit down and look after pouring the wine. When everything was on the table, Tim, once again, toasted 'the sleeping infant' and they all raised their glasses.

"Now, let's eat," he said. "I'm starving." Terri and Alison looked at each other and giggled. "What's the matter?"

"Nothing," said Alison. "We just said the same thing, that's all."

"Well, you're the culprit, you and Ian. What's wrong with your car, anyway?"

"The battery light was on," Ian told him. "Must be the generator, I suppose. We were only down the street from the apartment when we realized and figured it best to take it back so that there wouldn't be any trouble starting it to take it to be fixed. Alison's going to take it to the Canadian Tire by the mall on Monday as long as it starts okay and I'll go and fetch her if it's not done by the time she needs it to get home."

"I've done that before with my own car," said Alison. "It usually works out okay and it's convenient. The service managers – they have women there, two, anyway – come into the store so I've been going there for oil changes and things for a while. Terri does, too."

"Ah-ha," said Terri. "I prefer to go to people who buy our stuff because I feel more comfortable about not getting gypped, not that I'm accusing everybody else of cheating me, but women do tend to get taken when it comes to car repairs..."

"You can say that again," said Moira. "If I had a dollar for every time I've been talked into getting something done to my car which didn't really need doing, I'd be, if not rich, pretty well off, at least."

"Well, my reasons for going there aren't so noble," Alison admitted. "I just go to people I know because I can't work up the courage to got to people I don't know. I have to cross my fingers and just hope whatever's wrong isn't something that mean's it has to go to a dealer or something like that..."

"Don't worry," said Ian. "If it is, I'll drive your car over when I get home from work and then take it to what's it called, the dealer down the road. They'll be closed but you can put the keys in a slot and call them the next day."

"Cars are more trouble than they're worth," remarked Tim. "So let's talk about something else. That was good," he added, moving his empty salad dish and spooning some rice onto his plate. "Here let me do yours, Terri."

"Thanks," Terri said holding up her plate.

"Mark? You go ahead and help yourself to the chicken, Terri."

"Is that the Bombay Butter Chicken, Mom?" asked Alison and, not waiting for a reply, continued. "Your going to love this, everyone. I found the recipe in a magazine and made it for us one day when I was feeling ambitious."

"Yes, it's really good," agreed Ian.

"I cut back a bit on the spices," said Moira. "Because I wasn't sure how Terri and Mark felt about them and I know Tim doesn't like things too spicy."

"I thought you said you weren't getting fed, Ian, last week

when we had lunch," Tim observed, relinquishing the rice to him.

"It was a Sunday," grinned Ian, then responded to Alison's questioning look as he spooned rice onto her plate. "It's okay. It was nothing derogatory. Tim's just teasing. Alison's a great cook and our freezer's always full of frozen portions that she makes up for days when it's not convenient to cook."

"It's the only way to go," Terri nodded. "If you don't get into the habit of making extra and freezing things, you end up buying frozen entrées and eating too much salt. Talking about evenings, Alison, I can come in to close up now if you want to take a break. Mark can manage Daniel for a couple of hours or so and it'll be nice for you and Ian to have supper together again, maybe even go out to supper. You've been working every evening for five weeks now. You must want a break."

"Mom came in and did it a couple of times, so I have had a break. If you're sure, I might take you up on it one day next week, but what I'd really like is for you to come in and go over the accounting. You can bring Daniel in as we planned..."

"Oh, I will. I was going to suggest we try it on Wednesday or Thursday this week and see how it works out."

"That's good. I don't want to compound anything I may have done wrong. I'm going to have Natalie close up next Saturday – you know, not go in at all and see how it goes. I'll be as close as the phone if she needs me. I was thinking of trying it today, but then Mom invited us all for supper, so I didn't want that to get messed up if I'd ended up having to go over to sort something out after six. I did have her do everything today and last Saturday, too, so she should be okay without me being there next week. What d'you think?"

"It's actually probably a good idea to get her started doing it now if we're going to at all. Christmas hours will be starting on Saturdays next month and I think we'd both feel better about her depositing cash and locking up, etc. at six rather than nine." She broke off, looking from Tim to Ian. "What are you grinning at?"

"Nothing, nothing," said Ian. "Okay, I'll be honest. When we had lunch last week, Tim and I were talking about how you girls – ladies – had to learn to delegate." Then he added. "That was after the bit about me not getting fed, only I didn't actually say that,"

"Hey," said Alison. "I'm not sure I like all this talking about us that you seem to have been doing."

"They're right though, Alison," Terri mused. "About the delegating, I mean, not whether or not Ian gets fed. I'm sure that was just a joke. Now that I've experienced what's involved in looking after a new baby, I know that I won't want to be working the hours I have in the past and I know, for sure now that I can't count on Daniel behaving if I bring him with me as we planned. And you can't pick up the slack indefinitely."

"Well, we've made a start. Amanda's now opening every weekday morning and Natalie's supervising the part-timers and opening up on Saturdays and, next week, she gets to close up, too. Then, if you can come in six to nine, say Wednesday and Thursday the next couple of weeks, I can work with Amanda in the mornings and put Christine on for the afternoons and you can go through closing procedures with her. How's that?"

"Sounds like we'll be able to retire."

"Hardly that, with Christmas shopping coming up, but having two people able to close up will certainly solve a few problems. We'll even be able to go on holiday for more than a few days eventually."

"I'm glad you said that and not me, because Mark and I really want to go to England for Christmas."

"My parents..." explained Mark. "They naturally want to see Daniel."

"But, of course you must," put in Moira. "Ian and Tim and I can always help Alison if she needs us and there's Stella, too. That'll be so nice, and you'll be able to see your aunt, too. And, now that we've got all the big business problems settled, who's for crème brulée?"

Chapter Ten

"Do you really think it necessary?" Tim asked.

"Yes, I do. I was watching her when they were talking about it. I thought maybe you were, too, with the way you changed the subject so niftily."

"No, not really. I just don't like car repair conversations. They depress me. Are you sure you just haven't exaggerated the anxiety by mulling it over all day yesterday?"

"No. I just know when something's triggering it. Anyway, I don't need to be in the office until this afternoon so I'll just call her and offer to go with her. If I'm wrong, she'll say so. You, my love, on the other hand, ought to be on your way." She put her arms around him and kissed him goodbye in the open doorway. "Good luck with the presentation."

"Thanks. Let me know what happens."

Tim walked over to the garage and she waited until he'd backed his car out and down the driveway before closing the door and going to the kitchen phone. It was seven forty-five. She didn't imagine Alison would be taking the car yet, since it meant being at the store even before opening time and she would be there until nine this evening. But she'd better call now, just in case.

The phone rang a few times and she couldn't decide whether Alison's anxiety was preventing her from answering or if she was in the shower or something. Ian had left, obviously – probably to walk over to get the bus into the subway since he was working downtown just now, apparently.

"Hallo there. It's me," she said, when Alison finally answered. "I thought you might like company taking Ian's car in this morning. We can go and have coffee or brunch or something so that you're not stuck at the store all morning as well as all afternoon and evening."

The relief in Alison's voice was audible and Moira knew she had been right.

"That'll be great, Mom. I'd really appreciate the company. Are you sure you have the time?"

"I don't need to be in the office until after lunch and I'm not too crazy about you driving it over there. I didn't want to interfere when you were telling us about it on Saturday but – well, what happens if it stalls and there's not enough juice left in the battery to start it again?" She decided to make it sound as if her worry was over the physical problem of a car breakdown rather than Alison's likely panic attack in either the event of there being one or at the Canadian Tire Store, when she got it there, if one of the people she knew was not working this morning. Going in there cold was not the same as mentioning to the service manager, who she knew, that she needed to bring her car in and being told when to bring it over.

"I'm sure Ian would never have taken me up on the offer if that was likely. I mean, there's no reason for it to stall, but I would feel happier if someone was with me. What time were you thinking?"

"I have to get a shower and dress, so how about if I get over there in forty-five minutes to an hour?"

"That sounds good. We parked it in the visitors' parking, in case it ended up having to be boosted, so I'll meet you there."

"What were you going to do if it did needed boosting?"

"Ian said to just leave it if it didn't start and he'd look after it this evening."

"Well, that's what we'll do. I'm too chicken to use booster cables, anyway, and I'd be afraid of you getting them the wrong way around, too."

"I know how to do it, Mom, but I'm like you and would rather not. But the whole point of turning back and getting my car on Saturday evening was to make sure that it *would* start all right. Anyway, I'll see you in a while."

"Okay. See you shortly."

Moira hung up the phone. Well, she'd managed to handle the situation without putting her daughter on the defensive, thank goodness. Alison, perfectly aware that she was fighting anticipatory panic was probably trying to psych herself up to deal with communicating the problem with the car to the service people. Past experience, however, in trying to help Alison through phobic reactions had shown her it was better not to mention the real reason for offering to come with her.

She quickly put her coffee mug and Tim's breakfast things into the dishwasher and turned on the rinse cycle, then ran upstairs to shower and get dressed. She rather wondered why Ian hadn't come up with some reason for not taking Alison up on her suggestion that she look after the car. He was usually so keen to protect her from anxiety-producing situations, too eager sometimes. Maybe he just thought that since she had become so accustomed to the mall and its environs that it really wouldn't be a problem. True the mall did not intimidate Alison the way it would have done had she not worked in the store and become very familiar with it, but Moira knew that there were still days when it was the hardest thing in the world for her daughter bear the critical scrutiny which she, as a social phobic, perceived she was being given, however many times she told herself that nobody was interested in what she was doing. She also knew that, however well she had arranged the work schedule at the store, the pressure of Terri's absence was causing Alison a fair amount of stress and lowering her resistance to the panic and anxiety that would always threaten her in such circumstances.

A short time later, she was pulling into the driveway to the apartment building and spotted Alison walking towards the visitors' parking area. She tapped her horn lightly. Alison turned and came round to the driver's window.

"If you want to wait here while I pull it out, Mom, you can follow me," she said.

"Sure. Which way are you going, just in case you get out of my sight at some intersection or something?"

"I thought the way I usually go would be best. Up to Burnhamthorpe, get on 427 and up to 401 and along, then back down. We won't be stopping and starting with traffic lights since it's mostly highway."

"Right. Good thinking. You go ahead and I'll be right behind you."

Moira waited while Alison started the car, then followed her out to the mall in Mississauga without incident. They went to the service counter together and Moira could tell by the way

Alison tensed that neither of the women she knew was among the personnel writing up repair orders.

"Morning ladies," said the rather too cheerful young man who was the first service person to become available.

"Morning," said Moira.

"How can I help you?"

"I - we," Alison took a deep breath, "my battery light's on. We think it's probably the generator. You have me on the computer, but for my own car. This is my fiancé's."

"Phone number?"

She gave him her number at the store.

"Fraser?"

"That's right. This is – here, it'll be easier for you to get everything from the ownership," Alison said, handing him the car's ownership certificate and the man busied himself keying in the order.

"Right," he said, finally. "Here we are." He handed back the certificate. "And this is the right phone number?" He pointed to the screen.

"That's right."

"Okay. We'll just wait for it to print out and, if you'll just give me your key..."

Alison handed over the key and signed the repair order when he tore it off the printer.

"We'll call you just as soon as we know what's going on," said the service man.

"Thanks," said Alison, turning to go.

Moira smiled at him and followed her. "Now let's go and get that coffee," she said. "And I don't know about you, but I could do with a muffin or, maybe a bagel... What about Tim Hortons?"

"D'you mind if we get it to go, Mom? Eat it in the store. In the office?"

Moira, who had suggested Tim Hortons, thinking they could use the drive-through if, as she half expected, Alison didn't not want the added anxiety of eating in a restaurant, nodded and they made their way to her car.

By the time they reached the store with coffee and toasted bagels, Alison was, once more, in control of herself. She tapped on the door and signalled to Amanda who was busy with pre-opening chores, to let them in.

"Hi. You're early," said Amanda.

"I had a car problem to look after. We're going to have our breakfast in the office," Alison replied. "You remember my mother?"

"Hello Amanda," said Moira, "I don't really mind if you don't – remember me, I mean..."

"Of course I do. Hello. It's a little belated but I'd like to say how sorry I was to hear about your mother. I don't know what I'd do if I lost my mother..."

"Thank you. It's something we have to expect when we get into our fifties. You have a way to go yet..."

Amanda smiled.

"Getting closer all the time, though," she said. "Did something happen this morning?"

"Nothing awful. I just followed Alison over in case anything went wrong on the way. It's Ian's car, not Alison's. Probably needs a new generator. I'm just quoting everybody else. I'm no mechanic. How are the children getting on at school this year?"

"Oh, fine. They both seem to be doing really well."

"I'd better follow Alison through before our toasted bagels get cold." Moira excused herself. "See you later."

"This is Christine, Mom," said Alison when she reached the storage area, where Christine was fetching some cartons to take into the store. "Christine – my mother, Moira Fraser."

"Hello Christine," said Moira. "Nice to meet you. Are you liking it here?"

"Oh, yes. It's great here and I love the products. It's so nice to be able to sell something that you really believe in. And it's such a nice place to work and what really impressed me was the time Alison and Terri took teaching me all about everything –"

"Come along, Mom," called Alison from the office. "Your toasted bagel's going to be pretty cold and soggy."

"I'll let you get back to work, Christine, and go and eat my breakfast. Nice meeting you," laughed Moira.

"Nice to have met you, too," said Christine, carrying her boxes through to the store.

"She tends to talk a lot," explained Alison when they were settled and able to eat their bagels. "It's hard getting away from her sometimes. She's good with the customers, though and that's what counts."

Relieved and happy to see Alison in store manager mode, Moira sipped her coffee and unwrapped her bagel.

"She's the one who you're intending to have close up?"

Alison nodded, chewing her bagel.

"She seems dependable. Really likes it here, by the sound of things."

"It's not just the closing up, though, in the evening – the students have to be supervised, too. Apart from Natalie, they're all fairly recent. We tend to lose them with the school year because they get full time summer jobs or, even if they stay, they start university somewhere else. We have one girl who's going to Sheridan and two high school girls, not all working at the same time, of course. One on Monday, Tuesday and Wednesday and two on Thursday, Friday and Saturday, along with whoever's supervising – up until now Terri or me. Natalie's managing Saturdays fine now, though, which has actually created extra hours for the others. I mean, I've only been coming in, basically, just to close up, so she's *replacing* Terri or myself which means somebody has to replace her. So, I suppose that's really three students on Saturdays."

"So, it's costing quite a bit more in wages, with Christine, too. And I imagine you're having to pay both Amanda and Natalie more. Can you afford it?"

"That's Terri's department, but she says we should be okay, though now that she's talking about working fewer hours and we'll be paying more out permanently, I'm not so sure. Seeing how we do over Christmas is the key to that, I guess. To tell the truth, I'm a bit worried about it. Natalie's pay is not really more because when we suggested she had the experience to supervise the other girls on Saturdays, she agreed on the condition she *only* worked Saturdays. I imagine the raise gives her enough money for her needs without having to put in more hours which can be better put to use studying. But, altogether, all the extra pay works out to almost as much as one of our salaries – Terri's or mine, I mean – and, if Terri works less and we continue paying it out, we're not going to be able to meet the bank loan payments."

"Maybe that's what she means by *'okay'* – paying less to the bank. You have the collateral now to spread that out more."

"I'd prefer to get debt-free."

"That's not the way businesses are run today. You're still building, anyway. The store – the whole mall – is less than three years old."

"I just hate paying the interest to the bank, though. Maybe we should have paid the bank loan instead of paying you and Dad back. I wouldn't have minded paying the interest to you, but Terri insisted that our money, yours and mine, too, get paid back first."

"You can't blame her. If it had been the other way around, you'd want to even the playing field as soon as you could, too."

"When you put it that way, I see what you mean."

Moira stood up and threw her coffee carton and wrappings into the waste basket.

"I'd better be on my way. You're going to have a long day."

"Oh, I'll be leaving them to it." Alison nodded in the direction of the store. "I have to get up to date with the bills if Terri's coming in this week to start getting it all entered properly."

"Okay, I'll leave you to it, then," Moira said, picking up her purse and turning to the doorway.

"I'll walk you out," said Alison. "And, Mom –"

Moira turned back to her.

"Thanks – thanks for helping me."

Moira hugged her. "You're welcome, dear," she said. "If you don't have time to go over to pay them, tell Ian to come over in your car before closing time."

"I'd already figured on doing that as a contingency plan," Alison grinned. "Anyway, Cheryl or Sue will be working by the time it's ready and either of them would expect me to go over."

Moira smiled. "Okay. Look, don't worry about coming through with me. I want to pick up some of that lip balm I like while I'm here. It won't be long before the winter weather starts drying us out! So, I'll see you later. Have fun with the bills. Bye-bye."

1994

Chapter Eleven

"But you'll like the big school, Daniel. I know you will."

"How do you know?"

Terri was surprised at her son questioning her reassurance. Must be a new stage, she thought. How *did* she know?

"Well, Daniel. It's the same big school Mommy went to and it was fun meeting new friends and having a new teacher. You'll see."

"I don't want to see. I like *my* school and I don't want to go to the big school. In any case," Daniel continued challengingly, with his head to one side, "Becky will need me to look after her."

"Becky doesn't need to be looked after. There are teachers to do that. You didn't have a big brother to look after you when you first went to nursery school, did you?"

"I don't remember."

"Well, you don't have one, not like lucky Becky. She has you."

"Yes, she is lucky, isn't she?"

"Ah-ha."

"She needs me to beat up kids who make fun of her."

"Why would kids make fun of her, Daniel?"

"She doesn't talk right and she wets her pants."

"She's only two. Actually, she hasn't wet her pants for a long time and the nursery school doesn't take you if it's likely. Anyway, *you* didn't talk right and *you* wet your pants sometimes when you were two."

"No, I didn't."

"Yes, you did. And so did Tristan and so did Michael but you're all grown up now and ready for junior kindergarten in September. You can stay at the nursery school if you like but Tristan and Michael and all your friends will be at the big school."

Daniel looked at her as if he didn't believe her.

"It's true, Daniel. When kids get to be four, they go to junior kindergarten at the big school and you'll be four in September –"

"Tristan's already four. I went to his party."

"Yes, that's right. And he'll be coming to your party in September and you'll all be going to the big school by then."

"Will a clown come when I have my party, like at Tristan's?"

"That can be arranged," said Terri, "but it's only June now and your birthday's not until the middle of September, so we'll talk about it later. Right now we're going to see how this kindergarten looks. Now hold my hand while we cross the road."

"Will Tristan be there?"

"Daniel, you know that Becky's at Tristan's house and we're going to look after his baby when Crystal takes him to see the school this afternoon."

"Why?"

"Why what?"

"Why is Tristan going this afternoon?"

"Because they're doing it alphabetically which means in order of the letter your name starts with and we begin with 'H' and –"

"'H' makes huh–huh–huh for Havers and he's 'P' – puh–puh–puh for Parsons. He's a 'P' – pee–pee–pee. Mommy, why's pee–pee a letter?"

"Don't be silly, Daniel. Now, come along and stop talking if you can't walk and talk, too."

Terri was beginning to wish that she'd driven over. It had seemed a good idea to walk since that's what Daniel would be doing every afternoon when the new school year began. She was actually beginning to question the wisdom of the entire venture. It was all very well for the school to have orientation mornings for junior kindergartners-to-be, but would a three and half-year-old remember much about what he saw in June when he started school in September? Well, at least it would get Daniel used to the idea that he was not going to be at the nursery school when his little sister started going there.

The school now bore little resemblance to the way it had looked when she and Alison started kindergarten. A large modern extension, dwarfing the original building, had been added to accommodate a student population significantly increased due to the nearby condominium apartment development. The kindergarten area was quite separate from the rest of the school and housed in a large pod with two separate classroom areas and various play areas common to both. Senior kindergarten classes were in session with children in one area of the pod busily making play dough animals to be housed in a large model farmyard and children in the other area making Father's Day cards. The school vice principal showed them around then set Daniel and the other five children in the group of visitors to work on constructing a fort with the large plastic cubes and tubes in the *building zone* in the care of a teaching assistant, while she taught their parents 'a thing or two about the junior kindergarten program'. The children obviously liked the idea that their parents needed to be taught and giggled shyly before applying themselves to their task.

By the time the fort was built and the parents brought up to date on today's two-year kindergarten programs, it was story time for the senior kindergarten students and the six three-and a-half and four-year-olds were invited to sit with the 'big' kids to listen to the story on the large Styrofoam mat in the centre of the pod. Daniel and a little girl with whom he had quickly become friends kept whispering loudly to each other and giggling. Terri was wondering whether she should intercede when the teaching assistant quietly sat on the mat between them.

Eventually, after the story and a round of chanting *Alligator Pie*, the regular students were taken out to the playground and next year's junior kindergartners' orientation session finished with the children each being given a colouring book called *Justin's First Day at School* to take home to colour.

Walking home again, Daniel said that it seemed like a *'pretty interesting'* school and that he wouldn't mind going there next year after all, as long as Becky could manage all right on her own at nursery school. By the time they reached their neighbour, Crystal's, house to pick up Becky, he was bursting to tell Tristan about what a *'cool place'* it was.

"Can we go and get Tristan?" he asked Crystal.

"School's not finished yet, Daniel." Terri explained. "You're going to go with Crystal to pick him and Michael up, remember? When it's time."

"If it's not time, why didn't I go?"

Terri was wondering how to explain that it would have been too disruptive for the other children for him to go to nursery school for the last half hour or so when she was interrupted.

"I just made fresh coffee so stay and have a cup," Crystal invited, "and fill me in."

"I'll have the coffee, but I'll spoil the experience for you this afternoon if I tell you everything," laughed Terri. "Where's Becky?"

"In the sandbox. Here, we'll take it out on the patio," Crystal said, pouring coffee into the two mugs she'd already put beside the coffee maker. "If you want cream, you know where it is. And there's orange juice there for Daniel."

Terri fetched the cream for her coffee, poured orange juice into a beaker for Daniel and followed Crystal outside to the table on the patio, Daniel trailing her.

"Now you drink your juice," she said, handing the beaker of juice to him, "then go and play with Becky."

Daniel drank some juice and put the beaker on the table.

"Okay, but we have to go soon."

"It'll be soon. Now, go along. I think the *building zone* sold him on it," she told Crystal, watching Daniel take a meandering course across the lawn to the sandbox, chanting *'Alligator Pie'*, "that, and a certain little blonde he took a fancy to. He spent the entire walk there making an argument for not going then couldn't wait to get back to tell Tristan how *'cool'* it is. I don't why everything's *'cool'* all of sudden."

"He got it from Tristan, I'm afraid, and *he* got from the new baby-sitter we had when Rod and I were at his brother's wedding the other evening. She doesn't seem to know that there are other adjectives. Just about everything is *'coo-ool'*".

Becky, engrossed in shovelling sand into small piles failed to look up as Daniel, still singing, joined her. He told her they'd make the piles into alligator pies. She looked a little doubtful but didn't object.

"So how was the wedding?" asked Terri.

"Oh, it was really beautiful, you know. Made me wish I'd thought of having a chapel wedding in the evening. I mean, this time of the year, there's still plenty of sunlight for photos and everything. 'Course we were married in October so it wouldn't have worked but, anyway, it was a really nice wedding. Did you have a summer wedding?"

"No," Terri replied, "Christmas time. I'd been in England for four years and a Canadian winter wonderland wedding seemed like a romantic idea. It was at the church near our family cottage which is very picturesque in the snow, but the day turned out slushy and awful so it didn't work out exactly as I imagined it. There's a farmer up there who rents out a sleigh with horses for special occasions but there wasn't really enough snow for it to run properly so we just used it for the photos and went from the church to the reception by car instead. Then, would you believe, we went to the Laurentians for our honeymoon and were snowed in by a blizzard?"

"That's funny. Romantic idea, though."

Becky, who had decided she'd had enough of watching Daniel make alligator pies from her neatly piled sand, struggled to her feet and started towards them. Terri went over and picked her up and sat down again with her daughter on her lap.

"Were you a good girl for Crystal?"

"Yes, Becky good. Right, Crystal?" said Becky.

"You were good, Becky," Crystal told her. "Ryan wasn't, though, was he?"

"Ryan cry, Mommy."

"He seems all right now?"

"Sleeping," explained Becky, with that patiently exasperated expression that two-year-olds exhibit in the face of adult stupidity.

"Oh. Yes, that's good because we're taking him home with us, remember? He's staying at our house while Crystal takes Tristan to the big school this afternoon."

"Michael, too."

"Right."

Michael was a neighbourhood three-year-old whose mother was the third member of the pool of mothers who took care of each others' children when their respective mothers were working. All three worked part-time hours which they arranged so that one of them was always available to take care of the children and walk the three boys to and from the nearby nursery school which they attended in the mornings. The system worked well for both mothers and children.

"It's amazing how much that school has changed," Terri said.

"That's right... you went there, didn't you? I'd forgotten you told me that. It must have been a bit *deja vu* for you."

"Well, they hadn't come up with the idea of junior kindergarten orientation mornings then. Junior kindergarten, either, come to that."

"I meant just taking Daniel to the school like your mother did you."

"Actually I was too busy explaining that Becky wouldn't need him to stay at the nursery school to look after her to even think about it," said Terri. "I think this orientation thing must have started with junior kindergarten. We just went the first day and got on with it, didn't we?"

"Yeah, I suppose so. I don't really remember. I'd better go and see about transferring Ryan to the baby carriage for you."

Terri stood up and put Becky down.

"Daniel," she called. "It's time."

"Yeah? Good, let's go."

"Just wait while Crystal gets the baby. Do you have to go to the washroom?"

"No." He changed his mind when she looked hard at him. "Yes."

"I thought so. Go along."

"Becky, too," piped Becky.

"Okay, come along."

She took Becky's hand and they followed Daniel through to the powder room in Crystal's front foyer.

By the time she they all returned to the patio, Crystal was settling the baby in the baby carriage. "Everybody ready?" she asked, gently rocking the carriage.

"Yes," said Daniel. "Let's go."

"Looks like we're ready," Terri grimaced, taking the baby carriage from her and pushing it towards the side gate as Daniel ran ahead and Becky trotted after him. Crystal closed and locked the patio door, then went ahead of Terri to open the child-proof gate.

"If Mommy's going to push Ryan, you'd better hold my hand, Becky," she said. "Daniel –"

"Daniel," Terri joined her cry. "Get back here and walk with the rest of us."

Daniel was already down the street outside their own house. He stopped and waited for them to catch up with him.

"Daniel," Terri said, crossly, when she reached him, "you walk with Crystal. I'm going to stand here and if you run off on her, you're going to come straight back here and wait in your room until she comes back with Tristan."

"And Michael," chimed in Becky, coming up still holding Crystal's hand.

"Yes, Becky, and Michael, but I'm talking to Daniel and you mustn't interrupt. Now, Daniel, you can go along with Crystal to fetch the boys while I get the lunch ready, but you don't run off like that again. Okay?"

Daniel nodded and looked at the ground.

Crystal grinned over his head at Terri who smiled back.

"Come along then, Daniel," she said, letting go of Becky's hand. "You go in with Mommy, Becky." Daniel took her other hand and they started off along the road towards the church where the nursery school operated.

* * * * *

"You go and watch the game, dear," Janet said, "Ian will be wanting to get off home, I expect, won't you, hon?"

Ian looked up from stirring his coffee and nodded.

"Yes, Dad, I'd better pass on watching the game with you or I won't be able to tear myself away and get on home."

"S'pose you're right, son. If it goes into extra innings and you've got to drive home..."

"If it were a Thursday, I wouldn't mind a late night. You can get through Fridays on a few hours sleep..."

"Know what you mean. One of the great things about retirement, I'm finding, is not having to worry about how you're going to be feeling tomorrow..." Ralph patted Ian's shoulder and made for living room. "Pop your head around the door and say good night before you go."

Ian was having supper with his parents, as he quite often did when Alison was working in the evening, and which Janet encouraged, though not to the extent that it would appear possessive. At least, she hoped not. She knew that Alison was the last person to think so, but other people might see it as implied criticism of the fact that she was not home to make supper every night of the week. Ralph, for one, she thought, wryly. But, then, he could never be made to understand that times change and, nowadays, women had careers, too. Least of all would he ever understand that Alison's store was her lifeline, something which had very vividly been made apparent to Janet this week and something which she wanted to tell Ian about, once Ralph was engaged with the Blue Jays.

"Let's take our coffee outside. It's cooler now, I think," she said to him.

"Good idea."

Ian carried his mug out to the back veranda. Janet followed and they sat down facing the riotous peonies and roses in bloom around the lawn.

"So, you're really going to become RVers," Ian said, putting his mug on the arm of the Muskoka chair and flexing his own arms as he put his hands behind his head.

"Oh, it's only for the three weeks. I think we'll survive that, don't you?"

Ralph had been talking about flying to Edmonton, renting an RV and travelling the Alaska Highway for years and they were, finally, going to do it this summer. Janet was half looking forward to it, the Edmonton part, anyway, because their younger daughter lived there with her family, and half dreading it because Ralph was not the most patient person in the world and tended to get sulky when things went wrong, not that he'd admit to it, and lots of things could go wrong with rented RVs when you weren't very familiar with them.

"Of course you will. You'll love it."

Janet wasn't so sure. "Well, let's hope so," she said. "It'll be nice visiting Susan while we're there." She put down her coffee and stood up. "There's something I want to show you. It just came into the library. I'll be back in a minute." She went back into the house.

Janet had started volunteering at the local branch of the public library the previous winter, mainly to get out of the house which, since Ralph's retirement, had seemed less comfortably hers. She enjoyed it so much she couldn't think why she hadn't done it before – or even gone back to work part time years ago over Ralph's objections. She'd loved her job at the Central Library and had intended going back to work as a cataloguing librarian again when the children were older. As it turned out, with Ian arriving as a bit of an afterthought, by the time she could have done so, comfortably, she'd been out of the work force for nearly twenty years and everything had changed so much that, in the face of the dual challenge of needing to relearn the job and getting past Ralph's objections, she'd convinced herself that the children needed her to be home. By the time the girls were married and Ian was in high school, computers were beginning to make working in a library look even more complicated and she was unlikely to provide much competition for a recent graduate even for an entrylevel job. Now, despite the adult volunteer position consisting mostly of re-stacking books and helping people find titles three mornings a week, she found the new technology to be less complicated than it had appeared and wondered if the truth of the matter was that she'd lost confidence in herself through being out of the work force. Maybe young women today had it right when they went right back to work after maternity leave, not that there had been any such a thing when she had first become a mother. Oh well, you couldn't go back... She picked up her shoulder bag which was lying in its usual place, when not in use, on one of the kitchen bar stools which were never used because they always sat at the table in the breakfast area.

Janet went back outside, pulling the small book from the bag as she went.

"Here," she said, holding it up for Ian to see. "It's a book of poetry by a girl who had social phobia. Like Alison only worse... she died. Suicide."

Ian took the book and she stayed silent while he read the first few pages, including the introduction by the girl's mother which explained that, by publishing her daughter's poetry, she hoped to bring attention to the need for people to better understand mental health disorders instead of abandoning victims to their self-imposed exile.

"She means like you – you and Terri learning about social phobia so that you could stay in Alison's life instead of interpreting her fear as rejection and running out on her like the rest of her friends did. I guess her daughter had no Ian or Terri to make her feel that life was worthwhile... It's such a dreadful waste – she was obviously very talented. Some of the poetry has an almost scary maturity when you consider that she was only a teenager..."

"I didn't think you really understood Alison's problem."

"I didn't," Janet admitted. "It just all fell into place when I read that book. It made me very proud of you and, if I'm honest, a bit ashamed of myself for sometimes having wished you would move on and find somebody who appreciated you..."

"That's nothing to be ashamed about. All mothers think that once in a while. And I'm nothing for you to be proud of. I get just as frustrated as you do with making excuses when Alison's fear prevents her from socializing or eating out or what have you, but I love her... Anyway, it was the store more so than Terri or I that got her back to the land of the living before the agoraphobia really set in. I think, in a way, it's like acting –"

"You mean she was able to create a different self as the store owner – the expert, the person shoppers must come to rather than having to initiate communication herself and feel that she's being criticized."

"Yes, that's right. How did you know?"

"The girl in the book – she won prizes for drama. I imagine she was so good because it was an escape from herself, being someone else, not having to work at not feeling scared of everyone."

"Alison won a best actress award at drama camp once when she was a kid. She was in some Hart House production at U of T before I met her and was involved in a production, at one point, after we started seeing each other but it was when I was at Laurier and I don't remember what it was. I, maybe, didn't know in the first place." Ian paused, then continued, thoughtfully. "I hadn't thought of her role in the store as acting, but I suppose it is really. Anyway, it works. The success of that store, and they have the highest sales of any of the Canadian franchisees, apparently, is mostly due to Alison, especially in recent years. Of course both she and Terri worked like dogs the first couple of years to get it going, but Alison's been putting in mostly fifty hour weeks for more than six years now, except on the rare occasions when we take a holiday and the couple of times when she's been off sick. I wish she would slow down but, perhaps, she just can't without risking a relapse."

"I think, perhaps, that moving from one environment to another, whatever the circumstances, is a lot harder for Alison than any of us realize, except for Moira. I remember how, when I first knew her, I used to think that Moira was such an overprotective mother. Alison was in her twenties, for goodness sake, but it was really just that she always made herself available for whenever Alison might need a bit of support. I don't think it's been so obvious since Alison moved in with you..."

"She does still seem to be able to sense when Alison might need a bit of moral support... better than me, anyway. I sometimes just don't think until afterwards..."

"I'm sure your being there for Alison has meant a lot more to her than you'll ever realize. She'd hardly have stayed with you this long... *and*, finally agreed to a wedding date, if it didn't."

Janet was happy that Ian and Alison were getting married at last. She'd have liked her son to have a big wedding like those of his older sisters but, after having referred to Alison as *Ian's fiancée* for more than four years, it would be nice for her to be her *daughter-in-law* instead, at last. The City Hall ceremony, next month, would take place with just parents present, and Terri and Mark standing up for them.

"Well..." said Ian. "I hope so. I'd better be on my way. It's supposed to be my job to take the pups for a walk when Alison's working although she'll likely to beat me to it tonight."

Moving into the house they had purchased during the winter, had led to Alison thinking it might be nice to have a dog again and they had bought brother and sister cocker spaniel pups from her cousin Jackie's wife, who was a breeder and trainer. Alison took them to the park in the mornings and the evenings when she wasn't working. He sometimes went along, too, but when she worked in the evening, he walked them mostly along the streets adjacent to their house because he thought they should get used to walking on the side walk and crossing the road, both things Alison avoided doing by herself.

"I appreciate your understanding, Mom," he said, rising and picking up their mugs to carry into the kitchen.

Stacking the dishwasher after he'd gone, Janet thought of the times when she had been nervous about things like a job interview, meeting people Ralph worked with for the first time, meeting his parents all those years ago, for that matter – all the usual things that people got anxious about. But, if you had to deal with feeling that nervous on a daily basis – well, however did you manage?

Chapter Twelve

Alison smiled at the woman with the Jack Russell.

"Hello," she said. She'd been going to add something about walking the dogs before the daytime heat became too unbearable but couldn't manage it. Still, she thought, she'd managed to be the first person to speak, at last.

She had passed the woman several times along the path through this part of the park since the puppies had become old enough for walks. In fact, there were several dog walkers who regularly used the path. Her heart had pounded she'd been so shaky the first few days that she'd had trouble holding the dog's leashes. She had known, when they first bought the puppies, that they'd require more exercise than their small back yard afforded and, after a few times walking them with Ian during evenings when they'd both been home, she had managed to psych herself up to taking the puppies along the road, past the half dozen houses between their home and the park and throw sticks for them on the grass just inside. She knew dogs were supposed to be leashed, but nobody was around in the small area between a townhouse development which backed onto the park there and the treed area which had been preserved when the area was developed in the late seventies. Eventually, she'd steeled herself to walk them along the path through the trees and could now do so without heart palpitations except when somebody approached from the opposite direction. The first few times, she'd actually turned and gone back but, inevitably, the day arrived when a man out jogging approached from that direction, too. She'd kept going and nodded in response to his hearty *'Good morning'* and hurried the puppies on towards the safety of home.

Most people on the path at eight in the morning were either jogging or walking dogs. The joggers she could soon manage with a tight smile and nod but meeting dog walkers, naturally, involved the dogs needing to exchange greetings. Fortunately, their owners were mostly in a hurry to get back home and off to work so the meetings generally necessitated little more than perfunctory greetings and remarks about the weather to which Alison, first responded with nods and tight smiles but, more recently, had managed to steady her breathing enough for a monosyllabic reply. She reminded herself that this was how it had been at the store, when they'd first opened, and that, after several weeks of keeping at it, she'd even been able to breathe normally and stopped sounding as if she was having an asthma attack every time she served a customer. It had been exhausting, of course, but soon she'd even been able to handle being in the store alone in the days before things had taken off and the store had become too busy, at most times of the day, for one person to manage.

Because she opened the store some mornings and went in during the afternoon at other times, the meetings with other dog walkers were not a daily event and she found that later in the morning, she, invariably had the path to herself. However, she had also become more used to the short exchanges with the early morning people, now, and could manage them without any panic.

The woman with the Jack Russell had taken to stopping for short conversations beyond comments on the weather. The first time it had been to ask the puppies' names and Alison had indicated first one, then the other and told her that they were Felix and Fanny. The woman said that her dog's name was George, then laughed and said he was not a female masquerading under a man's name but that it gave them a connection through Chopin to the Mendelssohns. Alison relaxed enough to laugh, too. The woman had then urged George past the puppies and she said she must rush if she was going to get to work on time. Then, the next time they met, the woman had asked how old the puppies were and how their training was coming along. Alison had managed to reply, in sentences, without losing her breath or her voice. Today, she had determined that she would be the first to speak.

"Hi," the woman replied, not noticing that Alison had been going to say something else before she stopped and pretended to be busy unravelling Felix's leash from Fanny's. "They're saying it's going to be even warmer than yesterday," she continued. "Do you have air conditioning where you work?"

"Oh yes," Alison replied, then surprised herself by continuing, "I have a store in a shopping mall, a favourite place for people to get cool in this kind of weather."

"I imagine so. Great for business."

"Unfortunately, they mostly just browse..."

"Oh well, at least it's cool. I teach. I'll be glad when school's over. Just a few days now, thank goodness, and no more long days in a hot stuffy classroom. Better run. 'Bye..."

"'Bye."

Alison felt pleased with herself. That was the key; just to keep at it, whether places or people you had to ride the fear and get past it, then you could be normal, and she'd been quite normal, having a few words of conversation with another dog owner in the park. While she was feeling confident, she would make herself go to the nearby convenience store when she got home. In the four years that she had lived in the apartment, rather than brave unfamiliar territory and people, she had always driven over to the *Mac's Milk* near her parents' house which she had been going to all her life. Mostly, though, she tried not to run out of anything. Ian, thankfully, liked grocery shopping. Well, maybe not liked exactly, but didn't mind it, anyway, and they generally did the week's shopping either together or, if she was working, he would go by himself on a Saturday. Anyway, now that they had bought the house and moved further away, she must break the habit of driving miles out of her way to pick up a quart of milk or whatever. There wasn't really anything they needed, but today was definitely the day to make a start. Buy herself an ice cream bar, that's what she'd do and eat it walking back, without being afraid that somebody might be looking at her. She would do it. She had the confidence and the time this morning. She had taken the dogs out early because of the heat not because she was working this morning, so she had lots of time to walk along the road and around the corner to the store. She'd done so with Ian and was, therefore, able to visualize herself at every step of the way. Visualization, she found, helped to prevent the real thing from making her anxious.

She came back to earth with a start when the puppies both started whining indignantly. They had been wrestling each other after their Jack Russell friend left and now had the leashes so completely twisted around themselves that Felix could scarcely move.

"Oh you poor pups," she cried, "here I am standing around daydreaming, miles away, and you've got yourselves all tied up."

She stooped and sorted the leashes out, glad that there was nobody around to witness her stupidity. She calmed and petted them and began to walk through the trees towards home, the puppies trotting ahead of her. They were pretty smart pups, already house-trained and would sit and lie down when instructed. The best thing, she had to admit, was that the required daily walks were just what she needed to force her out to face the world... well, the park and the people in it and occasional sightings of neighbours, anyway, she thought, smiling at her own hyperbole. Charlie and Angel were virtually senior citizens by the time her problem had started and, while she did walk them sometimes, usually with her father, it wasn't strictly necessary and they had both become a bit arthritic before their deaths and not terribly enthusiastic about it. These puppies needed to be exercised regularly unless she wanted to risk their destroying everything in sight when left in the house by themselves and it was forcing her to get out and interact with people, if a few nods, 'good mornings' and short conversational exchanges could be called interacting. Whichever way you looked at it, she was improving. It was all very well to rest on her laurels, in so far as overcoming her fear to become half of the successful partnership at the store was concerned, but she'd been resting on them for six years now, while resorting to avoidance behaviour in almost everything else. It was amazing that Ian was still bearing with her. How did he have the patience to live with a woman who scarcely went out, other than to go to work and, once in a while, to dinner at *The Centennial Bistro*? Well, she went to her parents' house and Jackie's, Uncle John's, and to Ian's parents' and, sometimes to Terri's, although she wasn't too crazy about having to face all those neighbours who always seemed to be dropping in there, and to Derek's and Karen's place. And they'd been wilderness camping a few times and cross country skiing, things like that which didn't involve meeting many other people. Still, it wasn't fair on him and now they were getting married... she really must try harder.

* * * * *

Terri heard the back door being locked and unlocked as she was brushing her hair at the mirror in the store's small washroom. She called through the half open door to Alison.

"How's that for timing? I'm just making myself look respectable and I'll be right there."

They were having a late lunch together as they sometimes did after lunch time customers had gone back to work and only one person was needed to serve clientele made up mostly of mall workers also taking late lunch hours.

"We had quite a run on the mists this morning – your coupon in the flyer..." Terri continued, putting her hairbrush in her purse and zipping it closed.

"That's good," Alison replied from the office where she'd gone to check for phone messages. "Hope they bought other stuff, too, though."

"Some. Are we going Greek or vegetarian?"

"I don't mind really. I'm just having salad, anyway."

"Okay, let's go to *Goldie's*, then. There's nothing here that won't wait until we get back."

Goldie's, a vegetarian restaurant with a wine and beer licence, was one of the two restaurants in the mall that they frequented. Both were small and comfortable for Alison who couldn't handle the food court – other than to pick up the occasional take-out meal to bring back to eat in the office – or the steak and roadhouse franchise locations in the vicinity.

They were soon seated in *Goldie's* with a glass of the house wine to sip and a basket of hot rolls to nibble on while their salads were being prepared. The restaurant's décor leaned towards the psychedelic ambiance of the sixties hippie culture favoured by its middle-aged owner whose teen and young adult years had coincided with that era and seemed to have left a lifelong impression. Goldie was given to flowing Indian cotton skirts, shawls, beads and, quite often, even to flowers in her waist- length faded blonde hair. On her first visit to their store, partly to introduce herself and her soon-to-be opening restaurant and partly to investigate their products, she and Alison had established an instant rapport which did not happen very often for Alison. Terri rather suspected that a less confident, more vulnerable Goldie, hidden behind the successfully generated competent restaurateur image, subconsciously recognized a kindred spirit in Alison and vice-versa. Whatever the reason Alison's feeling comfortable with Goldie soon expanded into Alison being relaxed in Goldie's restaurant which was a relief to Terri because nobody likes to supposedly relax over lunch with somebody who's too tense to eat.

"You look pleased with yourself, today," Terri said. "What's the expression? I know – *'like the cat that swallowed the cream'*."

"I do?" Alison responded. "Well, I do feel a bit like that. I set myself some challenges this morning and met them."

"Like what?"

"It probably sounds silly to you, but they're big steps for me. It's what they call exposure therapy really, I suppose. I've managed, over the last few weeks of walking the dogs in the park, to progress from turning the other way and running home quick when I meet people to actually smiling and acting normally, well, close to normally... Anyway, one woman – she's about our age – started stopping to chat, nothing in-depth; she has to get back to get off to work. You know me – I just about managed a few monosyllabic replies... So, this morning, I decided I was going to be the first to speak and I was. I intended to carry on with something about the weather but didn't manage it, but I did communicate in sentences when *she* did the weather part."

"That's great. And I don't think it sounds silly..."

"Then, it made me feel so good about myself that I went to the store. I've never told you this but I have a major problem with going into a convenience store. I can manage a supermarket better than I can a convenience store, silly as it sounds –"

"Not really," said Terri. "The clerks in convenience stores always act so wary, probably because the job makes them so vulnerable to hold-ups and stuff, that most people feel their every move is being watched –"

"So somebody with a phobia about being watched would feel even worse. You're right. Anyway, I've been known to drive over to our corner store where we've been going since we were kids, just to get a carton of milk rather than go, by myself, to a nearby one that I don't know very well. Well, now that we've moved even farther away from it, that is *really* stupid, so this morning I made myself go to the *Mac's Milk* around the corner."

"Lunches coming up, ladies," Goldie called, coming towards them with a large salad plate in each hand. "Terri's favourite *Sautéed Mushroom Salad with Sun-dried Tomatoes* and *Spinach with Dried Fruit and Warm Honey-Mustard Vinaigrette* for Alison." She placed their plates in front of them. "D'you want topping up? I know, I know – no way, one's got to work and the other's got to drive home."

"You said it," Terri laughed. "Every kind of mushroom in this – how do you manage it?"

"Oh, I have my sources – my trade secrets, as they say and don't worry, there's none of the funny ones there. So how's business with you two?"

"Well, if you were thinking of using the body mist coupon in the flyer, you'd better hurry," Terri told her. "Both the lilac and the lavender are already gone..."

"You didn't tell me things were that bad," said Alison.

"Why would you run a coupon and not have enough stock?" asked Goldie.

"To be perfectly honest, we had no idea that people would fall over themselves for body mist. It doesn't usually sell that fast. Has to be Alison's brilliant copy..."

"That brings us to something I've been going to ask you for ages, Alison..." said Goldie.

"Ah-ha?"

"Would you consider doing some ads for me?"

"I suppose I could. I don't know if I'm really any good, though..."

"Of course you are," said Terri. "You've just run us out of body mist." She turned to Goldie. "Half the flyer ads Alison writes for our store get included in the advertising kits the company sends out to all the franchisees. I've been trying to get through to my charming husband that they should be paying her. There's a percentage comes out of their gross sales for those kits, so the company is getting paid for stuff they are picking up free from us. But Alison here has just been sitting back letting it happen for several years now, *and* we still have to pay *our* percentage for the kits. You know why? Because the company's accounting system can't handle something that's not cast in stone."

"Take no notice of her, Goldie," said Alison. "It's not me that's brilliant, anyway. I mostly just pick my father's brain..."

"Your father?"

"He's the creative partner at Lyndstrom, Fraser and Gates," explained Terri.

"The advertising agency. Makes sense. Anyway, can we talk about it, Alison? My advertising, I mean?"

"Sure. Not right now though. I have a store to run this afternoon. I'll come over tomorrow afternoon when Terri's student master. How's that?"

"Great. You can have lunch on the house."

Alison grinned. "Sounds good. If I think what you want is beyond me, I'll tell you though. Terri has more faith in me than I deserve..."

"But, if those body mists are walking off the shelves..."

"Probably the heat – lavender's very cooling. I guess you put in an order?" she asked Terri.

"Yeah. An emergency one. They might even show up this afternoon."

"I'd better get back then."

"What do you guys do if there's only one of you there when there's a delivery?"

"We always try to have two people in the store and take time-outs during slow times," explained Terri. "Back when we were starting, and we couldn't afford daytime staff, we had the partitioning built so that you can see through to the store entry area all the way from the back door so that, if you're by yourself, you can walk backwards till you get to the back door, keep glancing over your shoulder while you see who it is, then release the lever for the receiving bay tell the delivery man to bring the waybill through to you, then – if you have customers, you ask him to close the doors and go and lock the receiving bay as soon as you can..."

"Walking backwards?"

"Don't laugh. It works. 'Though there hasn't been the need for a long time, so I don't know how good we'd be at it now."

"And Amanda was never trained to do it, so I'd better go," said Alison, getting up, "just in case they do come through with the delivery, though it's hardly likely. I'll see you tomorrow, Goldie. It *is* your turn to pay isn't it, Terri?"

"If you don't remember, maybe I should say no... But, yes, I think it is."

* * * * *

Alison was still feeling good about herself when she arrived home that evening. Neither Ian nor the pups were in evidence so she decided to walk down to the park and see if she could spot them, although the long June evening was definitely drawing to a close and, unlike her, Ian did not take the same route all the time.

As it happened, she met them just as they were about to leave the park.

"Hi. I thought I'd come and meet you," she said, rising to her toes to exchange a kiss with Ian when she reached him. "Hello, Fanny. Hello, Felix. Did you have a good walk?" She bent down to pet the puppies. "Do you feel like walking a bit more?" she asked Ian. "It's such a lovely evening."

"You sound happy," Ian said, as they set off along one of the paths.

"I am. It's been one of those really *right* days." She took Fanny's leash from him with one hand and grasped his hand with her other one.

"And a really *right* day, I take it, is one where nothing goes wrong?"

"Right. *Really* right."

They laughed and Alison proceeded to tell him of her triumphs of the morning, the success of her flyer advertising and Goldie's request for her help.

"Sounds like we should celebrate," Ian suggested. "I didn't eat yet. I was late so I though I'd better get these guys out before they went hairy for lack of exercise. Do you fancy going out for a late supper at *The Centennial Bistro*?"

"Why not? No, I have a better idea. We walk through to the other end of the park and see if the fish and chip shop is still open. We should just make it. And we can get fish and chips to go and sit over by the fountain and eat it. Doesn't that sound more romantic on a summer's evening?"

"Well, it'll be a bit greasy and we'll have to share with the dogs and there'll be no wine..."

"We can have a glass of wine when we get home, 'though

beer might go down better by then. Okay?"

"Okay."

Later, with Ian sleeping soundly beside her, Alison lay awake in that state of wakefulness that happens when a day has been too nice. She rather wished her mind would turn off, but her thoughts kept running through all the things she had to feel happy about. She thought about their up-coming City Hall wedding and wondered why she had taken so long to agree to it. It hadn't really been very fair to Ian since he was the one who had had to brave disapproving parents when he'd talked her into moving in with him back when Angel died. It was Angel's death, following so closely on Charlie's, that had finally prompted her to make the move. Her parents' house had seemed so depressing without the two white poodles. She'd felt a bit guilty moving in with Ian for all the wrong reasons... but she had loved him all the time really, hadn't she? It was just that she had been so absorbed either in feeling sorry for herself or, later, in the struggle to conquer the fear and make the whole store project work. She'd been selfish but, then, mental health problems made you selfish. She was glad he understood and was so willing to learn more about her disorder all the time. He probably knew more about it now than she did, in fact. She must remember to get that book his mother had shown him. Janet had had to take it back to her library but she'd noted down the title and the ISBN. Maybe their own branch of the library had a copy... she always felt so self conscious checking on the microfiche reader – computer, now, of course... No, no, she thought, no negative thoughts – not now, after having had such a positive day...

Chapter Thirteen

"Perhaps we should get a dog of our own again," Moira said, watching Alison's cocker spaniel puppies race across the lawn after the ball she'd just thrown.

"We never actually had one of our own," Tim replied, "Technically Charlie and Angel were Alison's..."

"Okay, smart-ass. Perhaps we should get a dog to live on our premises again."

"Then we'd have three of them when we're baby-sitting these two."

"How often is that?" asked Moira, coming back to the lounger on the shady patio which she had vacated to throw the ball for the puppies, who had now forgotten about it and were wrestling each other instead. "This is the first time we've looked after Felix and Fanny, other than that weekend when Alison and Ian went camping."

"They're only – what is it? Seven, eight months old and this is the first time Alison has been persuaded to forget about that store for two entire weeks since they opened it. Maybe she'll find out what she's been missing..."

"Well, I hope she does..."

"Then, we'll be baby-sitting her dogs all the time."

"All the time!" Moira retorted. "I take it you don't think it's a good idea to get a dog again?"

They were relaxing over a drink in the garden on a hot Sunday afternoon in late July. Moira sipped her ice-filled pina colada and replaced it on the table at her side. Arranging their schedules around looking after the puppies had made the week a little hectic and Moira rather wished she'd believed Alison's declaration that they were housebroken and she wouldn't have needed to rush home to let them out. Instead, she'd worked around not leaving them alone for more than a few hours and it had turned out not to be necessary. The puppies were as good as her daughter had said they'd be. Not getting an answer from Tim, she glanced over at the neighbouring lounger and realized he was asleep, with the section of the paper he'd been reading over his face. She picked up her book but found herself watching a squirrel which had run down the trunk of a tree and was bounding across the lawn to the birdbath. She wandered if his progress would wake one or both of the now sleeping puppies...

"Anybody home?"

She started as somebody called from the driveway and jumped up to investigate. It was Terri with the two children in one of the new recycled plastic children's wagons. Daniel was already scrambling out as Moira opened the gate.

"Hi Aunt Moira," he said, "Mommy says Felix and Fanny are here. Hey, I see them. Come on, Becky."

"Well, hello... Daniel," Moira replied to his departing back. "I thought it sounded like you, Terri. Bit of a long walk on a hot afternoon wasn't it? Come on in and have a cold drink."

"We went to the playground and I thought we'd take the long way home and see if you were here and how the puppies were getting on. Actually, I thought you might like Daniel to play with them – mutual working off of excess energy kind of thing..."

Daniel was already running across the lawn to the puppies, both of whom were already bounding towards him.

"Come *on*, Becky," he shouted back to his sister.

Terri pulled the wagon along the path to the adjoining patio and helped Becky to climb out. Becky's attention was immediately drawn to the newspaper over Tim's head. She stood beside him with her thumb in her mouth.

"Be*cky*," Daniel yelled again.

"I think Uncle Tim's asleep under there, Becky," said Terri. "Although how he can sleep through your brother yelling for you, I don't know."

She led Becky over to Daniel and the puppies on the lawn.

"Pipe down a bit, Daniel," she said. "Uncle Tim's asleep on the patio. Didn't you see him?"

"No. I wasn't looking. Felix, drop it. Drop it."

He was trying to pull the ball out of Felix's mouth.

"Here," said Terri, picking up a rubber bone. "Throw this and he'll drop the ball as he runs to get it."

Daniel threw the rubber bone and the puppies both ran after it, Felix dropping the ball as he went.

"Okay. Mommy's going to sit with Aunt Moira on the patio, so you play nicely now and don't tease them. They have sharp teeth, remember?"

Daniel, who had previously experienced Fanny's sharp teeth, nodded solemnly. "We'll just throw things," he said.

Becky picked up a knotted rope dog toy and Felix immediately grabbed one end of it and pulled. Becky held on to her end and laughed delightedly.

Terri walked back to the patio.

"I'll go and get you some drinks," said Moira. "Is Becky all right with the dogs?"

"I think it's okay. I'll keep my eyes on them."

By the time Moira returned with a *Bacardi Cooler* and glass filled with ice for Terri and plastic beakers of orange juice for the children, Tim had revived and was telling to Terri about how well the dogs had adapted to their temporary home.

"... and, if they have, the neighbours haven't told us about it," he was saying as she placed the tray on the table.

"About what?" she asked.

"If the dogs howled when we left them."

"They're used to being alone when Alison and Ian are working. I was more concerned about their bathroom habits, but no accidents so far, touch wood," Moira said, touching the wooden tray. "You like the pina colada, don't you Terri?"

"Yep, I'm the one."

"And there's orange juice for the children when they're ready for it, and some cookies. And there's ice cream, but I'll leave that up to you... I don't want to spoil their dinner."

"Let's just wait and see if they get fidgety," said Terri. "Looks like Daniel just remembered the playhouse. Is there anything in there they shouldn't be into, Tim?"

Daniel had tired of throwing things for the puppies and run down to the end of the garden to the old playhouse. Tim had built it for Alison and, despite more than a quarter of a century of sun, rain and snow, the structure was still sound, although the bright paint that had once covered its walls was no longer in evidence.

"The door's lying on the floor, but it's not as if it can fall over on them or anything. It came off its hinges a while ago, so I just shoved it inside," Tim said.

"Probably just as well. It's very warped. Remember how Daniel got stuck in there last year, Moira?"

"I mostly remember being worried sick that he wouldn't stay back far enough and would get hit when I forced it open."

"Did she tell you about this, Tim? You were away or at your office – somewhere, anyway – and Daniel managed to close the door, despite being told to leave it open, and it stuck. Moira wanted to go down the street to the playground and find a kid old enough, but small enough to climb through one on the windows and keep him back, but I told her that he'd stay back as long as he could see me at the window – the shape of me, anyway, that stuff's so weathered you can scarcely see through it any more."

"The windows are stuck shut anyway," said Tim.

Moira grinned. "Oh, I was going to cut out the plastic but I expect it would have shattered and it would have taken forever to get the edges smooth enough for anybody to climb in without getting cut to pieces. Anyway, Terri told him to stand in the corner and I shouldered my way in."

"Well, it seems to have been a traumatic experience he's forgotten about."

Daniel had pulled the wagon through the open doorway and was calling Becky over.

"Why don't you put the little picnic table in there for them, Tim?" suggested Moira.

"Oh, don't go to any bother. We'll be on our way once they get cranky," said Terri.

"It's no bother," said Tim. "It's just sitting on the end of the workbench at the back of the garage. Might be a bit cobwebby, though. I don't remember the last time I moved all the junk there." He rose and picked up the tray. "I'll take their drinks down there."

The puppies jumped up and followed him as he made his way over to the side door of the garage, placing the tray on an adjacent wooden bench. He came out with the child-size picnic table and a cloth with which he proceeded to dust it off.

"He shouldn't go to all that trouble," said Terri.

"Don't worry," Moira replied. "It'll get him into gear to clean up the rest of the eyesore at the back of the garage."

Terri nodded, appraisingly. "So, there was an ulterior motive, then..."

Moira nodded as they watched Tim place the tray on the table and carry it over to the playhouse. Daniel obviously spotted him and ran out yelling to Becky that they were getting a table for their house. They watched Daniel, on Tim's instructions, pull the wagon out of the playhouse so that Tim could slide the little picnic table in there, instead.

"Has Alison called?" asked Terri.

"Yes, the night before last from Vienna. They'd been to a dinner theatre place..."

"Really? That's great. I thought she'd have Ian ordering from room service all the time."

"No. She's been trying really hard the last few weeks. I think having the dogs and the necessity of having to get out with them on a daily basis has got her into working up her courage to face other unfamiliar places. She said she didn't do as well as she hoped on the flight and I imagine they have been using room service to some extent, but it's Ian's honeymoon, too, and she doesn't want to be drag on him. Anyway, the play was a farce, so they were able to follow it fairly well, she said, despite not understanding a word."

"Well, I'm really happy to hear that everything's working out. I know she's determined to make it work for Ian and even went back on imipramine to keep her from relapsing, but... well, that stuff really only stops her getting depressed. It doesn't really do much for panic, does it?"

"The idea is more to help you keep your spirits up so that you keep working on your problem, I think," Moira said.

"There's a lot more information coming out on these problems, isn't there? I read an article in – well one of your competitors' magazines, actually – about a woman with what was described as irrational panic disorder but it was the same sort of problem as Alison's except she became totally agoraphobic and didn't leave her house for years."

"You don't need to sound so apologetic about reading my competition. They're not exactly competition, anyway. I mean none of our publications has a mandate to be thought-provoking so they don't get into that kind of editorial. Sounds shallow, but the target audience wants cosmetics and clothes rather than to challenge the intellect, so what do you do? Anyway, I read the article and it *is* good to see mental health generally getting talked about instead of being swept under the carpet. I don't think mental health is likely to be talked about as easily as colds and flu and digestive problems in the foreseeable future, though."

"No, I suppose not, but it might help prevent misunderstanding... Anyway, I should be rounding up my kids and getting home. I'm supposed to be on call for the girls at the store, so let's hope nothing urgent's happening. Alison was saying we should get cellular phones to make it easier for the girls to reach us at the weekends. You know, the new mobile ones, not just for in the car..."

"It's probably better to wait a bit until the prices come down," said Moira. "But you're right, they do make life easier, I'm told."

"What on earth is Tim doing in there with them? I'd better go and see."

"Probably telling them a story or something. Don't worry about it. Mark's at home, isn't he? He's probably more interesting for the girls to call, anyway..."

"Ha ha. What time is it?"

"About a quarter to five or so, I should think. Would you like another drink?"

"In view of your crack about my student employees setting their caps at my husband, maybe I will. I should call him, though, and let him know where we are."

They both rose and Moira went in to get them both another cooler and Terri used the phone, which the Frasers brought outside during the summer, to call home. When Moira came back out, Daniel was running towards the patio with the dogs at his heels.

"Becky's fallen asleep, Mommy," he told Terri who had finished her call and was hanging up the phone.

"So I see," she said as Tim, stooping, emerged from the playhouse carrying the sleeping Becky. "What were you doing in there?"

"Uncle Tim was telling us a story about two little girls called Terri and Alison who used to play in the playhouse long ago..." said Daniel, making it sound like the first line of a fairy tale.

"Hardly *that* long ago!" interrupted Terri, looking challengingly at Tim, who grinned. "Just for that you can stand and hold her."

"Put her down on the lounger there, honey," said Moira. "So what did the two little girls do in the playhouse then, Daniel?"

"I didn't get it, but now I do. It was you and Alison really wasn't it, Mommy?"

"Yes, Daniel," Terri agreed, "but I don't imagine that Uncle Tim's story really happened to them..."

Daniel looked puzzled.

"Did you or Alison have a doll called Mrs. Beasley?" he asked.

Terri looked at Tim who had placed Becky gently on the lounger and was arching his back to counteract the bent posture required to get both himself and Becky out of the playhouse.

"I think I'll go and get another beer," he said, exaggeratedly backing towards the door until he reached it and quickly stepped inside.

"What's happening, Mommy?" piped up Daniel. "Why's Uncle Tim pretending to be a scared little kid?"

"Mrs. Beasley was a doll on a television show we used to watch when we were children, sweetheart," said Terri. "Mommy and Alison both wanted one for Christmas but Santa didn't oblige because he never brings things that mommies and daddies don't want their children to have. Anyway, Mommy and Alison used to pretend they had a Mrs. Beasley doll who lived in the playhouse..."

"... and she came to life and gave them Oreo cookies and Smarties whenever they wanted and never made them eat yucky broccoli and carrots and let them watch television, even in the middle of the night..."

"Yes, Daniel, but it was just pretend. Anyway, I thought you liked broccoli..."

"Well I do, but it is a *bit* yucky..."

"Great," said Terri, glaring at Tim as he came back out.

"It's okay, Terri." He turned to Daniel. "You'd better tell your mother the rest of the story, Daniel, before she gets really mad at me," he said, sitting down and leaning back in the chair.

"Mrs. Beasley said she could only come to life if they were good and did what their parents said and ate their broccoli and carrots and all the other yucky things, but they didn't and when they went to the playhouse there was only Mrs. Beasley the doll and she didn't come alive. So the next day, they were really, *really* good and Mrs. Beasley was alive again when they went to the playhouse. And now I'm going to play with Felix. Come on, Felix."

Daniel ran off with both dogs at his heels.

"A veritable tale with a moral," said Moira.

"Right," agreed Terri. "Sorry I misjudged you, Tim. I guess the real pretend Mrs. Beasley wasn't as smart as the one in your story."

"Guilty conscience, eh?" Tim laughed.

"All these years later? Right!"

"I never could figure out what kids saw in that ugly doll, anyway," said Moira. She indulged in a moment of nostalgia and saw the playhouse the way it was the winter of the Mrs. Beasley period, with ivory walls, green trim and red roof. Tim would shovel a path to it each time a fresh snowfall necessitated shovelling the driveway and walks and the two little girls, promising they would come in if they felt cold, would run down to the playhouse and play their game. Eventually, Alison had disputed something that Terri, speaking for Mrs. Beasley, said for them to do and an argument had broken out, ending with Terri saying she was going home. When Moira told her that it was a bit inconvenient for Tim or herself to take her home at that moment, she said it was more inconvenient for her to stay because Alison was mean. Alison, meanwhile, was getting cold out in the playhouse and decided to come in. To explain the argument to her parents, she had to tell them about Mrs. Beasley coming alive, by which time, both she and Terri had forgotten what the argument was about and said they wanted to play dress-up instead.

"She was a rather silly looking doll wasn't she?" said Terri. "I remember reading somewhere that she actually gave some kids nightmares. I think you and my mom were probably right about not wanting us to have one. I think *Family Affair* ended around that time, anyway, didn't it?"

"I forget. It seems to have been in reruns ever since. I take it all's calm on the store front?"

"What? Oh yes. Mark said he's been working all afternoon and wasn't answering the phone but the only call was from Shelley, the girl who's baby-sitting for us tonight and she left a message, on the machine, saying for Mark not to pick her up as she's out and will be dropped off at our house."

"Oh, where are you going?"

"Barbecue at Scott's. The posh kind. They're having it catered. It's to impress some bank types who are up from California. You have to work pretty closely with them down there apparently. Adam and William are up at the cottage with my parents."

"Well, I hope it all works out and that you have a good time, too."

"Thanks. I'd better wake Becky up. If she sleeps any longer, she'll be a problem for Shelley. Where's Daniel? Did he go back into the playhouse?"

"I think so. Looks like Tim's in dreamland there, again. I'll go down and get Daniel while you get Becky organized."

Moira walked down to the playhouse where she found Daniel sitting at the little picnic table playing with some action figures which he had, obviously, brought with him in the wagon. The puppies were asleep on the floor beside him.

"Hey there, Daniel," she said. "Time to go home."

"Oh-oh. I'm busy..."

"I think Mommy needs you to bring the wagon up, so how about I help you put your toys in and you can pull it up to the patio?"

"Okay, but they're not toys. Well, Becky's are toys. These –" he held them up as he spoke, "– are Batman and Robin, don't you know that?"

"Sorry, of course, I see that, now. I couldn't see them in the beakers –"

"They're batmobiles, not beakers," said Daniel. "But they can be beakers again now, if I have to pack up. Can I come and play with Felix and Fanny again soon?"

"Well, they'll be back at Alison's house next week, but I'm sure she'll need you to play with them some time. Come along now and let's put everything back in the wagon."

By the time she and Daniel had the wagon back on the patio ready to go, Terri had taken Becky, who was wide awake again now, to the bathroom and was coming back out.

"Well, looks like you're all ready to go," said Tim, stirring himself as Terri settled Becky in the wagon. "Are you getting in there, Daniel?"

"No," replied Daniel. "I have to help Mommy pull."

"Oh, I see," Tim said, looking at Terri who shrugged.

"Have a nice time tonight," said Moira, "and let me know if anything comes up at the store during the week – if I can help, I mean."

"Oh, thanks," said Terri, "but everything's running pretty smoothly. Summer's the best time for one or other of us to be away since the students are available to work in the daytime and we have a pretty experienced crew at the moment. Well... thanks for the drinks."

"Thanks for the drink and cookies, Aunt Moira," said Daniel, Becky joining him part way through the sentence.

"Oh, you're welcome. Come back and see us again, soon." Moira scooped up the puppies as Terri opened the gate. "Bye bye, now."

"Bye," chorused the children. "Bye, Uncle Tim. Bye, Felix. Bye, Fanny."

Terri grinned.

"Bye. See you later," she said.

1997

Chapter Fourteen

So he had an ulcer, Ian said to himself, as he came out of the doctor's office and headed to his car. It wasn't so surprising really. Half the people he worked with had them. It went with the territory. All the years you spent being the fall guy for people who blamed systems and software, rather than admit to their own ineptitude when their computers began spewing out nonsense, eventually told on you, he supposed. Although, as the doctor pointed out, there was the genetic factor in that his father had been suffering with duodenal ulcers for years.

He unlocked the door and got into his car and started the engine before getting out again to brush snow off the windshield. A thin layer of ice remained and he decided to wait for the car to warm up a bit before getting underway. Better to ensure having a warm windshield when there was sleety snow around. He pulled the pamphlets the doctor had given him from his inside pocket and skimmed through one of them while he waited, then gave up because the light was bad and the type small. Basically what it came down to was taking *Tagamet*, cutting back on the coffee and avoiding spicy, fatty and acidic-type foods until the *Tagamet* had done its job, though it probably wasn't a good idea to indulge in those, period, not that he ever really did, anyway.

The doctor had explained that the bland diet and lots of milk and cream that used to be the mainstay of ulcer treatment was now outmoded and medication to protect the ulcer from the digestive juices while it healed was the way they were treated now. He wondered if his father knew that. He'd been drinking milk for his ulcer ever since Ian could remember... it was probably habit and he'd hardly be likely change at this stage of his life. He'd been retired for five years now and probably didn't even have an ulcer any more...

He stuffed the pamphlets back in the inside pocket of his jacket and got out of the car and brushed snow off the windshield again, this time the ice coming off with it, before carefully manoeuvring his way across the parking lot and out onto the road where other drivers were slowly progressing homeward on the slippery surface. He hadn't really expected to be in rush hour traffic but supposed the bad weather had sent people, those who could leave their workplaces, anyway, on their way early. It had certainly put paid to any idea he had been harbouring about going back to the office. He was going home. He was glad Alison wasn't working tonight, although he wasn't quite sure if he was glad for his own sake or hers. You always felt so helpless when you were waiting for somebody who was battling bad driving conditions. He'd give her a call next time the traffic came to a complete stop and it was safe to use his cell phone since, come to think of it, she probably felt the same way.

It was almost an hour and a half later – a journey that usually took twenty minutes – before he finally drove the car into its place in the garage next to Alison's. His whole body felt stiff from concentrating on keeping the car from skidding. He flexed his shoulders a couple of times as he got out, then picked up his briefcase from behind the driver's seat, and made for the door to the house.

Alison opened the kitchen door as he came into the mud room between the garage and the kitchen, the two dogs at her heels.

"So you officially have an ulcer," she said, giving him the hug which he knew she thought he needed to help calm down after the stressful drive. She was right; he was feeling more relaxed already. "That means bland everything, doesn't it? Like, steamed or boiled things with no seasonings... Milk to wash it down..."

"It's not like that any more. Things have progressed in the last few years. Here, I have all the literature," he said, breaking away from her and pulling the literature from his inside jacket pocket. "You just have to take some medication, although I didn't stop to get it."

"I suppose another day is hardly going to make any difference. I was about to steam cod fillets for supper, though..."

"What?"

"Just kidding." Alison took the pamphlets. "I'm making a veggie lasagne. I just put on a scratch sauce to simmer, so I won't be actually putting it together for a bit. I'll make a cup of tea while you're changing. Kettle's on. Say hello to the dogs, though, before you do. They're both looking thoroughly miffed at not being greeted first."

The spaniels had given up competing with each other for his attention and were sitting looking at him with mournful eyes. He bent and scratched their ears.

"Sorry, guys. First things, first."

The dogs followed him upstairs, watched him with their soulful spaniel eyes as he changed into jeans and a sweatshirt then followed him back downstairs. Even after three years, those eyes still tended to make him guiltily wonder what he had forgotten to do for the two of them.

"You know, dogs are really the worst control freaks," he said as he came back into the kitchen. "These two truly believe that, if they give me the evil eye long enough, I'll take them for a walk. I just know it. Well, I have news for the two of them," he bent down and scratched their heads, "nobody is getting a walk tonight. There's 'break your leg as soon as look at it' ice out there."

"I think they're just looking for their supper, actually," said Alison. "I took them for a walk before it got really bad." She was sitting at the kitchen table reading the ulcer literature. "I poured our tea. Do I have the honour of your company or are you about to open your laptop."

"I didn't bring anything home to do," Ian said, sitting down. "I will admit that I did intend to go back to the office after the appointment but –"

"Weather wasn't permitting. I wasn't implying that you were becoming a workaholic..."

"But you think I am?" He sipped his tea.

"No, no... Well, not exactly. It's just that it says here that getting stressed out with work-related problems isn't good for people who are ulcer-prone."

"I don't get 'stressed out'. I just sometimes have a lot to do... I shouldn't have given you that stuff. I haven't even read it myself, except for a bit when I was waiting for the ice on the windshield to melt, but the light was bad and it was hard to see."

"It's okay. There's no need to get 'stressed'," she grinned. "It's up to you. Not my problem, ma-an... Actually, I'm a bit stressed myself..." she finished her tea and poured another cup. "D'you want topping up?"

He shook his head.

"What's the problem?"

In Alison, stress was likely to become full-blown anxiety and with it, the additional stress of trying to handle it without letting him or anyone else down.

"Well, you remember that community cable – whatever it's called – producer who did that program on the store? Local success stories or whatever they call it?"

He nodded, but she didn't continue immediately. The local cable television station had featured the store in a weekly program a few months before. Alison had arranged the work schedule so that she wasn't working on the day the crew shot footage in the store but she had forced herself to participate, with Terri, in the live studio interview portion of the program. It might have looked a little less than a *bona fide* success story if Terri, a member of the family that owned *Envirodermics*, had been interviewed by herself. Ian had gone along to the studio with them and knew how hard it had been for Alison. In fact, but for her phobic history, the severe chest pains brought on by her anxiety might, quite easily, have been mistaken for a heart attack, had she told anybody, but him, about them. Miraculously, she had appeared only slightly breathless and, as prearranged, had left Terri to answer most of the questions.

"Alison?"

"Sorry. Yes, well, the producer woman evidently figured out that I have an anxiety disorder. She has a brother with panic disorder and well, my own little panic attack that evening wasn't as unnoticed as we thought. Anyway, apparently, she's now working at the CBC – community cable is mostly a starting point for people waiting for something better to come along – and she's renewed acquaintance with people she went to Ryerson with, and one of them is developing a radio segment on anxiety disorders for the national morning program. They're looking at a sort of round table discussion format, except that it's not exactly round table because everyone's in different studios. Of course, the problem now is that they're having trouble finding participants. I mean, did they think people with anxiety problems were falling over themselves to let the world know who they are or something?"

"Maybe they figured radio would be pretty much anonymous..."

"Whatever... Anyway, the cable woman – I shouldn't keep calling her that – her name's Shauna and she's talked her brother into participating, apparently, and they have another man, a peacekeeper in Bosnia who got traumatized. So they need a social phobic, preferably a female to balance things out ..."

"...and you think you should do it?"

"I said I would. At first, I said I'd have to think about it, but I knew that if I did, I'd scare myself out of it, then she – the CBC producer, *her* name's Sally – said she needed to know by the end of the day or they'd have to reschedule or drop it all together. So, since I couldn't see letting an opportunity for something to educate the public get dropped because I was a scaredy cat, I said I'd be there and went and took some Xanax."

She laughed, albeit a little panicky. He reached across the table and took her hand.

"I think it's... well, really brave of you. I mean, going on national radio's enough to make anybody nervous. I guess, that's not exactly what you want to hear..."

"It's okay. I know what you mean. I couldn't *not* do it, though, could I? After all that you and my parents and Terri have done to help me pass for a normal person –" she grinned. "– I can't refuse to help other people when I'm given the opportunity. A program like this will go a long way to make people under-stand – family and friends of people with anxiety disorders, I mean – and be helpful, instead of not knowing what to do, drift-ing away, whatever..." She jumped up and rushed to the stove. "I forgot to stir the pasta sauce." She stirred the sauce tenta-tively. "Bottom feels a bit sticky, but I don't think it's ruined or anything. I may as well finish it and put it in the oven. I don't suppose you mind dinner a bit early, do you?"

"It's not all that early," Ian said. "Want me to do the salad?"

"Sure, if you like. I have the lasagne noodles that you don't have to boil first, though. That's why I said it would be early."

Alison set about putting the lasagne together while he took the lettuce crisper out of the fridge, along with the other ingre-dients which were all washed and ready to use.

"I'll call my mom and tell her when I've got this in the oven. Not that I've got a lasagne in the oven," she giggled. "I mean about the radio. You will be able to come with me, won't you? It's first thing, so I thought, since you're working in the office this week, I could drop you off there, afterwards, and come and pick you up at the subway in the evening. Does that sound okay?"

"Sure, except that you haven't told me when..."

"Didn't I? Thursday. We have to be there by nine to... well, for me to get acclimatized, I guess. It'll be broadcast here at ten thirty, but everything's done an hour earlier because it's national..."

"... and the Maritimes are an hour ahead. Right. Thursday morning's no problem. But I'll get the bus from the subway. You'll be working and I don't want you driving back and forth from the store just to pick me up."

"We have two students working on Thursday evening, so it's not a problem for me to leave for the three quarters of an hour it'll take if it's freezing cold..."

"Well, let's not worry about it now. I thought you wanted to call your mother. How come you haven't told her yet?"

Alison leaned over the oven to slide the lasagne in.

"I thought my husband should know about my radio debut first," she said straightening up. "Seriously, I think I just didn't want to tell anybody, until I was actually face-to-face with somebody in the flesh, in case I started excruciating over it once I got off the phone. It's a lot easier to be courageous in front of somebody than by yourself, you know."

"Not being the courageous sort, I wouldn't know about that..."

"Idiot." She picked up a piece of the red pepper Ian was chopping and reached up to kiss him on the cheek. "Thanks," she said. "I love you."

* * * * *

Terri couldn't believe that Anna was asking for her advice. Her elder sister *gave* advice. She didn't ask for it.

"Anna, Mom's going to be concerned for you. She's not going to judge you. Even if she were, it's not as if you're at fault. Colin's the jerk who's to blame." She realized immediately that she'd said the wrong thing. Rule number one when a couple breaks up: don't criticize either one to the other in case they get back together again. "Look –" she put the kettle, which she had been about to fill, down on the counter "– I think a *drink* drink would be more appropriate than tea. How about I make us both a rye and ginger ale – or coke, whichever?"

Anna nodded and blew her nose.

"Ginger ale or coke?"

"Coke, please. But not too much rye. I have to drive home, remember."

"I was hoping Heather would keep the kids busy over there for the best part of an hour," said Terri, going into the living room to the small corner drinks cabinet. She picked out a bottle of *Canadian Club* and returned to the kitchen. "That's plenty of time. Anyhow, why don't you and Heather stay to supper? Mark's at some meeting and won't be home until late, so it's just me and the kids. Daniel's friend, Michael, is staying over, and... well, having supper with a bunch of little kids'll be a nice change for you."

Terri had got the call from her sister, asking if she was going to be home for a bit just as Daniel, Michael and Tristan – it was Terri's turn to baby-sit – came home from school. Terri explained that it was her baby-sitting day and she'd be home, but with a houseful of kids. So, Anna had brought her younger daughter, Heather, with her and Heather, who was twelve and doing the Y baby-sitting course, had been happy to practise her skills by taking all five children – Tristan's little brother, Ryan, in the wagon – over to the ravine beside the golf course where there was a gentle slope which the younger children in the neighbourhood used for tobogganing. Other children would be there with parents or baby-sitters at this time on a comparatively warm winter afternoon and both Daniel and Tristan took their positions as big brothers seriously so Terri knew she could count on their cooperating with Heather.

"Right! Well..." Anna was responding to the invitation to supper as Terri got ice and a can of Coke from the fridge and glasses from the cupboard, "there's Kate and Jon..."

"They're old enough to get their own supper once in a while," said Terri. "And let's face it, with no Colin; they don't have to worry about being told they're doing everything wrong." Oh, hell, she thought as soon as the words were out of her mouth, there I go again...

Anna, to her surprise, grinned. "Well, that's true. Thanks. They both have after school activities today, but I'll call later and tell them we're here and they can defrost something in the freezer for supper.

Terri brought their drinks to the table, handed Anna hers and sat down.

"So," she said, holding up her glass, "to turning forty. That's when life begins, they say."

"Okay," Anna took a deep breath. Her fortieth birthday was next week. "To turning forty." She clinked her glass against Terri's and took a sip. "Although men seem to have a better deal than women at these new beginnings," she added a little bitterly.

"I won't argue with that but I will continue with our previous discussion. You have to tell Mom, Anna. She'll be so upset if she thought that you didn't value her enough to confide in her first. We won't mention that you told me..."

"It's not as easy as that, Terri. You don't understand. I was always the good kid growing up – not arrogant with them like Scott or wild like Derek – the one who always did as she was told, looked after Derek and you, and Alison, too, half the time, never had problems at school, grew up and did the traditional thing with getting married... I'm just not the one who they'd have expected to–to–"

"To have your marriage break up... Like, Derek and I would deserve it because we lived with our partners without getting married first..."

"I wasn't going to say that and it's not what I think –"

"No, I was just putting myself in the position you see Mom and Dad in, but you're wrong, Anna. Mom, especially, doesn't think that way now. She thinks it's good that people have more options today and that marriage and divorce aren't black and white like they used to be. We've talked about it. She knows that growing up in the Depression, then the War and the uptight fifties made her generation think that way. Believe me, she'll understand. Anyway, how are you *not* going to tell her?"

"Obviously I have to tell her. She's hardly going to think Colin just disappeared into thin air. I just thought I'd get used to the idea myself a bit first. The children, too."

"Heather doesn't seem too upset."

It was her niece who had told Terri that her father had left home and moved into an apartment downtown. Anna had gone straight to the bathroom when they arrived.

"None of them seem to be too upset really," said Anna. "Kate thinks it'll be nice to stay at his place when she and her friends go to concerts and things, instead of coming all the way home on the TTC in the middle of the night."

"That's how teenagers are. They always see the things that benefit them most."

"They've only ever been to things that somebody's parents have dropped them off at and picked them up. They're only fourteen!"

"Well, she can dream, can't she? And it won't be long before they will be. Look at Jon. It was only three years ago that he was fourteen and you'd hardly put restraints on him now, would you? But we're getting a little sidetracked, here. What are Colin's plans with the kids?"

"Well, let's face it, they're all old enough, by law, to make up their own minds about when they see him and he says he'll pay child expense and the education plan contributions, etc. Jon says he doesn't want to see him. It was Jon who told me about the girl. I think he sees it as an embarrassment. Her being only a few years older than him, I mean."

"Where does she fit in, anyway?" asked Terri. "I mean, I can see Colin, in male menopause, falling for a younger woman, but he's always been so, I don't know, old-fashioned, really, that I hardly see him moving in with her."

"He's not, as far as I know. He wants a divorce because he wants to marry her. None of the usual stuff with Colin!"

"You mean the *"needing space"* and *"wanting to find myself"* bit?"

"Right. He said he was sorry but he'd met someone else and hoped I'd understand and would cooperate with a divorce. He didn't say anything about her, but a friend of Jon's saw them having dinner in a downtown restaurant one evening and, quote, *it was obvious what was going on with them,* unquote was how he put it. Jon only told me about this on Sunday, after Colin had gone. He said the kid told him just after Christmas but he didn't want to upset me in case it all blew over. He hasn't been on very good terms with his father lately, but I figured it was just his age..."

"It sounds to me as if the kids will all deal with it in their own ways. Look on the bright side. There's that. Then you're a teacher and have a life outside of your family, you don't have the problems that mothers with younger children have, like having to hide your true feelings about their father in front of them, half their salary going to pay for day care and not having the kind of money which he persists on spending on them, hardly ever being able to get out and do adult things, outside of working, I mean, because of lack of money... all those things..."

"You seem to know a lot about it."

"Michael, the little boy you met before Heather took them all to the toboggan hill? His parents split up a year ago and his mother's having an awful time... she's a nurse and was working part-time so she was able to get full-time hours once a position became available but we're talking twelve hour shifts. Try arranging childcare around that without a partner!"

"Okay, I see what you mean. I really don't have it so bad." Anna, pensively, finished her drink. "Is that why Michael's staying over?"

"Yeah. Mostly, she tries to arrange shifts around when he's at his father's on the weekends, but when she's stuck either Crystal, my other neighbour, or I have him stay over. With shift hours, she's still able to take her turn in our baby-sitting pool, so it all works out. Let's have another drink – just weak ones, again – and we can relax for a bit before the kids come back..."

The telephone rang and Terri answered it, holding the two glasses in her other hand.

"Hello... Oh. Hi, Crystal. They're not here at the moment... No, I didn't dump your kids somewhere. My niece has taken them all over to the toboggan hill... Yes, Ryan, too. Don't worry, she's reliable. She knows she's to ride with him, and Becky, too. Yeah, I know you let her go on her own. So do I, now, but I couldn't expect Heather to be able to watch them all at once, so they just took the two long toboggans... Right. They should be back soon. Come round anyway. Oh, okay, put your laundry in... If you miss them on their way back, I'll bring them round. See you."

She rinsed the glasses and began making them fresh drinks.

"That was Crystal. She'll watch out for the kids on their way back, so we'll have two less sets of wet coats and boots to deal with. Did you hear Alison on the radio last week? It was on the evening repeat."

"Yes," Anna replied. "I meant to call you over the weekend, but... well; I ended up with other priorities. It's funny, isn't it?"

"What is?" Terri asked, handing Anna her glass and sitting down again.

"How you never realize what's really happening until afterwards. I mean, Alison was always around – my little sister's best friend – only child, doting parents, Ontario scholar..."

"The last person you'd expect to have anxiety problems."

"Exactly. It made me think, listening to her and the other participants. You never know what might trigger some kind of a problem..."

"Don't start worrying about Colin's behaviour impacting on your kids, Anna. Alison's problem is basically genetic. Her grandmother was agoraphobic, only Moira never even realized until way later. She thought her mother just avoided going out because her father was a drunk – it's a long story and I don't even know all of it... but there are no recluses in our family, so don't start worrying about your perfectly well-adjusted teenagers." Terri held up her hand as she finished speaking. "I think I hear the pitter patter of tiny feet, the gleeful shouts of happy children, etc. Or, more likely the whining of somebody who's been out in the cold for too long. Anyway, our *'happy hour'* is over."

Chapter Fifteen

"Look, it's getting late and you have to work in the morning and I've got plenty of help with Susan and the girls staying over, so why don't the two of you be getting along home?"

Janet was glad that Ian had stayed so long but she knew the day had been an ordeal for Alison. Of course a funeral was an ordeal anyway, but the unrelenting stress of not being able to escape a crowd of in-laws, many of whom she scarcely knew, for such a long period of time, was that much more so for a social phobic, as she could see from Alison's exhausted white face. She guided Ian over to where Alison was putting used paper napkins and other litter into a plastic bag because she didn't trust herself to collect up plates and glasses without dropping something.

"I'm just telling Ian to take you home, Alison, and leave the mess for my granddaughters to look after," she said. "Good idea? You've both been wonderful, but you're tired and have to go to work in the morning. Susan and the girls can sleep in."

Alison looked relieved and Ian looked as if he suddenly realized the pressure he'd been putting his wife under while trying to be a dutiful son to his bereaved mother. Janet smiled. "Look," she said, "you needn't worry about me. I'm all right. Really.

And I've plenty of company. Are your coats upstairs or in the closet?"

Her thirteen-year-old granddaughter, Leanne, came over to them.

"Are you guys leaving now?" she asked. "Grandma says she'll bring us over to your store tomorrow, Alison. Do you give discounts to relatives?"

Alison's taut features relaxed a little. "Depends on how much you're spending," she said, grinning slightly.

"Well, there's me, my mom *and* Kaylie. We want to get some more of that relaxing body mist that was in the gift basket you sent us for Christmas. We all use it and it's almost all gone."

"Alison's tired, Leanne," Janet said, "Your coats are upstairs?" Ian nodded.

"Run up and get their coats, Leanne," Janet continued. "Maybe that'll earn you your discount. I don't think she means to be rude," she lowered her voice, "it's just the flight, having to share a room, going to the funeral home, then the funeral. Neither of them has been to one before, so both girls are a bit overwrought, I think."

Alison shook her head. "It's okay. Terri's nieces are the same. I think it's just some kind of status symbol to say your aunt owns the store and you get a discount. I'll just go through and say goodnight to Susan and Kaylie."

Alison went through the living room to the kitchen as Leanne came back downstairs with the coats.

"Thanks Leanne," said Ian, taking his coat.

"Here, I'll hold onto Alison's," said Janet, taking Alison's coat from her granddaughter. "She went to say goodnight to your mom."

"I'd better get back there, too," Leanne was halfway across the living room. "Or, Kaylie will start whining about me not doing my share."

"Are you sure they're not going to get on your nerves, Mom?" Ian asked, putting on his coat.

"They're no problem. It's a bit like being back when your sisters were that age with all the squabbling, except the things to quarrel about are a bit different today. And they don't have a little brother to complain about."

Ian smiled. "Well, I'll pick them up tomorrow after work and take them home so that they can catch up on their e-mail as I promised. Will you and Susan be coming?"

"When you said the girls could come over and use the computer, Susan and Linda arranged a girls' night out. They thought we'd go somewhere nice – somewhere new that we haven't been to before. Linda's looking after it. Pat's coming, too."

Pat and her husband, Roger, had come from Halifax for Ralph's funeral and were staying with Janet's daughter, Linda, who lived not too far away in Nobleton.

"Are you sure you're up to it, Mom?"

"Ian, for goodness sake stop asking me if I'm sure I'm up to everything. I'm bereaved, not incapacitated."

"Sorry, Mom..."

Alison came back, followed by both Leanne and her sister, Kaylie.

"What's wrong?" she asked.

"Nothing, dear. You two run along now and thank you for all your help. Here, I'm seeing you off and forgetting to give you your coat."

Alison took the coat and hugged her tightly.

"I won't do an Ian and tell you what to do," she said. "But I do suggest you and Susan sit down and have a nightcap while you leave these two capable young ladies to finish cleaning up."

"Yes, we can finish up in the kitchen, Grandma," the girls chorused.

"Mom's already got all the leftovers wrapped up and put away," added Kaylie. "And we're just stacking the dishwasher."

"Okay, girls, you look after things," said Alison. "You know what – if you're coming over to the store tomorrow, why don't we time it so that you can come home with me instead of Ian picking you up later?"

"That's a good idea," Leanne said.

"Is that all right with you, Janet?" Alison had her coat on by this time and took a couple of steps backward to the door, looking from Janet to Ian. "Ian?" She opened the door.

"Fine with me," Janet said.

Ian nodded. "Sounds good," he said. "They can take the dogs out for us and earn their supper. Goodnight, Mom."

Ian hugged her and turned to follow Alison.

"See you tomorrow, girls." He called through to the kitchen. "'Night, Susan. See you later."

Susan shouted something about having her hands in the dishwater, so goodnight and she'd talk to him later. Janet and her granddaughters watched Ian and Alison get in their car and drive off.

"Okay, you two, do as Alison said. Off you go and get your mother out of that kitchen."

"Sure, Grandma," said Kaylie. "Let's go, Leanne."

Leanne looked as if she was about to tell her older sister to stop bossing her around but then must have remembered that they had just buried their grandfather and quickly hugged Janet and followed her sister.

Janet went into the living room and looked at the plant displays that Linda had brought back from the funeral home because she thought it would be better to keep the living plants rather than let them go with the cut flowers to the cemetery. Janet wished she'd taken them home with her. She really didn't want them. Maybe she'dfeel differently later. She went over to where she'd placed all the cards in a basket on the table by the window, picked up a bunch of them, started to read the messages then decided she needed her glasses and put them down again. She turned away restlessly as Susan came into the room carrying two glasses of brandy.

"Here we are, Mother," she said. "You and I are going to sit down and relax. The girls are tidying up the kitchen. Now, where are you going to sit?"

Janet sat down on the loveseat, taking the proffered glass and watched her younger daughter sit on the adjacent sofa. The middle child, Susan was the one who always tried so hard to please. She was rather glad that Linda had suggested Susan and her daughters stay here, while Pat and Roger stayed at her house, although she suspected that the decision had more to do with not really wanting two young teens around, having survived the ups and downs of adolescence with her own children who were now both doing well at university, than with whatever level of affection she had for her aunt and uncle. Anyway, Susan and the girls had provided more enjoyable company for her than Pat and Roger would have done, during the days since Ralph's death.

"Alison looked ready to drop when she came back to say

goodnight to me," observed Susan. "They needn't have stayed so long."

"It was Ian. I told him stop worrying about me and take her home in the end," Janet said, sipping her brandy. "I appreciate –" she broke off "– mm, that does feel good. Anyway, where was I? Oh, yes, I appreciate his concern but he knows how hard it is for Alison to be around so many people all afternoon and evening..."

"I was surprised she came back to the house. I expected her to go home from the funeral. She's only ever stayed at anything long enough not to be rude before. Well, to be honest, I thought she *was* rude at times, but that was when I didn't understand that she actually had a psychological problem with being around people and places she wasn't really used to."

"I think she felt it her duty, as my son's wife, to stay in this case," Janet realized, as soon as she said this, that she'd said the wrong thing.

"Not like your second daughter's husband who didn't even show..."

"Sorry, dear, I didn't mean to rub it in. I told you before, I think Peter was right not to take the time off and you shouldn't hold it against him. And for him to have flown all the way from Edmonton just for the day would have been a really silly waste of money."

"You're right, that wasn't one of my better ideas. Anyway, I apologized about getting mad at him and he... well, he's not stupid. He knew I was upset about Dad and everything. So, all's quiet on the home front now. Would you like another one of these, Mom? It'll help you sleep..." Susan didn't wait for Janet to reply. "Hey, you guys," she shouted in the direction of the kitchen. "How about getting up to bed. You must have finished in there by now. One of you bring the bottle of brandy in here on your way, please"

"Is it all right for Fluff to come up to our room, Grandma?" asked Leanne, coming into the living-room carrying the big Persian cat.

"You can take him up with you, Leanne, but I expect he'll come into me, once I come up. He thinks the bottom of my bed's his own, you see."

"You said that before, but he was still with me when I fell asleep. Do you remember that time – a long time ago, when Kaylie and I stayed with you when Mom and Dad went to Europe – and Fluff was still a kitten and he kept running up the back of Grandpa's chair and sitting there and batting Grandpa's paper when he was trying to read it and losing his balance and crashing onto Grandpa's lap and ripping the paper?"

"Fancy you remembering that. You couldn't have been more than five years old."

"I was six. I started grade one when we went home."

Janet suddenly realized they were all three looking at the chair which Ralph had always sat in, reading the newspaper and watching television. She wondered how to break the spell and was grateful when Kaylie finally came in with the bottle of brandy.

"Here's the bottle you wanted, Mom," Kaylie said. "Can I pour it?"

"Give Grandma hers first, then."

"Not too much, dear," Janet said, holding up her hand as a signal for Kaylie to stop pouring and Kaylie moved on to her mother.

"Thanks, Kaylie," said Susan. "Now just leave it on the coffee table and off you both go to bed, please."

"'Night Mom, 'night Grandma," Kaylie hugged both of them and left the room. They heard her going up the stairs. Leanne was still holding the cat and staring at her grandfather's chair.

"Leanne..." said Susan, "off to bed now."

"Yes, okay. G'night Mom," Leanne turned towards her mother. "Look, can you hold Fluff for a minute. I need to hug Grandma."

She deposited the cat in Susan's lap and stepped around the coffee table to where Janet was sitting on the loveseat.

"Grandma, I'm so sorry about Grandpa..." She started to cry.

Janet put her arms around her and they held each other tightly.

"It's all right, Leanne. There's no need to cry. You'll always remember little things like Fluff and Grandpa's paper, but they're memories you have to learn to treasure, not get upset over."

"I know that's what you have to do. The minister said so, too. But it's going to be awfully hard, don't you think?" asked Leanne, pulling a tissue from her pocket and blowing her nose.

"Yes, but he didn't say it would be easy."

"It'll be harder for you. I only knew him for thirteen years and only saw him on holidays but you lived with him for years and years... Look Grandma, I think it might be best if you sold that chair or gave it to the Salvation Army or something."

"Leanne..." admonished Susan.

"It's all right, Susan," said Janet. "I think she's probably right. Anyway, Leanne, you just take Fluff now and get up to bed. Mommy and I'll be up very shortly, too. It's nearly midnight and it's been a long day for all of us."

"Okay. Goodnight."

Leanne hugged Janet again and got up to take Fluff back from her mother.

"Poor Fluff, getting jostled around. Come along now and we'll get up to bed. Goodnight Mommy."

"Goodnight Leanne."

Susan watched her walk to the door murmuring to the cat.

"Maybe I should have left her at home with Peter," she said, after listening for Leanne to go up the stairs. "Perhaps she's too young..."

"No, I think you were right to bring them both. It's the natural order, isn't it? Experiencing the death of our grandparents prepares us to handle the death of our parents, then our wives or husbands. We're the lucky ones when we deal with death in its natural order. It's much harder for people who have to experience death out of turn when children die and things like that. So, it was best to bring them. Alison was telling me that she was their age when her father's mother died and she said it made her see her father as a person, her grandmother's son rather than as *her* father, if you see what I mean."

"That's sort of the way I felt when *your* mother died, although I was quite a bit older, but I'm not sure it works the same way with grandfathers, though. I mean I was grown up when Grandpa Byrnes died, and more conditioned to the fact that he would die, and too young to be much affected by Grandpa Shaw's death and scarcely knew him anyway. What I mean is that I won't hold my breath for them to start seeing me as a person just yet. Teenagers surely couldn't survive the scorn of their peers if their mothers were really anything close to being regarded as people, could they?"

Janet laughed. "Come on now. Being the mother of teenagers isn't that bad. I don't remember too many really bad problems when you and Linda were young."

"Well, you had two built in, unpaid baby-sitters for Ian. You *had* to be nice to us."

"That's not fair..."

"I'm only kidding." Susan grew serious. "You are feeling okay, Mom?"

"Now, don't *you* start... Acting like Ian, I mean. Of course I'm okay, getting quite sleepy, with all the brandy you've been plying me with, in fact. So, let's drink up and get to bed."

Chapter Sixteen

"So, now, Terri's worried about her father dying," said Alison.

"Why? There's nothing wrong with him is there?"

Moira felt relieved to be coming to the end of 400 highway. She much preferred driving on smaller roads, and in early May, it was still too early in the year for Highway 69 to be wall-to-wall vehicles, heading north for the weekend, on a Friday afternoon. She and Alison were on their way to Sudbury for the fiftieth birthday party her sister Pauline's three children had arranged for their mother. Even as she told her niece, Claudia, that they'd all be delighted to come, she'd known Tim would find some excuse not to go and she hadn't been at all certain whether Alison, whose resolve to fight her social phobia tended to wax and wane and was hardly something one could predict several weeks in advance, and Ian would attend. As it turned out, it was Ian, not Alison, who had politely declined because he wasn't comfortable going away for a weekend and leaving his mother so soon after his father's death. He had been dropping by his mother's house each day, to the point, Alison had told her, that his mother was getting more than a little exasperated. So, by the time the first weekend in May arrived only she and Alison were driving up Highway 69 towards Sudbury.

"No. It's just that she figured out that he was older than Ian's father by two or three years and, well... just started getting worried that he might die."

"They're two completely different types. Ralph Shaw was a typical uptight candidate for a heart attack, not that I knew him well and I don't mean to sound derogatory, but he was. Paul's a much more relaxed kind of person."

"I know. I said the same thing. It's awful, both my husband and my best friend being totally obsessed by death. It's a relief to get away for a couple of days."

"Well, it's understandable with Ian. He just lost his father, but I can't see why it should affect Terri. She hardly knew Ian's father..."

"She only ever met him at our wedding. She knows Janet more. It's just the idea of someone our age losing a parent, in an age-related way, I mean, that's obsessing her. She even said that I should be feeling bad about not giving him a grandson to carry on his name, which is none of her business, but I just agreed that it was a pity and changed the subject. She's being very irrational. I hope she gets over it soon."

"Talking about being irrational, you're going to have to feed Ian tranquillizers or something if he carries on like that. He'll drive his poor mother around the bend. By the way, I thought we'd stop when we get to Parry Sound for coffee and you can take over driving from there."

"Sure. That's fine. It's not just his mother he's driving round the bend, believe me. You're right. I don't mean about tranquillizers, necessarily, but it's got to be something psychological and he should have somebody to talk it out with. Janet's looking into going to one of those bereavement groups. She says that she isn't really having any problem coming to terms with it herself, but she's worried about Ian. She figures his being overly concerned about her is really the only way he's able to express his own grief but he can't see it, so she thinks if she pretends she needs him to come with her, he'll be exposed to the different ways people deal with grief and, well, get over it. Does that make sense to you?"

"I think so. There's no guarantee it'll work, but it's worth a try. Are his sisters like this, too?"

"Good Lord, no. Janet would really have a problem on her hands if they were all suffocating her, wouldn't she? No, Linda, the one who lives in Nobleton, just sees her mother about the same as she normally does and Susan lives in Edmonton."

"Oh, that's right. I'd forgotten," Moira said. "Moving on to our own family, I thought that we'd give Claudia a call and let her know we're in town once we get settled in the hotel, then order a room service dinner and just sit around and watch television until we get sleepy, okay?"

"Fine with me but we can go to the restaurant if you like. Don't worry about me. It's the banquet hall tomorrow that'll be a major effort. I'm sure I can handle the hotel restaurant..."

"I was thinking of myself as much as of you, to tell the truth. I just think it'll be nicer to be able to relax in the room than sit in the restaurant."

"Okay, we'll do that then."

They lapsed into silence.

Moira thought about the up-coming party. Pauline's three children had gone to a lot of effort. They'd even persuaded

Hal and his wife, Maureen, to come, leaving their three children in the care of Maureen's parents in Vancouver. John, with whom they were staying over for a few days first, was driving them up to Sudbury early tomorrow morning. Along with John's son, Jack, they were all booked into the same hotel as Moira and Alison for the night and would all meet for a drink and light supper before going to the party. She was surprised that John's live-in girlfriend wasn't coming but John had said he and Jack, whose wife couldn't come, would share, when he'd arranged with her to book the rooms for them all, so she hadn't questioned it. They had been together for more than ten years now so she was sure Pauline must consider her family. Maybe she, like Tim, just wasn't crazy about a weekend with John's family. She was glad Jack was coming. He and Alison always got along well as children and, perhaps, catching up with one another would leave less time for Alison to get panicky. It was a pity he was intending to leave before the brunch at Claudia's house on Sunday, but they could always plead that they should be on their way themselves if Alison started to feel uncomfortable.

It was seven years ago, when their mother died, that she and her brothers and sister had last all been together. She hadn't even seen Hal in all that time until the night before last when John and Grace had brought the two them over to supper. It was odd to find that your little brother was now a middle aged man. Made you feel your age, she thought ruefully.

"What are you shaking your head about?" asked Alison.

"Was I? I was just thinking how old I must be if Hal is middle-aged."

"Is that a riddle?"

"What? No, I just mean that my little brother, who was born when I was twelve years old, just seems so much older than he did when I last saw him which, of course, translates as I must be looking older myself."

"Not necessarily. It could be that late fatherhood, and playing catch-up with having three of them, one after the other like that, has taken a lot out of him. How does Maureen look?"

"Well, she's younger anyway, not much older than you. Funny, isn't it? Claudia's kids are older than her uncle's."

Claudia, like her mother, had married and had her two children early. At age eighteen and seven years younger than Moira, Pauline had almost beaten her to motherhood, Alison having arrived just a few weeks before Claudia, and had very handily beaten her to grandparenthood.

"You're from a family of extremes," said Alison.

"Extreme opposites in that particular branch - there's Claudia, the schoolgirl bride while her brother and sister are eternal students."

"I don't think they intend to be eternal students. They just both went off on a couple of tangents and had to start over when they found they wanted to do other things. It'll be nice to see Jackie again. I never seemed to hit it off with the Sudbury cousins, but Jackie was always fun to be with. Maybe it was because we were both only children while Claudia, Brian and Marie were like some kind of impregnable united force whenever I saw them. Even then, Claudia always wanted to play Barbies instead of doing something intelligent. She was as empty-headed as her namesake."

Claudia had been named after the character in the Rose Franken books, which her mother had discovered and read voraciously in her early teens which, Moira rather thought, had been what led her to an early marriage, although Vince was hardly a replica of the fictional Claudia's husband, David.

"I didn't know you'd read those books."

"I haven't. I just know they're about a dippy rich girl called Claudia who marries a dependable type and lives happily ever after. They're long out of print, surely."

"Oh, I imagine so. There'd hardly be a market for them now. She didn't live happily ever after though. There was the War, and her husband had tuberculosis and their son, Bobby, was run over and killed."

"*You* read them?"

"There wasn't a heck of a lot else to read in our little public library back then."

"That's your excuse. Well, at least I didn't get named Claudia. Are you sure you don't want me to take over the driving?"

"Do I look as if I'm getting to zombie-state, then?"

"No... Well, a bit..."

"Thanks a lot. We should be at Parry Sound shortly, so start looking out for a restaurant and we'll take a break and then switch over."

* * * * *

Alison let herself into the house after her mother dropped her off, not expecting Ian to be home. She'd phoned earlier to let him know they were on their way home, but there had been no reply. The dogs weren't there either but the porch lights, hall and kitchen lights were all on indicating that he had come home and had taken the dogs for their walk. It was already dark so she hoped he hadn't let them off their leashes in the park. Fanny, particularly, had lately been displaying a marked tendency to wander off, ignoring calls to come back. He'd obviously been at his mother's for supper again. She sighed. Maybe Janet had forced him to take her out for supper, though. Or, better still, maybe Janet had finally got through to him. She had told Alison, before she left to go to Sudbury with her mother, that she figured that a rude awakening looked to be the only way to make Ian see sense and let her get on with her life her own way. They'd agreed that any such action would have to come from Janet since Ian would only interpret Alison's telling him to give his mother some space as some kind of jealousy or something born of dependency feelings of her own.

She took her overnight bag upstairs and unpacked it, putting most of the clothes into the laundry bin. She was about to start running a bath when she heard the kitchen door open and ran downstairs. The two spaniels came charging towards her and she started to pat them and tell then how she had missed them when she realized Ian was right behind them. She stood up and he held her tightly in a fierce hug.

"You didn't miss them half as much as I missed you," he said. "I'm sorry, Alison, I should have come with you. My place was with you. Mom gave me hell..."

"It's okay. My Dad didn't go either. He says more then a couple of hours with Pauline and Vince and he's ready for the nut-house. Things worked out all right and it turned into a nice weekend for Mom and me doing a together kind of thing without the two of you."

"That's not exactly what I mean." He loosened his grip on

her and put his hands on her shoulders instead. There were tears in his eyes. "My priorities have been out of whack the last few weeks. I-I'm sorry."

Alison hugged him again. "It's all right. Your father died. You had every right to turn into an unreachable idiot for a bit..."

Thank goodness, she thought. Janet really had straightened him out.

"Where were you?" she continued. "There was no answer when I phoned and your cell was switched off."

He sat down on the stairs and pulled her down beside him. He absently patted Felix with one hand and put the other arm around Alison.

"I was at the gym, trying to make up for lost time. I went into the office this morning – I've got a lot to catch up on there, too – but I kept worrying about you up there, with all those people you hardly know, and couldn't concentrate beyond going through my in-tray, phone messages and e-mail. Then I came home and made a sandwich for lunch and called my sister Linda to apologize for accusing her of not caring about Mom when all she was doing was trying to get me to back off and let Mom find her own way. Then, I must have been so exhausted from thinking about all my transgressions that I fell asleep watching the game on television and didn't wake up until nearly six – don't even know who won. Then I couldn't remember what time you said you'd be home so I called Tim and he told me you probably weren't much more than halfway home yet and would probably be stopping for supper. So I had a light supper and went to the gym. Then, of course, when I got home, I realized the dogs were well and truly overdue for a walk. Then Fanny took off on me –"

"I did mention to you, the other day, that it was not a good idea to let her off – not that we're supposed to, in the park, anyway – I really don't know what's got into her just now."

"She finally came back. Thought we were going home without her, I suppose, and was afraid of missing her supper."

Both dogs pricked up their ears and looked from Alison to Ian and back again.

"Oh," said Alison, getting up. "The poor dogs must be starving."

"Me, too."

"And me. We did stop for supper but just a sandwich because we'd been to the brunch and weren't terribly hungry. I'll make us both toasted cheese and tomato on bagels and you feed the dogs, okay?"

She went into the kitchen. Ian followed her and they both set about their tasks.

"D'you think this open bottle of wine is all right?" Alison asked, putting the cheese away. "It's been sitting in the fridge for the last week." She picked up the bottle.

"It might not taste as good as it should, but it'll be drinkable. I'll look after it." He took it from her, got two wineglasses from the cupboard and poured the remainder of the bottle of wine into them, let out the dogs, who had finished wolfing down their supper and sat down at the kitchen table. Alison slid the bagel halves with their cheese and tomato toppings out from under the grill and onto plates. She brought them to the table and sat down opposite him. Ian raised his glass.

"To us," he said.

"To us," Alison touched her glass to his. "I'm so glad you're back again."

"I was really behaving like a jerk, wasn't I?"

"A very self-righteous jerk, but a jerk all the same."

"Sorry. I'm over it now. My mother straightened me out. She more or less turned me out yesterday. Said I should be up in Sudbury with you and she was ashamed that I didn't know enough to put you first when there was absolutely no need for me to be going there every day. Did I really think she was so dependent on my father that she needed me to stand in for him? And a lot more of the same."

Alison decided it was best not to respond but to wait until she could say something positive.

"The worse part is that, subconsciously, I really did think that. I mean, he tended to have all of us under his thumb with being so much the *my way or the highway* type that the three of us, my sisters more so than me, I guess, tended to go along with his opinion, or decision on whatever, to his face, then go our own way. Anyway, I knew Mom did that, too, but sort of forgot and saw her as being too devastated to make her own decisions." He paused and concentrated on eating for a few minutes. "Anyhow, let's put it to rest. As Mom says, if she really needs me, she knows where I live." Alison smiled and he caught her eye, making them both laugh. "So, let's talk about *your* weekend. How was it?"

"Oh, I managed not to disgrace myself," Alison replied. "Jackie, was there and we both always got on better with each other than with the Sudbury cousins. He said to say hi and tell you that they'd never come back to live in the Toronto area again. Ottawa's a much nicer city. The move hasn't hurt the kennel business at all and a couple of previous customers have driven up there rather than go somewhere else. Talking about cities, Sudbury's much improved these days. I hardly recognized it. Of course, it's been years since I was there. My Aunt Pauline was very disappointed that you weren't there. She said, once she realized that it was a surprise party and not a dinner out with her kids, that she immediately thought she would finally get to meet my husband, and to see my father again – it's been all of fifteen years, she told my Mom, why was he always working so hard? So it was a great disappointment that neither of you were there and wasn't I getting to look like my grandmother – when she was my age, when they were children..." she broke off. "Don't look at me like that; she really does go on just like that."

"Oh, I'm sure she does. You're brilliant at picking up people's mannerisms. I love you. Let's go to bed. You shove the dishes in the dishwasher and I'll let the dogs in."

"I was about to run a bath when you came in. I've been travelling all day and you're fresh from the shower at the gym, except for taking the dogs to the park."

"So, we'll have a bath together. Come on. Let's go."

* * * * *

"So, Alison had no problem?" Tim said, carrying a tray with two mugs of coffee and a plate of cookies on it in from the kitchen. He put it down on the coffee table in front of where Moira was sitting on the sofa and sat down on the adjacent chair.

"She was fine at the party. I think she sort of adopted a long lost cousin – niece, whatever – persona, and just stayed in character. She, obviously, couldn't carry it over into the brunch at Claudia's this morning, so stayed with me and made it through.

It took her a while to wind down in the car, but that was okay. I was driving..." Moira picked up her coffee and took a sip. "Wow, this is a little strong for going to bed. We'll be awake all night."

"Good, though, isn't it?"

"It is. You went shopping in Kensington Market, I take it? What else did you get?"

"Oh, all sorts of things. I went a little crazy like I usually do there."

"Just as long as there aren't all kinds of vegetables that I'll have to freeze because we'll never get through them all before they go off..."

"Wrong time of the year for that. I got lots of asparagus, though. But we can just have that every day. It's not something you get tired of."

"Right."

"So, Pauline and Vince were suitable surprised?"

"Actually, it was a genuine surprise party. I was –"

"– surprised?"

"Ha ha. I thought they would have guessed something was going on, but it seems everybody involved managed to keep quiet. There were lots of their friends and neighbours there, too. You'd have thought somebody would have inadvertently or, even, intentionally, dropped a hint."

"What did your brothers think of it?"

"Well, you know John's not the most family-oriented guy..." She took a bite of a shortbread cookie and chewed it. "And Hal hasn't seen any of us since my mother died –"

"He saw me two years ago when I was in Vancouver."

"– any of us who were there. I think what I'm trying to say is that, allowing for the fact that we're not the closest family in the world, it all went pretty well. John made a speech with anecdotes about Pauline being a nuisance of a little sister, with he and I having to watch her when we'd rather be playing with the other kids, that sort of thing. Hal came at it the other way on – Pauline having to watch him when she'd probably have preferred to be off playing with her friends. Most of what he said was true, but John rather embroidered his memories to make us sound like a normal family."

Tim knew what her childhood had really been like. She'd told him years ago when she tried to explain why she didn't want to be married. He'd eventually convinced her that her marriage wouldn't turn out like her mother's, least of all if her marriage was to him, and talked her into it. She was glad he had. Theirs had been a good marriage based on respect for each other. True, Tim tended to pull stunts like pleading too much work to take time out for family functions like Pauline's birthday party, but he was always there when her own insecurities began to show like way back when her fear of marriage was threatening to destroy their relationship. When she'd had that ectopic pregnancy and nearly died. When Alison's anxiety problems began and she'd been afraid she'd failed somehow as a mother. Yes, he'd always been there when it mattered. That didn't mean she had to let him off lightly, though.

"Pauline accepted the fact that you couldn't get away, but I think Vince and the kids thought it was an excuse. What are you going to do when we retire and you can't use pressure of work to get out of visiting my family?"

"Oh, I expect I'll develop something incapacitating like a bad back or – what is it old men in Victorian novels always have – gout."

He put his foot up on the coffee table, feigning horrendous swelling.

"That'll be really credible," Moira said, but couldn't help smiling.

"You're not really mad, are you?"

"Not now. Alison and I had a good time really and it was nice doing something together. It was sort of fortunate in a way that she ended up on her own, too."

"So, I'm forgiven?"

"I didn't think you even recognized that you needed forgiving."

"Low blow. But I make great coffee. I'm worth keeping, aren't I?"

"Oh, well worth it."

"Good. So, how about we have a real weekend getaway next weekend? Bermuda? It's a contra – that travel agency account."

"Really? Sounds like a great idea. Definitely has a more romantic ring to it than Sudbury. First flight out on Friday morning?"

"'Fraid so, but it's worth it when you get there."

"Oh, I wasn't complaining. I just need to know in advance to get organized. It looks as if I'm starting summer hours early this year what with taking last Friday afternoon off and now, the whole of next Friday..."

"Why worry? They need you more than you need them at this point of your career, don't you think?"

"I don't know about that," laughed Moira. "The new breed of young women, falling over themselves to become magazine publishers, are pretty aggressive. They don't have much respect for age and experience. Their world is a dog eat dog one."

"Sounds just like this year's crop of design graduates. It's the way they're getting taught that does it. Makes them think they're more valuable than they are. I mean, I'm all for creating confidence in kids, but the schools go overboard with it these days. I'm at the point of refusing to even read the stereotypical resumes they're taught to send out telling me what great assets, for God's sake, they'll be to the firm."

"Exactly. You have the advantage of owning a large share of the company, though, which makes them dependent upon you for work. You don't have to work with the constant feeling that you're perceived as a dinosaur. Anyway, Friday shouldn't be a problem. To be honest there isn't another group publisher who even works on Friday but, then, they're all men while at the publisher level they're mostly women at the moment, so I'm the most obvious target for them. You know, I'm seriously thinking of retiring and becoming a consultant..."

"That bad, is it?"

"Well, yes... I'm tired of it, I guess. Consulting would give me the challenge of getting things off the ground again instead of picking up the pieces after people who are not really qualified to do their jobs. What do you think?"

"It might be a good bridge to retirement. Lots of people in the industry do that now but they mostly get leaned on for charity contra-type projects – you know, your bill becomes a tax receipt instead of being paid."

"It's not as if we have expensive tastes and need the money and it would make a change from the huge chunks the government has been taking out of my salary all these years. Anyway, I'm only at the thinking-about-it-stage..."

"Maybe it's time for me to be thinking of winding down a

bit, too. Time for us to get out and see a bit of the world, maybe, before we get too old and befuddled..."

"I'm feeling befuddled already just now. I'm going to fall asleep in a minute, I think," Moira said, standing up and stretching sleepily. "A weekend in Bermuda is just what we need. I can't wait for next weekend."

Chapter Seventeen

"So he's going to go with her to the bereavement group?"

"Yeah. Janet straightened him out about hanging around her all the time but they've both decided that it will be as well to go to the group program she found. It's in one of the rooms at the library where she volunteers actually. That's how she heard about it."

It was the Monday after Alison's Sudbury weekend and Terri had picked up a pizza to bring to Alison's house for lunch. As usual it was a late lunch, during the early afternoon when it was reasonable to expect one person to be able to manage the store alone. Alison had filled her in on the events of the weekend over the pizza and they were now drinking coffee.

"She actually joked," Alison continued, "that it would, hopefully, ensure that Ian wouldn't overreact to her own death and give me a bad time again. I said she shouldn't joke about such things. Anyway, just being able to talk about it with other recently bereaved people should help them both to get it into perspective although, personally, I think he should be on an antidepressant. But, short of my slipping it into his coffee when he's not looking, that isn't going to happen, so let's hope the group will solve the problem. Now that we've mulled my weekend over thoroughly, how was yours? Mark get home okay?"

Mark and Terri's brother, Scott, had been in England for most of the preceding week on *Envirodermics* business.

"Yes," Terri replied. "That's why I invited myself to lunch. You're the only person I can really talk this over with..."

"What?" Alison asked. Then, when she didn't go on, asked. "Is something wrong?"

"Not wrong exactly. I just don't know how right it is. Maggie had asked them to come over to discuss 'the succession' arrangements."

"The what?"

Terri knew there was no reason for Alison to have given any thought to the subject; although she had known herself that it would come up sooner or later.

"Maggie, my aunt... They – she and my uncle – want to retire when she's sixty. That's a little over a year from now. So..."

"She wants you and Mark to go back to England?"

Terri nodded and they were both silent.

"Do you still want to go?" asked Alison, eventually. "I mean, when you first came back, I remember you saying that you were happier there, but that was before we started the store and you bought your house and had the children and everything..."

"I don't really know what I want. My first reaction was *no*. No *way*. But I think that was because of – you know, Ian's father dying and the thought that it could happen to my parents. I've been a bit obsessed with that, I know. After all, we're only talking a six or seven hour plane ride, whatever, so that's a pretty silly reaction when it's your husband's career you're talking about, right? And selfish, too, because Mark's father really has been ill. Mark popped up to see him while he was there and he's a lot better now. Anyway, I was glad I hadn't actually voiced my first reaction because Mark then said that it looked as if I was in a bit of a quandary just – and, here's the key – just as he was."

"You mean Mark's not crazy about the idea?"

"He sort of would like to live there again, but doesn't *not* want to live here." She shook her head when she saw Alison's puzzled look. "Sorry, I'm not making sense. What I mean is, he sees all the pros and cons but has no feel for what should work best. They discussed all the alternatives like entirely separating the North American interests from the U.K. and European ones so that the U.K. could be sold off and Maggie would retain major share ownership in North America and Scott and Mark would continue to purchase shares out of profits or however that's set up. In other words, *status quo* insofar as we're concerned here. The thing is that if Mark takes over the day-to-day operations over there, it would be under the same arrangement for him, or Scott and himself, depending on what kind of arrangement they worked out, to continue to accumulate shares according to profits, although Scott's too tied up with U.S. operations to have time for specific involvement in Britain or Europe. From her own point of view, whether she sells or Mark takes over, she's only concerned about maintaining an investment which will generate the money she needs as income, and to cover all her philanthropic interests which, as you know are huge and require *mega* dollars. The compromise position they came up with in the end was for Mark and me and the kids to go over for the next school year and see how things work out. On a personal level, I mean. We'd rent the house, maybe to someone on a sabbatical or something like that, and live in that furnished flat in Maggie's house, you remember?"

Alison nodded.

"So, in other words, there's a year to make up our minds," Terri summarized, " and Mark nominally retains his head of Canadian operations position and gets to junket back and forth, as needed."

"What about you?"

"That's what Mark said. Maggie suggested that, since you and I have been so successful, I might like to work with the franchisees... consulting, sort of..." She could see what Alison was thinking and, knowing she wouldn't actually say so, nodded and said. "I know, same situation I found myself in ten years ago with a made-up job."

"It *is* different now, though," Alison said. "I mean, you'd be able to work part-time hours around the children and school and dancing lessons –" they both grinned at this because Terri had just gone to her mother for help, after attempting to make Becky's costume for her first ballet recital and failing miserably – "like you do with the store and..."

"And I should be looking at the big picture."

"Yes."

Terri sighed. They both knew that, however much she valued her relationship with Alison and the store, it couldn't be allowed to come before Mark's interests and those of *Enviroder-mics* as a whole. They also knew that the success of their store was not due to either one of them individually but to the fact that Alison's creativity complemented Terri's practicality and *vice versa*. Worse, though neither one was about to mention it, was the fact that while the store had been, and still was, Alison's lifeline in keeping agoraphobia at bay, it could equally well become the impetus for her plunge right back into reclusion if she couldn't handle the pressure of operating it on her own.

Alison sat contemplating her empty coffee mug for a few minutes, then looked up.

"Maybe it really is time we moved on," she said over-brightly. "Want another coffee?"

"Please," Terri said, pushing her mug cross the table, knowing intuitively that Alison would take the mugs to the coffee pot rather than bring the coffee pot to the table, to give herself a moment to regain her poise. "We don't have to sell the store," she said when Alison put their re-filled mugs of coffee back on the table and sat down. "You managed everything on your own both times when I was on maternity leave."

"That was a little different – you were right *here* when I messed up the ordering or couldn't manage the payroll, not on the other side of the ocean. I can manage staff and train the part-timers and come up with, sometimes even brilliant, ideas for promotion, but administration gets me stressed and... well, you know..."

"What about offering Amanda a share in the business and have her look after ordering and inventory?"

"Two things that come to mind immediately. She only wants a job to help out with the family finances, not a career. She doesn't mind short spells of managing the store but definitely wouldn't want to do it full time. And, secondly, if you and Mark decide to go the staying in England route and we do sell, another partner could turn into a major problem."

"You're right. I'm being selfish. It might have worked if we still had Christine – remember her?"

"She went into partnership in that bulk food store."

"Yeah, she was really into a career once she dumped her husband," Terri laughed. "I want to keep the store so much, Alison, but it's not something you can really do as an absentee partner, is it? I suppose some kind of stopgap arrangement like that could work if we knew that we were definitely coming back to live. And, it's not just that I want to find a solution just for my own benefit. I know you want to keep the store, too."

Outside one of the dogs scraped at the kitchen door. Alison stood up and turned towards the kitchen door. "Have to let them in before they do any damage," she said. She had put them out when they first sat down to lunch. Felix and Fanny now came bursting in and rushed to Terri to be petted.

"All right that's enough now," Alison said, closing the door. "Go and lie down." The dogs gave her what Terri thought was a very regretful glance and went over to the dog pad in the corner of the kitchen where they both flopped down. Alison sat down again. "Look," she said, "the store is our partnership. It works because we complement each other. It can't work any other way. It *is* time to move on, Terri. Look, I realize you're worrying about me and I appreciate your concern but, actually, I sort of have the answer. I'm going to have to spend more time on the website as time goes on. Rod wants *Envirodermics* to get into online selling which is only just beginning now but is likely to be huge in a few years..."

Terri was not entirely familiar with the internet. Alison had begun experimenting with web page design and had taught herself how to code because it interested her in the same way that graphics software had interested her when her father had first started using it in the eighties. Through Tim, whose company had been handling *Envirodermics* advertising since the need for the objective approach to communications taken by an agency was required had become evident a few years before, and his account executive, she had convinced Scott and Mark and, eventually, Maggie, that they needed a website. Tim and Alison had come up with a basic design and Alison had created Canadian pages in English and French, her father's firm providing translation, and pages for U.S. products and currency. In the U.K., the same pages had been customized for British and Europeans, respectively. Alison worked with people there by e-mail, and with Rod Parker who was the North American retail marketing manager.

"... so you see, I'd have to spend more and more time working on it. And people in the mall, who I've been doing flyers and newspaper advertisements for, have been asking me about websites, too," Alison was saying. "In fact, I really do have another career to develop, Terri –"

Terri, to her mortification, felt a lump in her throat and tears spring to her eyes. She buried her face in her hands. "I don't want it to end, Alison," she spluttered. "It was so great working together. You know, we've never even had a serious quarrel and it's ten years almost to the day since we first started putting it all together..."

"It's been the best partnership there could be, but your place is with Mark in England. Cheer up. You loved living there before. You'll love it again."

Terri looked up. "How's that for a switch? I thought I was supposed to be the practical one," she said. "But you're right. It *is* time to move on."

"It's time I moved on physically," Alison said, looking at the kitchen clock. "It's almost time for Amanda to leave. She'll kill me. Come on, let's get going."

* * * * *

Driving home, Terri let the tears which she had fought back, sitting at Alison's kitchen table, flow. She was crying for herself as much as for Alison. She knew that underneath her friend's bravado there was sheer terror at the idea of losing her security blanket which is what the store was for her. Terri felt dreadful. Why did this have to happen just when Ian's being such a prick, she thought, then was immediately ashamed of herself knowing that none of us exactly chooses how we react to the death of a parent or anyone else, for that matter. Alison had said that he had seemed to be pretty much back to normal last night, but she was afraid that depression was getting a grip on him. She, if anyone, would be able to recognize that if it were the case.

There was time for everyone to get used to the idea of selling the store before it actually had to be done. As Mark had said, there were plenty of prospective franchisees looking for their kind of location. Maybe, if she started cutting down on her own hours in the store now, Alison would have a chance to get used to her not being around. It was not as if manpower was a problem with the school year ending. If they could find another managerial person to work in tandem with Amanda... And, surely, if it became a matter of taking more managerial responsibility or not having a job at all, Amanda would be amenable to putting in more hours... Living nearby, it had proved quite convenient for her to be on call, for the student part-timers, during the occasional weekend when both she and Alison had been away. But, then, Alison really did seem to be planning on cutting back her own hours in the store, anyway, as the amount of time she needed to work on the website increased. And she was genuinely committed to working directly with

Envirodermics on that and had even joked about it being an ideal job for a social phobic since you worked through the internet and hardly ever actually had to see anybody. But Alison knew that avoidance of people was also the worst thing a social phobic could get into. She'd been practically housebound once and wasn't about to get into that situation again. How was she going to beat it this time? She *needed* to continue with the store.

I've got to stop this, Terri told herself sharply. Alison was aware of the situation now. It might scare her, but she'd figure out what was best to do for herself. Even though she'd said that it was time to sell the store and move on, she might see that, if she could find some reliable help in managing it, it would be better not to for the time being. Terri reached the corner of her own street. She turned into it and pulled into her own driveway and blew her nose, realizing that she had no memory of her drive home as she did so, and checked her eyes in the rear-view mirror to make sure she didn't look as if she'd been crying. She had to go to Crystal's house to fetch Becky. She'd tell Crystal she had to get back home right away because she was expecting a phone call. She just couldn't handle telling Crystal that they were going to England to live, not after all the emotion involved in telling Alison. She'd only end up crying again in front of Becky and Ryan. This was ridiculous. She must get a grip on herself. She and Mark had been happy in England before. New experiences would be good for the children... everything was going to work out... fine.

2001

Chapter Eighteen

It had been the first time they'd flown across the Atlantic since they were in Europe for their honeymoon. While on that trip, despite being extremely vigilant about taking her medication because she didn't want to spoil his honeymoon, Alison had had one full blown panic attack at the airport and a couple of less severe ones during the flight and was so tense by the time they touched down at de Gaulle that he thought he'd have to carry her off the plane. This time she was taking only a natural source relaxant because, she joked, she'd be able to knock herself out with a couple of strong drinks which would be better than spending the entire journey getting more and more stressed. In actual fact, since discovering something called cognitive behavioural therapy, via the internet in the last year, and finding out how it actually worked and, because there were no therapists actually offering it yet in the GTA, working with it by herself, she was now maintaining a higher level of control over her problem than ever before. Ian wasn't thoroughly familiar with the way it worked but, as Alison explained it to him, while she had always a great advocate of exposure therapy, forcing herself to face down her fears, she had been missing the cognitive part, the therapy to correct the fearful thought processes. She seemed to have got it right by working with books on the subject, and they were in London at last.

"Ian! Alison! Over here!"

He recognized young Daniel's voice, as they came to the end of the green channel and out onto Gatwick Airport's arrivals concourse, and swivelled the trolley around almost knocking Alison over as he did so.

"Sorry, honey. They're over this way."

Alison had already regained her balance, spotted Terri and the children and gone ahead of him towards them. Normally, coming out into the huge cavern full of people, meeting other people and scrutinizing each person coming through from Customs, immediately provoked a panic in Alison, medication or no medication. Ian was so surprised he stood quite still and watched as she and the children, with Terri close behind, reached the end of the barrier at the same time.

"I-an," called Daniel.

He'd grown so much since the year before, when they had last been in Toronto staying with Terri's parents, that Ian wondered if he'd have recognized him if the kid hadn't seen them first. And Becky had grown, too. Terri, of course, looked just the same as always. He realized other travellers were having to skirt around him and he was, consequently, getting more than a few dirty looks so he quickly pushed the trolley along to join in all the hugging, welcoming and being welcomed.

"Mark's driving around in circles instead of parking – short term parking is sometimes hard to come by here," Terri explained. "We just have to go through there to get to the Perimeter Road." She indicated a tunnel-like passage ahead of them.

"Yes. Come on, let's get out of here!" cried Becky.

"I can't wait to show you our house and everything at last," Daniel told them. "You haven't seen where we live and we've lived there for more than two whole years now."

"You should have come to visit us before," Becky chimed in. "We've been to Canada every year since we started living here and you've never come here. Daddy's been even more times."

"So's Mum," said Daniel. "She went with him when we stayed with Nana and Grandad Havers, remember."

"Yeah, but we like it there, so that was okay."

"I didn't say it wasn't."

Ian pushed the trolley along, in the wake of Alison and Terri, with the children chattering on either side of him.

"Your Dad has to be in Canada for business," he said. "We don't have that excuse to hop on over. So, how's school?"

"We broke up last Friday," Becky told him.

"That the same thing as 'finished'?"

Becky stared at him.

"You were too young," explained Daniel. "We said 'finished' not 'broke up' when we went to school in Canada. He knows really." He turned back to Ian, "Ian, my dad says you'll be able to fix our computer. *Will* you?"

"Depends what's wrong with it."

"It keeps hanging."

"Oh. I should think I can fix that. Windows 98?"

"Um. Yeah. I think so. It's an old one from Dad's office. We think there's bits of stuff from the software it had in it, for whatever it was being used for, that didn't get removed properly and Dad says you're an expert on that kind of thing. Are you? I mean, I only lived in Canada until I was turning seven so I was too young to know you were an expert."

"Your dad just means that I work with computer systems putting that 'stuff' in and taking it out for businesses. Does this passage or tunnel, as your mother called it, ever end? It seems to go on for ever."

"I think we're nearly there," said Becky. "Mummy's stopping for us to catch up." She ran to where Terri and Alison had stopped to wait for them at the top of a ramp.

"He says he can fix it," she was telling her mother as Ian and Daniel reached them.

"Fix what?" Terri asked, taking Becky's hand as they started to walk down the ramp.

"The computer!"

"For heavens' sake, Becky. You make it sound as if we begged them to come over just to fix your computer."

"It's okay," Ian laughed. "Looks like the great outdoors is finally ahead of us. Mark must be pretty tired of driving around in circles by now."

"It's not been that long. We always do this when we pick somebody up. We just keep tabs on the arrival time and can estimate pretty closely how long it'll take for whoever we're picking up to get through customs," Terri explained as they emerged from the terminal. "And, here he is... coming now."

Mark pulled up in a Rover SUV, the passenger side window rolling down as he did so. "Door's are unlocked," he shouted.

"Come on," said Daniel and Ian followed him to the back of the vehicle where he opened the door and scrambled into the set up seat and helped Ian line the luggage up beside him. Terri motioned Becky and Alison into the back seats, leaving the passenger door open for Ian.

"I can take that off your hands," said an outgoing passenger who had just unloaded his luggage from the car ahead of them.

"Okay, there you go," Ian handed the trolley over, slammed the rear door, hearing the click as Mark pressed the power lock, and ran round to get in himself.

"You see, we have it down to a tee," said Terri, as they drove off.

"Welcome to our local airport," said Mark. "Excuse me for not helping, but it's quicker to let you get on with it and Daniel's quite the expert now. Sometimes things get nasty when somebody behind thinks you're taking too much time. How was the flight?"

"It couldn't have been too bad because I slept most of the way," said Alison.

"You did? I can never seem to sleep much on a plane."

"I cheated."

"I'll say she did," said Ian. "Two fast vodka and tonics, wine with dinner and she was out like a light."

"Good for you, Alison. Hope you don't end up with a headache."

"Come on. There's no need to make it sound like I'm some kind of inebriate." She changed the subject. "How far is your house from here?"

"We first get onto the motorway..." Becky began.

She continued explaining the journey to Alison, with promptings from Terri and interruptions from Daniel. Ian turned to Mark.

"So how are things?" he asked. "Been up there on Wordsworth's lakes yet this summer?"

This was the way he and Derek had jokingly put down Mark's native Cumbria when they camped and canoed together in Northern Ontario.

"No," returned Mark. "We've been waiting for you. You're going to experience Wordsworth's lakes for yourself. We probably won't be able to walk about much because of the FMD restrictions. My parents are expecting us all for a few days next week. It'll cheer them up. My father's retired now and it's my brother who actually runs the farm, but losing the sheep was almost as bad as if he were losing his children." He lowered his voice. "Alison's up to it, isn't she?"

"Oh, yes. Everything seems to be fine at the moment," said Ian. "I just hadn't expected you to go to that much trouble, although I suppose it's no different from driving up to Huntsville from Toronto, or Haliburton, whatever..."

"Well, it's a bit far for us to go up there a lot but we try to take the kids up to see them as much as we can. And they like to meet real Canadians. They don't count Terri. She's almost British again now, anyway."

"Did I hear my name taken in vain?" asked Terri from the back seat.

"Not in vain, love. I was just telling Ian that my parents don't see you as a Canadian any more and like to meet the real ones."

"My name is Daniel and I am Canadian," yelled Daniel in parody of the *Molson* rant, which had been at the height of its success last summer when the Havers children had been visiting the land of their birth.

"My name is Becky and I am Canadian," Becky shouted.

"Okay, okay, I submit," said Mark.

It was obviously a regular point of contention. Ian smiled. He heard Alison laughing with the children. It was good to see her so relaxed. Seven years ago she had been so determined not to spoil things for him when they had gone on the European tour for their honeymoon that it had ended up being something of a nightmare of stress, tension and anxiety for her although, once she grew used to the tour bus and fellow travellers, she had managed to enjoy that part. She had just not wanted to attempt an extensive trip again but had 'practised' a few times when they had flown to the Bahamas and Cuba for long weekends. He had expected, after Terri and Mark bought their house in England, that the idea of flying over and staying with them would not present too much of a problem for her. However, as it turned out, a great deal of her energy was expended in adjusting to the changes taking place in her working life, in gradually spending less time in the store, up until it was sold, and more time in the office set up for her at the *Envirodermics* head office, as the website she managed for them evolved into an online store, and she was afraid that it would put her under too much pressure. Her self-administered cognitive therapy during the last year had greatly reduced the stress of exposing herself to new and uncomfortable situations and, at last, she had felt ready to tackle flying to England and staying with Terri. Seeing how well she had managed the flight, he rather wished they had come before but, after his own brush with clinical depression when his father died, he could well understand Alison's caution in taking things a step at a time. There was always the chance of the anxiety being too much for her to overcome and the temptation to take the easier route in avoiding new people and places, with its inherent risks of depression and agoraphobia.

"Last lap," said Mark, breaking into his thoughts.

Ian hadn't really been paying attention to the passing scenery but now took more notice. They were climbing a steep hill. The road was narrow and the hedgerows on either side grew right at the roadway's edge. There was no shoulder at the sides of the road.

"I hope this doesn't get too icy in the winter," he said.

"Not as a rule," Mark replied, "but, now and again it becomes a bit of a problem. This is the North Downs, by the way. We're not far from where Churchill lived. Chartwell. It's a National Trust property now. We thought you might like to visit it. Anyway, you can see for miles up here. It's a nice place to live and..."

"... having been brought up on the fells, the steepness isn't a problem for you anyway, right?"

"You said it. But, if you think this is steep and narrow, wait till you see the roads up there."

* * * * *

"It's amazing to think he was sitting here writing about the 'greenhouse effect' more than a century ago," Alison said. "How did he fit all that writing, painting and thinking into one lifetime?"

"Well, he *was* almost eighty when he died," Terri pointed out. "You forgot to say critic and revolutionary. Strange man... Of course, if you got to sit here all day, you could get inspired about all sorts of things. It's so beautiful"

"He was actually over fifty when he came here and was starting to go strange – I mean the fight with Whistler, the magazine and general self-indulgence."

"Sounds like it was his infatuation with this Rose that put him over the edge, then there was that other young girl... and he was seventy by then. I don't think he'd have been too nice a person, from a woman's point of view, I mean. Well, he wasn't exactly up to par in the first place according to his wife."

"He really loved this place, though. Listen to this –" she read from a brochure she had picked up before they sat down to tea on the terrace at Brantwood "– *Morning breaks as I write, along those Coniston Fells, and the level mists, motionless, and grey beneath the rose of the moorlands, veil the lower woods, and the sleeping villages, and the long lawns by the lake shore...* It just says it so beautifully. Can't you just see how it would have looked as he wrote that?"

Alison looked out over Coniston Water to the mountains on the other side. She was so glad she had talked Terri into the two of them visiting Brantwood this afternoon. The place had seemed to fill her with a sense of purpose even as the Gondola brought them across the lake from Coniston, when she still had no concept of the immensity of the huge collection of Ruskin's books and paintings that it housed. She had touched on Ruskin's work in a couple of university philosophy and sociology courses and, of course knew of his involvement with the Pre-Raphaelites, but had no idea of the extent of the man's impact. The fact that such eminent figures as Tolstoy, Proust and Gandhi numbered themselves among his disciples was mind-boggling and she had been completely ignorant of his own painting, as opposed to his support of other artists, and the pioneering conservation activity here on the estate.

"I can't believe you've never been here," she said. "You've been visiting Mark's parents just across the lake all these years and never visited Brantwood?"

"Come on, Alison," Terri replied, "it's always the same. It takes having a visitor to get you to a local tourist attraction. Have you ever been to Montgomery's Inn, the Bradley Museum, what's it called? – the Jalna place – Benares...? Outside of long ago school trips, I mean."

"Actually, I *have* been to the Bradley House since grade five. We took Mark's nieces, once, to the Victoria Day thing they have there. I know what you mean, but what about the walks around the estate here..."

"My in-laws are sheep farmers. You can hardly run out of places to go for a walk. Of course, you're not seeing it as it really is, with all these restrictions and next to no sheep. I *will* bring the children over here the next time we're up, though. I think they'd like it, but they're too young to appreciate going through the house. We've been on the Gondola several times and on the *Swallows and Amazons* cruise, and we've been to Hill Top, in the *off* season, and to Dove Cottage, but they didn't think much of that, although that was a while ago, now. Their grandparents always take them to all the tourist attractions when they stay here, without Mark and me, I mean, and they go on outings with their cousins. Last summer, Daniel went climbing with Brad and the boys for the first time."

"I suppose a lot of businesses around here are going to end up bankrupt," said Alison, changing the subject.

"People with huge mortgages on B&Bs, I imagine will. Snack bars and things like that, too. A lot of the farms, though, are owned by the National Trust and leased to the farmers so, under the circumstances, the tenants can hardly be thrown out. Not until the government aid programs get put into place and they see who's going to sink and who'll swim."

"The government has grossly mismanaged the whole thing according to your brother-in-law. Half the culling wasn't necessary and they should have made disinfecting boots and shoes at farm entrances mandatory when the first outbreaks came to light. And he thinks the footpaths should have been closed faster."

"Brad's not exactly Tony Blair's best friend" laughed Terri. "He's right about the disinfecting though. It was making everybody coming into the farmyard step into the disinfectant that saved his home flock. But it was winter and it wasn't like there were the number of walkers that there normally are during the rest of the year. So, I suppose, they didn't really see the danger."

"A lot of the farmers at home have been getting visitors to step in boot trays of disinfectant, apparently. Just in case."

"Yeah?"

"Mm. And they're even asking people, who have been over here, not to come around. I'll be afraid to even step on a hiking trail after being here, even if it's no where near a farm."

"Disinfect or just don't wear the shoes you've worn here. I like those sandals, by the way. Where did you get them?"

"They're just *Rockports*. I brought them online at half price back in the winter. Smart thinking, huh?"

"They look comfortable," said Terri, "and a lot more sensible than mine. I thought we were just going through the house, not traipsing around the grounds for miles. I think I'm going to find I have blisters when I stand up again and we have to walk all the way down to the pier to get the Gondola when it comes."

"I wonder why they called it a *steam yacht*. It sounds like a contradiction, doesn't it? I mean, you think wind power when you think yacht. It's funny to think of people sailing in it a hundred and forty years ago. This whole area is sort of full of images of the past in a more intrusive way than other tourist attraction. Maybe it's just me, being more used to Ontario lakes without ghosts of poets and reivers, and medieval castles and things. Or even high speed boats and their operators getting brought up after lying on the bottom for thirty odd years."

"What? Oh, Donald Campbell, you mean? Amazing when you think about him lying down there dead for most of the time you and I have been alive. Of course, it still hasn't actually been confirmed that it *is* him..."

"That's just technicality. Who else would be wearing his St. Christopher? It's hard to believe that the boat was a hundred and fifty feet underwater and half buried in mud all that time when you see the pictures in the museum. You wouldn't expect the paint to look like that. It's funny how Mark's parents and everybody all talk about the crash as if it just happened recently, isn't it? I suppose the older you get, the less time thirty-four years takes to go by. We were celebrating the Centennial that year, in Canada. I don't imagine it really seems like thirty-four years ago to our parents when there they were; toting us, as little toddlers, around to Centennial events."

"Don't," said Terri. "The last four years, since we came back to England to live, have gone by fast enough for me. I don't want to think about the rest of my life flitting by as fast as, according to you, it must have flitted by for my parents."

"No, you're right. It doesn't bear thinking about. Are you finished? If you are, let's walk down to the dock – pier, I mean. I see the Gondola out there. You could take your shoes off on the grass if they're bothering you."

Walking back down to the water's edge, Alison thought about the years going by faster as you got older and wished she'd known about cognitive behavioural therapy before she had lost all the years of her twenties and half her thirties being too afraid to travel and explore places like this. She shouldn't think of them as lost entirely. After all she'd been a partner in a successful business, earned a degree, she had a good marriage and worked at and on her own terms, a job she enjoyed. Each had taken a lot of hard work in fighting back panic to create 'safe' environments in which she was comfortable. Yes, even marriage because it involved new homes and neighbourhoods, new family members and their homes. Would any of those things have been easier if she had known about CBT? She thought so. This trip to England had been so easy compared to the terror she had experienced during their European honeymoon trip, despite being practically sedated in order to control the panic. Not that she didn't have to work now at controlling the panicky thoughts every time she felt, or thought she felt, a stranger's eyes on her...

"Hey, where are you?"

Alison suddenly became aware that Terri had stopped beside her and was waving her arms in a hailing motion.

"Sorry, I was miles away."

"And I was having a long conversation with myself –" She broke off. "Hey, how's that for timing?"

The Victorian steam yacht was nearing the shore as they reached the pier.

* * * * *

Becky felt cross. She would have preferred to have gone with Mummy and Alison in the Gondola but they said they were going somewhere that was boring for little girls. They didn't seem to realize that it was boring being left behind with a brother and three boy cousins who were all older than she was and who spent most of their time hiding from her even though they had been told, time and again, to let her play with them. Tommy, the youngest of the cousins, used to be her friend but seemed to think that, having turned ten, he shouldn't be playing with girls anymore. Just like Daniel who was fine when there was nobody else around but, when there were other boys, it was like, sister – what sister? The only girl cousins she had were way older. They used to baby-sit her and Daniel in Canada when they were little. In fact, all her Canadian cousins were way older: Adam and William were fifteen and sixteen now, Mummy said. She sighed, letting the swing which she had been twisting around spin itself straight and gave herself a hard shove to get it swinging the normal way. As she pumped it higher; she could see down the fell to the town and the distant lake each time she went up high and decided to keep swinging until she saw the Gondola on its way back across the lake with Mummy and Alison on board. The only trouble with that was that you couldn't really tell from here which boat was which. She stopped pumping and, when the swing was slow enough, she jumped off.

Crossing the lawn, to Nana's back door, she passed the vegetable garden and decided to ask Nana if she could pick some peas for dinner then remembered that they'd had dinner because, at Nana's house, you had dinner at lunch time which meant that it must be nearly tea time. She also remembered that she was supposed to go to Uncle Brad's and Auntie Claire's house down the lane for tea. Well, she was not going to have tea with those boys. She'd tell Nana and Grandad that the boys didn't like her any more and could she have tea with them. No, that sounded babyish. Maybe it would be better... No, there was the answer! One of Socks's kittens had got out again. He was batting at a bee in among the lavender plants and, luckily, not making contact.

"Here, kitty," Becky called softly, going down on her hands and knees on the grass as close to the lavender plants as she was going to go because of the bees and wasps hovering around them. "Come along, kitty. You'll get yourself stung if you stay here. Come on, I'll take you back to your mummy where you'll be safe." She picked up a twig and flicked it until the kitten pounced on it. "That's better. You mustn't go over there. Lavender means wasps and those wasps will sting you and you wouldn't like that, believe me. It happened to me once when I was too young to know better, just like you. And it really, really hurts." She picked the kitten up and ran on to the door. Bursting into the kitchen, she cried, "Guess who I found in the lavender again, Nana? The bad little black kitten."

"Oh dear," said Nana, "what am I going to do with that little devil? He must have slipped by me when I went out to get the washing in. Go and put him in the basket, love."

"He really is a little devil, isn't he?" said Becky.

"I don't think your mummy would like you saying that, Becky. It's not really a very nice thing for a little girl to say. And let's pretend I didn't say it either, yes?"

"If you think I should." Becky put the kitten in the basket with Socks and the other kittens. "Wow, that chocolate cake really looks good! Can I have tea here, Nana? I'd really like to have some of that chocolate cake."

"You're supposed to be having tea with the other children at Auntie Claire's house. But," she relented," I suppose those boys are being difficult again? What do you think, Grandad? Should Becky have her tea here?"

Grandad was already sitting at the kitchen table. He looked at Becky and then around the table. "Well," he said, "looks to me like there might be enough for one more person, since that's a little person, just, and wouldn't be eating more than a couple of sandwiches and some chocolate cake."

"Oh, no. I wouldn't eat more than that," said Becky, hurriedly, "and Nana's chocolate cake is the very best, isn't it?"

"It is that, love."

"Okay, Becky, you just sit down and I'll ring Auntie Claire and let her know you're here."

Becky sat at the table with Grandad and listened to Nana explaining to Auntie Claire about Becky rescuing the kitten from the wasps in the lavender. She felt a little guilty but she really had come in because of the kitten, hadn't she? It might have been a ready-made excuse, but it was still the truth.

"Auntie Claire was about to send the boys out to look for you," Nana said, putting the phone down and getting a glass and plate from the dresser for Becky. "Here you are." She put the plate down in front of her and poured some milk into the glass.

"Help yourself, now," she said, sitting down. "Are those boys giving you a hard time then, love?"

"Put it this way, Nana," Becky replied, "I just wish Uncle Brad and Auntie Claire had had a girl instead of all boys."

"They wished that, too, love," said Grandad, "but it's not something we have much say in, is it?"

"I s'pose not," Becky replied.

"But, you know, Becky," Nana said, "Auntie Claire really likes it when you and Daniel come up to stay. She gets fed up with there not being any girls, too."

"D'you think so?"

"I *know* so. She loves it when you and Daniel come up and, this time with the two of you sleeping over there, it's – well, it's almost like having her own little girl for a while."

Becky thought about this. "I suppose it must get a bit much for her with all those boys..."

"Oh, it does, love," said Nana, seriously. "It really does."

"Perhaps I should get back over there after tea, and she and I can play *Scrabble* or something."

"She'd like that for sure."

"Are Mummy and Alison having tea at that place they went to?"

"I think so. And your Daddy and Uncle Brad and Ian won't be back from Keswick until supper time."

"Ian and Alison are cool, aren't they?"

"Oh, yes. I suppose they are."

"Ian – he can fix any computer you know. He fixed ours when Daddy didn't have a clue what to do and Alison... she makes web pages, you know."

"I'm afraid Grandad and I don't know much about computers. We know how to use that old one of Uncle Brad and Auntie Claire's, that they gave us, so we can e-mail you and your mum and dad, but that's about it for us."

"Well, Alison – she writes up the code that makes webpages. And Ian, he's even more brainy. He sets up systems for big companies. I'm not sure what that means exactly, but it's very important in business."

"Well, love," said Grandad. "We're just old-fashioned farmers, retired farmers, at that. We leave computers and such to the new style farmer like our Brad, your Uncle Brad, that is. I must admit, he got that old thing of ours moving a lot faster, Ian did."

"Poor chap," said Nana. "Sounds to me like he's spending his whole holiday fixing peoples' computers."

"Oh, that's okay," Becky told her, "Alison says he's never happier than when he's playing with a computer but the trouble is you can't cite a computer in a divorce action. That was just a joke, though. Alison loves Ian more than anything in the world. She told me."

"Well, that's good," said Nana. "Now, if you're full of chocolate cake, and it looks to me as if you are, I think, maybe, you should get back over to Auntie Claire's and give her a break from the all-boy company."

"Yes, I think you're right, Nana. It must take a lot of patience to sit down to tea with those awful boys and nobody else," Becky said gravely, looking up from collecting the last crumbs of her chocolate cake with her fork to catch Nana's quick wink at Grandad. "Why did you wink at Grandad?"

"Wink? Oh, that – that's just our signal for 'More tea, love?'" Nana told her, picking up the teapot and pouring Grandad another cup of tea.

Chapter Nineteen

"Yes, Janet. I'm picking them up at around three. Is something wrong?"

Moira turned off the speaker and picked up the handset as she waited for Janet's reply. She took a sip of coffee but found that she'd let it get cold while she was putting together the working paper on re-launch ideas for a gardening magazine.

Janet was explaining that her granddaughter, Leanne, in Edmonton, had been seriously injured in a traffic accident and was being operated on. Janet had booked herself a seat on a plane that was leaving at four-thirty and wondered if Moira would mind giving her a ride to the airport since she had to be there around the same time. She could call a cab if it was inconvenient...

Moira realized that Janet needed moral support more than she needed a ride and said there was no problem in running over to pick her up first, but pointed out that she'd probably have to check in before Ian and Alison were through customs. Janet said she knew that and was only asking because Ian had told her that Moira was picking them up when she'd asked if he wanted her to. Moira said she'd pick her up at two and they'd have time to sit down and have a coffee in Terminal Two and she'd use the tunnel to meet Alison and Ian in Terminal One. She'd actually told Alison to watch for her outside the terminal because she hadn't intended to park unless the arrival time changed, but she'd have more than enough time to find them. Janet said it wasn't fair to make Alison and Ian cart their luggage all the way through the tunnel to Terminal Two when they didn't have to, but Moira said it they'd be used to it after all the moving sidewalks at Gatwick.

After hanging up, she turned back to her computer screen but decided to run downstairs and empty out the cold coffee and pour some fresh before getting back to work. They had converted Alison's old bedroom into a home office when she had started working freelance as a publishing consultant two years ago, since she'd needed something more permanent than the dining room table which was where she used to do any work she brought home. Going down the stairs she decided she had better run the dogs home before she went to pick Janet up. She had intended taking them with her but now she'd have to park the car so it wasn't possible. They were sitting patiently on the patio, waiting to be let in, and jumped up wagging their tails when they saw her change course and cross the living-room to let them in. She slid open the screen door and they both ran through to the kitchen to drink noisily from their bowls. Moira rinsed out her mug, poured fresh coffee and went back upstairs to work.

When Moira reached her house a few minutes before two, Janet was waiting on the front porch. She pulled into the driveway and flipped the trunk opener for Janet to put in her suitcase before getting into the car.

"I hope I'm not being a nuisance," Janet said as Moira pulled back out into the road and set off towards the highway. "I was pretty sure you wouldn't mind since you were going there, anyway."

"No, of course not. Have you talked to – it's Susan, isn't it? – since you called me?"

"They're at the hospital. She was calling me on her cell phone, but you can't have them on inside the hospital, so I was hoping she or Peter would go outside to check for messages before I left, but they haven't. Anyway I left a message with the flight information and said that I'll call again when I get there and I'd get a taxi to either their house or the hospital, depending on whether I get through to her or not..."

"And you still don't actually know what's wrong?"

"Susan said internal injuries and a broken ankle. They're removing her spleen and there's damage to the liver and diaphragm. There's no head injury as far as they know, which is a mercy. There's a woman comes into the library where I volunteer, you know – ?"

Moira nodded, not taking her eyes off the road as she turned onto the ramp to the highway.

"Well, she brings her head-injured son in. He was in a car accident ..."

"If Susan said there's no head injury, that must be what she's been told. The big problem with removing the spleen is the risk of infection, but that's usually taken care of with antibiotics. Anyway, let's not worry about what's *not* a problem. "

"Yes, of course. I'm being morbid. Better straighten myself out. I won't be much help to them otherwise."

"I'm sure they'll be glad of any help you can give and, I'm sure that Susan will appreciate having her mother to lean on."

They stopped talking while Moira negotiated the roads into

and around the airport to Terminal Two where she could park and see Janet off, then go to meet Alison and Ian when their plane landed.

"How old is Leanne?" Moira asked when they were finally sitting down to have coffee until it was boarding time for Janet.

"Seventeen. She and her friend were on their way to the swimming pool where they're lifeguards and they were just crossing the street and the car came out of nowhere. The other girl isn't so badly injured and was able to tell the police what happened. They sedated Leanne right away, but Susan said she was in terrible pain at first. Susan got there before the ambulance. It was only a couple of streets away from their house, she wasn't working today, you see, and somebody came and told her. Susan phoned me when they'd taken Leanne to be prepped for the operation and she could do no more than wait. She had only just been able to get Peter, her husband, know. He was at work and the older girl, Kaylie has a summer job in Calgary where she's at university. Susan started crying on the phone. Reaction, I guess. She hadn't really had time to think properly until then. She was outside and wanted to get back in there in case there was further news. I'd best go straight to the house if I can't get hold of either of them. I won't be much use carting a suitcase around the hospital and I know where the emergency key is kept from when I've stayed there before."

"I would imagine," Moira sought to reassure her, "that Peter will have got there by now and he'll probably look after picking you up at the airport. Or, even if they haven't been able to check for messages, they will have done by the time your plane gets in. I expect Leanne will be resting after the operation by the time you get there."

"Yes, you're probably right. I shouldn't be making contingency plans when there's plenty of time for them to arrange things. I should just try calling again both the house and her cell before I get on the plane, though."

"Do you want to use my cell phone?"

"No, it's all right. I'll just wait and it'll be something I can do when I'm waiting around in the departure lounge. You'll explain everything to Ian for me, won't you?"

"Of course. I expect he'll phone you later. It'll be upsetting for them coming home to such bad news..."

"Yes," said Janet. "They've had such a lovely time over there. Alison really loved it up there where Mark's parents live, in the Lake District. I always wanted to go there myself. In the Spring when all the daffodils are out. You know, Wordsworth's..."

"Alison has rather an overactive imagination. She tells me you can feel the presence of the Lake poets, Ruskin and the like. Even Beatrix Potter. But to each his own. Or her own, I suppose. They do seem to have enjoyed themselves, though. Both of them."

"Maybe she'll phone and talk to Leanne, when Leanne is able to, I mean. She sees Alison as a role model, you know."

"She does? Does she know that Alison has an anxiety disorder?"

"Oh yes. Alison explained it to her years ago. When Ralph died and the girls were here and spent quite a bit of time with Alison. That's *why* Leanne idolizes Alison. She thinks she's so courageous, always facing down her fears."

"I wonder if Alison knows."

"I don't expect she knows just how high in Leanne's esteem she figures, but they e-mail all the time and she gives her advice when she asks for it. Things like that. We all seem to need that sort of relationship in our teens, don't we? You know somebody younger than our parents but older than an older sister – a teacher or someone whose kids we baby-sit, that kind of thing."

"Yes. I suppose you're right. I hadn't really thought about it. I don't think Alison had anybody. Maybe I just didn't notice, although I don't really like to think so. I sometimes wonder if I was that person for Terri. I didn't realize at the time, but there have been things she's said in later years that have made me realize how much impact things I said or did seem to have had on her." Moira was silent for a moment. "You know, it's funny the subject should come up. I haven't thought about her for years but there was a social worker *I* went to with all my troubles. I knew that it was her job to look after me but I always liked to imagine she helped me because she liked me, too."

"Well, I expect she did," said Janet, obviously a little puzzled.

"You see," Moira explained, "I don't often talk about this but my father was an alcoholic, the violent kind and my brother and I, and my little sister, too, at one point, were put in foster care. Then he became sober and my little brother was born and our family was gradually integrated again. I was fourteen by then and quite happy in the foster home that my brother and I were in then, so making the transition was very difficult for both of us. John, my brother, never really made it. He turned sixteen and left home within a few months but that, of course, wasn't an option for me, although we talked about me coming, too, but were afraid the police might find something to charge him with if they found us and it would be difficult enough, at sixteen, for him to find work and somewhere to live. Vicki was my mentor and helped me to work out things at home and stay in school. She even got me my first part time job. Anyway, you're right.

We do all need somebody like that when we're in our teens. I'll let Alison know that it's important for her to call Leanne."

"I'm really sorry to hear about your having had such an unhappy childhood. I didn't know..."

"Of course not. Anyway, it wasn't really so unhappy and it's the way our lives pan out that makes us who we are, so I guess it was all meant to be. I hate to hurry you, but you, maybe, should be getting along to the departure lounge and I'd better get over to Terminal One."

"Yes, you're right," Janet said, looking at her watch. She stood up. "I feel better – not so panicked – being made to sit down and have this little chat. It's much appreciated, Moira."

"Oh, you're welcome. I'm glad it worked out that we had the time," Moira replied. "Your gate's just along that way somewhere, so good luck. I'd better get a move on. They should have landed by now but it'll probably take ages to get through customs. It always does. You take care, now, Janet. And give me a call later this evening and let me know how things are, okay?" She gave Janet a little hug and kissed her cheek. She was glad to see that she was a lot more relaxed now.

* * * * *

Janet truly welcomed the cool linen as she lay down on the bed in Susan's guest room. She wasn't really surprised to find out how tired she was. After all, the day had included two extra hours so she'd normally be asleep by now. The events of the morning and the dreadful news of Leanne's accident, booking her flight, calling Linda to tell her what she was doing, packing, arranging for the cat to be looked after and making sure she hadn't left anything switched on in the house were all things that felt as if they had happened in another life. Even getting to the airport in the afternoon and Moira's insisting they make time to sit down and have some coffee and calm down seemed to have taken place a long time ago. Moira, of course, had been right. Instead of feeling frazzled, she had been able to rest, even sleep, on the plane and arrive cool, calm and collected.

Peter had been at the airport to meet her and they had arrived at the hospital to find that Susan had been told that Leanne was awake and the operation was entirely successful but she would have to stay in recovery for the evening and probably overnight since *'outcome was highly unpredictable with injury and surgery of this nature'* – phraseology which sounded scarier than it was. It was recommended that they go home and get a good night's rest and yes, they'd be contacted if anything happened. They should all be able to see her tomorrow.

It was seven-thirty by then and Janet had prevailed upon her daughter and son-in-law to let her take them out to dinner at a restaurant which she knew they enjoyed from previous visits. It was close to ten when they arrived home and, after calling Linda and Ian to let them know how the operation had gone, as well as calling Moira as she had promised, Janet had unpacked her suitcase thinking that she was well and truly ready for bed.

Unfortunately her mind seemed to be going a mile a minute and, while she was very tired and felt content doing no more than lying in bed, the desire to sleep seemed to have completely disappeared. Her mind wondered restlessly over memories of Leanne and Kaylie when they were small and moved on to her other grandchildren, Linda's two boys who were older than their cousins and had both finished with university now and were involved in their careers. It was a shame that Ian had no children, although there was still time. Alison was thirty-six so she couldn't afford to leave it much longer, although people didn't seem to worry about having first babies after the age of forty these days. She understood Alison's fear of passing on what she thought might be defective genes to her child but, now that she seemed to have found a way to deal with her anxiety disorder, perhaps she wouldn't be so concerned about her child inheriting a predisposition to developing the same problems since she knew she could teach the child coping skills. Moira and Tim would love to have a grandchild, Janet was sure. They were regarded almost as a third set of grandparents by Terri's children. Maybe not so much now but they certainly had been before Terri and her family moved to England and she knew they always came to visit when they were staying with Terri's parents during the summer. And Tim was wonderful at creating unique activities for children. Alison's childhood memories made you feel almost envious. He seemed to have had endless patience in helping her to master things. That was probably why she had such tenacity and could work at things without getting discouraged. Ian said that Alison might get frustrated to the point of tears but she never gave up on anything she considered she should be capable of doing. It might take months, years, even, but she'd get there.

Janet thought about what Moira had confided during their conversation at the airport. It sounded as if *her* childhood had been pretty dreadful. You would never know it, though. She always seemed so poised and sure of herself – she had, after all, climbed the ladder in magazine publishing in the years when it had been almost entirely a man's field. You'd never know she was a battered child, which was clearly what she meant when she said she and her brother had spent a large portion of their childhood in foster care. She was from some small town up there in the lakehead, too, but seemed to have got herself to the city, and must have acquired an education somewhere along the way, before getting a job with the country's largest magazine publisher. And then, as Alison had once put it, the skinny kid from the sticks had snared Tim Fraser from right under the noses of the Havergal, Bishop Strachan and Branksome Hall alumni from whose ranks Upper Canada College old boys were *supposed* to select their brides back in the early sixties. Of course, when Alison had said that, she had thought she was just speaking figuratively, having no idea just how far Moira had actually come from her origins.

She really must get to sleep. Peter had talked Susan into taking a sleeping pill, saying that he'd be on the ball if the hospital called and there was no need to even think they would, anyway. If she had known it was going to be this hard to get to sleep, she'd have asked for one herself. She thought about going down to the kitchen and making herself some hot milk, but felt too comfortable to get up. They said lying down was as good as sleeping when it came to resting so, as long as she didn't get stressed over it, she'd be all right. Even if she was tired in the morning, well, Good Lord, at seventy-one, she was entitled to be, wasn't she?

Was she really seventy-one? It seemed like only yesterday that she was unsuccessfully trying to persuade Ralph to let her keep working until her first pregnancy was a bit further along but he wasn't having people think they hadn't enough coming in without his pregnant wife working. Linda would be fifty next year. How could fifty years have gone by so fast? Well, her mother used to say *'the older you get, the faster it goes, so enjoy it while you can'*. Mom had been in her grave for twenty years now. Lord, she was getting morbid. She must get to sleep.

Alison really seems to have loved the Lake District, Janet thought, her mind going off on another tangent. It wasn't too late for her to see it herself, was it? Maybe she could go on one of those seniors' tours? She could afford it. And she'd love to see Dove Cottage for herself... and all the daffodils. There would surely be daffodils at Dove Cottage in the springtime...

Now, that's what she would do – recite the poem to herself, like counting sheep...

> *'I wondered lonely as a cloud*
> *That floats on high o'er vales and hills,*
> *When all at once I saw a crowd,*
> *A host of golden daffodils...'*

But the effort of remembering what came next was too much, and Janet slept.

Chapter Twenty

"I didn't know Heather was going to be here," cried Becky, jumping out of the car and running up towards the cottage's wraparound porch. "Heather, you look so cool."

"And you look so English, little cousin," grinned Heather, coming down the steps to hug Becky. "Hi Aunt Terri, Uncle Mark and hey, you gruesome, Danny Boy."

"What?" asked Daniel, dodging her attempt to hug him.

"It's a joke. Gruesome – grew some, get it?"

"Right," Daniel said, doubtfully. "I'm going to find Grandpa." He ran round to the other side of the cottage.

"Bet you father loves that look," said Terri, referring to the spiked hair, lip ring and nose stud which her nine-year-old daughter thought made her cousin look so cool. She held Heather at arms length, then hugged her. "Is your mom inside?"

"Yeah. We decided to wait for you before we got on our way home. She and Grandma are out the back, but don't keep her talking long. I have to work tonight."

"I know. I'm surprised you waited."

"We wanted to see you – couldn't wait until you got back to Grandma's apartment. Let's help your dad unload the luggage, Becky. You over your jet lag?"

Terri made her way around the side of the cottage, using the route Daniel had taken, to find her mother and sister coming towards her, having been alerted by Daniel of their arrival.

"Mom! It's so good to see you. And Anna, I thought you'd be gone. It's so great to be here again."

Exchanging hugs and kisses, the three of them went up the steps and onto the back porch where Daniel was already regaling his grandfather with details of their journey, both their flight from London yesterday and today's trip north in the rented car. They sat down in the shade of the porch overhang and Terri nodded her agreement when her mother held up a glass and jug of fresh lemonade.

"You found everything all right at the apartment?" Stella asked, passing Terri the glass.

"Of course, Mom. What could be wrong?"

"Well, there's nobody to take care of it when we're up here like you used to do. Kate's been going over to water the plants since she got her driver's licence, but I had to give up on most of them."

"I thought that lady next door watered your plants."

"She moved. Anyway, it's not important. How are you? You're looking good. Come and sit down. Leave Mark to take care of the luggage. He knows where to go, should do by now, anyway. Is Heather helping him?"

"Yes, and Becky." said Terri. "What's Colin think of the new image?" she asked Anna.

"She decided that turning sixteen gave her free choice in the matter of seeing him or not and hasn't seen him since, but you're right – he'd have a fit. I keep telling myself it's just a phase and not worth fighting about. Like the phase little boys go through not wanting to be hugged by their aunts and grandmothers, etc."

"Yes, sorry about that. Daniel's driving me nuts, too. How long does it last?"

"With Scott, it didn't seem to happen but you must remember how Derek was. You're not that much younger than him and he was really afraid of being associated with his little sister in the minds of his friends. He'd cross the road so as not to have to talk to you and Alison coming home from school."

"I remember vaguely but it didn't seem to have much impact. I hope Becky remembers *her* brother's rejection of her that way, too. Mark's going right back after supper because Scott's called a big meeting for the morning so Dad's going to be the only male company for him over the next couple of days..."

"Dad'll cope he's already been through it with Jon and Adam and William, as well as Scott and Derek," said Anna. "Although William never really did the macho male thing, did he?"

"William's the happiest person I know. He always has a smile for everybody. How did he do at school this year?"

"He passed but didn't come up to his mother's standards. He's used to that, of course, and doesn't let it bother him. He's been volunteering at the city day camp most of the summer. Adam's been put to work in the warehouse, though, now that he's sixteen. He doesn't like work, does he Mom?"

Their mother laughed. "No, Adam hasn't exactly turned out in the mold of his father. He's – well, a trifle lazy, shall we say?"

"*Bloody* lazy, if you ask me," said Anna. "Jon ran into Jim, the logistics manager, one evening down at the SkyDome and he told him his cousin didn't exactly show the level of industry he did when he had that vacation fill-in job. He wanted Jon to see if he could mention it to Scott somehow since he could hardly complain about the boss's kid himself, but Jon said he was hardly in a position to offer an opinion."

"Jon was always a hard worker which puts Adam at a bit of a disadvantage, following in his footsteps," Terri pointed out. "I guess Jon's totally engrossed in computers now."

"Oh yes. He's either working or studying year round with the program he's in. He's really into it, too much so, really. He has hardly any social life."

"What's Kate doing this summer? I heard Heather's working at McDonald's and is expected there at four-thirty."

"Yes, we're going to have to go. I should make it all right if I use the 407. Kate's working at the day camp again. It was through her that William applied this year. Anyway, we'll have to be on our way if Heather's to get to work," Anna said, getting up and walking towards the steps. Stella and Terri followed her. "We'll have a proper chat when you're back in the city, okay? 'Bye, Dad. We have to be on our way. Nice seeing you, Daniel. Heather and I have to go."

Their father broke off the intense talk he and Daniel seemed to be having and followed his wife and daughters towards the driveway.

"'Bye, Auntie Anna," Daniel shouted. "I'm going down to check the boat, Grandpa, okay?"

"Sure, you go ahead," Paul told him. "I'll be right there. The gear's all in there ready for us to go and fish for our supper, but I'll count on you checking it over."

Heather was already in her mother's car, when they reached the driveway, with the door open talking to Becky who turned and ran towards them.

"Hi Grandpa. Hi Grandma," she cried. "Sorry I didn't come

round the back. Heather and I were helping Daddy take our stuff in."

"I don't believe it," Paul said, catching her hands as she ran up. "If it isn't my littlest granddaughter looking all grown up!" He lifted her into the air and set her down again in front of Stella.

"I don't think your father got much help out of either of you, did he?" Stella said, holding up two of several braids in Becky's hair. "You didn't arrive looking like this. It's your cousin's work, isn't it? Well, at least you're not squirming away like your brother when somebody hugs you."

"I love you, Grandma. Be careful of my hair, though. Hi Auntie Anna."

Mark came out of the house just as everybody finished hugging Becky and the round of welcomes began all over again.

"Mo-om," whispered Heather. "I'll be late..."

"Okay, honey," said Anna. "We really must be going. 'Bye Mom. 'Bye Dad. I'll call you, Terri."

They all began to walk round to the back of the cottage again after waving goodbye to Anna and Heather.

"Are you and your dad coming fishing with us?" Paul asked Becky.

"I don't think Daniel will want me to," she replied.

"Oh, we'll see about that. You have time to come out, Mark? You're staying for supper, aren't you?"

"Oh yeah. I'd stay the night and drive down in the morning, but Scott called a breakfast meeting."

"That was a bit selfish. He knew you were coming up here today."

"Well, never mind. I'll be back up for the weekend and I don't need to leave until nine or so. There won't be much traffic. Won't the fish be in hiding at this time of the afternoon?"

"Oh, the kids'll find some. Right Becky? See you later, ladies."

"I didn't unpack anything, Terri. The girls took off on me to do Becky's hair, so I just put the bags in the rooms and got all the kids' stuff out of the car in case they want any of it while they're here. And the duty-free bag and things are on the kitchen table."

"Thanks, love. I'll look after it later. I'm going to sit and have a drink with Mom right now. Proper drink, eh, Mom?"

"Do we have drinks in the boat, Grandpa?" asked Becky.

"Well, not the kind your mother's talking about, but there's pop and that flavoured water you like in the cooler."

"Come on, then. Let's go. If Daniel doesn't want me to come, that's too bad because you two do, don't you?"

Becky took her father's and grandfather's hands and they walked down to the dock.

"We'll go and sit on the front porch, Terri," said Stella. "The back one's starting to get the afternoon sun."

"We're going in first to make ourselves nice cool gin and tonics. We picked up a duty free bottle and a bottle of scotch, too, with Dad in mind..."

"He's not supposed to have it, you know."

"Why, there's nothing wrong with him is there?"

"No, but you have to watch your health when you're in your seventies, on the down slope to your eighties. You'll see when you get there."

"So, you don't want me to make you a gin and tonic, then?" Terri asked, getting ice from the fridge.

"I'm only in my seventies by a few months."

"So that's a 'yes'?"

"You know it's a 'yes'. There's an open bottle there. Leave yours until it's finished. Here, I'll get the glasses."

* * * * *

"The night's are definitely drawing in," said Paul, looking out at the dark lake that evening when he, Terri and Stella were sitting at the back of the cottage. Mark had left to go back to the city and the children were in bed. "How did Alison and Ian's stay with you go?"

"They all had a lovely time Terri was telling me this afternoon when you were out on the lake with Mark and the kids," Stella said before Terri could reply.

"Alison had no problem with her what d'you call it? Social phobia?"

"Not so's you'd notice. She's discovered this cognitive behavioural therapy, it's called, and doesn't need the medication any more. We had a great time. We went up to Mark's parents' place – they said to say hello, by the way –"

"Thought it was all closed up with the foot and mouth."

"A lot of the footpaths are, but the tourist things are open and they'd never been before, so there was lots to see. Alison got quite mystical about it. She can't wait to go back again."

"I can just see Alison at Dove Cottage. She'd being seeing herself back there with Wordsworth and Dorothy, and, maybe, Coleridge or Southey visiting," said Stella. "What did she think of Coleridge's opium pipe there on the shelf?"

"Oh, Mom, that's just what they were into then. It's no different than a poet smoking marijuana today, though modern poets seem to be more into the booze, don't they. Maybe song-writers are more the equivalent. Anyway, everything went so well that they're coming to spend Christmas with us which will be really great. It was tough for them coming home, though. Ian's niece – she's about Heather's age – was hit by a car. Ian's mother's still out in Edmonton, that's where his sister lives."

"Is she all right?"

"Ruptured spleen," Terri told her mother. "It had to be removed and the stuff around it had to be patched up. The big problem is that they like to get you up and moving as soon as possible after that kind of surgery – something to do with the organs healing properly, but her ankle was fractured, so it's pretty tough going, with the crutches and everything. She's pretty despondent and she's usually a perky kind of kid, apparently. Ian and Alison are flying out there tonight for the weekend."

"Really? That's a way to go for a weekend."

"Well, Leanne regards Alison as a sort of mentor, it seems, so she thinks she should help cheer her up and get her thinking positive again. Ian has to be back at work on Monday and his mother is coming home with him, but Alison will probably stay a few days more. She has her laptop and can do anything that's needed so they can hardly complain at the office. I mean she was keeping tabs on the website and was in e-mail communication with them all the time they were in England, so it's not a case of taking extra holiday time. She even went in with Mark one day went over some coding with the chap who does the day-to-day on the British product pages. So *they* owe *her*, if anything."

"That's really good of her, but she'll have to fly back by herself."

"Yes, it'll be a bit of a test, but she really has the anxiety under control now, so she doesn't see any problem."

"I'm so glad to hear that. Alison was almost like an extra daughter when you were kids so I hate to think of her having all those difficulties. It's funny, back then I would have thought she was the last child to be likely to develop self confidence-type problems in later life. She was always the best at everything, wasn't she? Always at the top of the class in marks, good at sports, always got the best parts in school plays. Remember when she was Alice? And in your ballet recitals. She was voted the student most likely to succeed in the school year book when she graduated. You'd left the year before and gone to England but she was going to university, so she was in the five year program. I remember Moira showing it to me."

"Well, she did succeed, Mom. Look what we did with that store. We were always the highest grossing franchisee after the first couple of years it took to get going. It was Alison who figured out how to bring people in. And look at her now. *Envirodermics-on-line* just wouldn't work without her. You've seen it – it's brilliant"

"Give yourself a bit of credit, Terri," said her father. "It was the two of you that made that store work the way it did. It's a shame those people who bought it don't have your acumen, but that's neither here or there. The two of you worked like dogs those first two years and you were both still working on school courses. Lucky for you that Mark had his work cut out making a place for himself in the company and didn't have too much time on his hands or you'd have had a divorce before you had a marriage. All you ever did was work and study. Bored the rest of us all silly."

"You know you still sound English, Dad, even after all these years," said Terri. "But, anyway, it's not that I don't give myself credit, but we were talking about Alison and the fact that the year book prediction *did* come true, despite her having to drop out of university and getting agoraphobic and everything. And those first years with the store were twice as hard for her as they were for me. She had to fight the urge to run and hide every day that she went in there, at first, until she was able to make it what she called a 'safe place'. That's how she's fought the anxiety disorder – by facing it down until she could cope with whatever was triggering it. It takes a lot of energy, not to mention courage."

"That's probably why this cognitive therapy thing you're talking about works for her. She's already halfway there with that pointing her thoughts in the right direction sort of attitude."

"It's actually called cognitive *behavioural* therapy – CBT – which basically means correcting your thinking and applying it to the situation. Apparently it's what they call evidence-based treatment in medical circles but there aren't many therapists who know how to work with it yet. Alison's talking about finding out from the Mental Health Association whether she'd be eligible to act as a facilitator or advisor on how to implement CBT for the kind of group programs they provide. They're the sort of thing aimed at people wanting to improve their lives voluntarily, rather than via professional recommendations. You know, people who've been through therapy but need some ongoing support that's not necessarily professional... that sort of thing, and family members trying to figure out how to live with each other's problems. She said, after Ian went through that bout with clinical depression after his father died, they both really came to understand the impact one person's problems have on another and she thinks it's an area where ordinary people would be much more helpful to families than some psychotherapist telling everybody what to do."

"She has a point there," said Stella. "You see a lot more relationships breaking down under that kind of stress than you do actually working things out. Want another drink, anybody. Or, how about a cup of herbal tea before we go to bed?"

"Sounds good. I'll have the green tea with mint," Terri replied.

"Another drink sounds more my line," her father growled to show his disgust at the very idea of green tea with mint. "But I think we'll have it inside. The bugs seem to be infiltrating the porch here and it's getting a bit chilly, too. Won't be long now before we start seeing signs of autumn..."

Chapter Twenty-One

"Kaylie got home just before I left," Alison told Ian as they reached his car. "You didn't need to park, you know. I was all set to watch for you on the road."

"I just thought you'd need a hug and that wouldn't be possible with all the cars, taxis and shuttle buses all fighting it out," Ian replied, opening the trunk and putting in her suitcase.

"You were right," said Alison. "I did. Thanks."

She turned back from opening the passenger-side door and threw her arms around him and kissed him.

"I needed another one," she grinned.

"Always, at your service, ma'am."

"I was feeling as if I'd pushed myself too much, you know," Alison said when they were in the car and negotiating the ramps to the exit. "Like, really starting to get palpitations and think people were looking at me when I came through onto the concourse. I was so glad to see you."

Ian hadn't needed to take her in his arms to know how tense she was. He'd recognized it as soon he spotted her and was glad he'd made the decision to park the car instead of picking her up outside the terminal.

"You've stretched yourself a lot during the last month. You

really shouldn't have stayed out there. It was nice for Leanne to have you there for a bit after Mom had gone home, but nobody expected you to go out of your way for her like that."

"I guess your mom telling my mom how Leanne looks up to me went to my head," Alison said. "Anyway, we had a good time and I was able to encourage her getting about on those crutches and, let's face it, who's better placed than me to help someone through feeling scrutinized? Susan let me use her car – I ran her into work first – so we were able to get out and about and I took her into the hospital for her physiotherapy and check up. But you're right, I was really feeling frazzled by the time I got on the plane."

"Well, this evening you're going to relax. I have the supper all under control so you don't have to lift a finger... well, except to make up with Felix and Fanny. They're pretty miffed at you for taking off again when you'd not been back much more than a week."

"Hey, you left them, too."

"I was back in a couple of days. They hardly noticed it."

"Oh, *right*."

"Actually I left picking them up until Monday evening. By the time I'd run Mom home and checked to make sure everything was all right there and that the cat hadn't starved to death while she was away, I really wasn't fit for conversation with your parents, so I called and asked if I could pick the dogs up after work the next day because I was dead on my feet and had to get to bed. Of course, that way I got invited to supper, so Monday without you was well taken care of, then of all amazing things, my sister Linda asked me to dinner on Tuesday and I went to my mother's on Wednesday. And yesterday, I went to

Derek's. I actually tried to put that off until you were back, but they insisted I come anyway."

"I'll have to go away more often, then you'll be the social hit of the season," Alison said dryly. "Actually, it's funny how people do that with men – think they're incapable of getting their own supper for a few days. In fact, you probably make the supper more than I do and, all the years, I had the store, we each had to eat alone half the week."

"Silly, isn't it? And a bit of a nuisance really because of having to get home to let the dogs out. I'd probably have done better to have left them with your parents. Well, we can get back to normal now and tonight, it's just you and me, right?"

Alison squeezed his hand. "Right," she said.

"Oh, Mom wants you to give her a call just to let her know that Leanne's continuing to progress. Don't do it now, though. You can call her while I'm putting the finishing touches to the supper, and after you've made up with Felix and Fanny."

"Wow, do I salute you, too?"

"Just keeping you organized. I guess, I missed you and don't want the evening to go wrong."

"I know. I missed you, too. And you're right, tonight's for us. Terri and Mark and the kids'll all be over tomorrow so goodbye togetherness. Becky can't wait to see the dogs again. Daniel's still doing his nonchalant, no-time for the sissy stuff act, but Terri thinks he's getting over it. She says he always gets like that after he's visited his cousins and it usually takes two or three weeks for him to get back to normal, but this time it seems to be taking longer. It doesn't seem like four weeks since we were there in the Lake District, does it?"

"The summer's gone fast this year. It'll be Labour Day a week

Monday. We'll have to stop at the store. I forgot to get milk," Ian said, as they reached their exit from the highway. "Were they still up at the cottage when you were talking to her? Terri?"

"No, this was yesterday and they were back at her parents' apartment. Why?"

"Oh, Derek was asking me. He's probably got hold of her by now, though."

They stopped to pick up the milk and, finally, arrived home.

"Here, you take the milk and I'll look after your suitcase," Ian said, as they got out of the car.

Alison went ahead to open the kitchen door and greet the dogs who were falling over themselves to show her how pleased they were to see her. Ian followed with the suitcase which he took upstairs and left in the corner of the bedroom figuring that it would be accessible if Alison needed anything but could, otherwise, wait until the morning to be unpacked.

"Okay, okay, that's it, guys. Time to go out," Alison was telling the dogs as he came back into the kitchen. "Did you have time to take them for a walk before you came to meet me?" she asked, letting them out into the yard.

"Yeah. I came home early so that I could have the supper ready to go. It was a bit of a skimpy walk but it'll have to do for today. I have everything ready for my stir fry and it'll be ready in exactly fifteen minutes. Pour yourself a glass of wine and leave everything to me."

"With pleasure," Alison laughed. "I'll call your mother in the den so that I don't disturb the gourmet preparations. And I said I'd give Leanne a call when I got home."

She poured them both a glass of wine and took hers into the den. Ian heated oil in the wok and took all the ingredients out of the fridge where he had left them ready and put the rice in the microwave to reheat. He'd known that the journey home from Edmonton was likely to prove a problem for Alison despite the control she had developed over her anxiety. He suspected that the journey probably seemed to have taken many more hours than it actually had done and that Alison, while hiding it well, was feeling pretty exhausted. He'd learned over the years that it was best to let her know that he understood in wordless ways, a hug or a squeeze of the hand having the capacity to communicate far better than asking if she was all right. Somehow action didn't communicate her old worry about her problems putting limits on his life, too, as blatantly as words did, and let her know that he was there for her without making her think that he thought she needed him to be.

Ten minutes later, he switched on the coffee maker and put ice in an ice bucket with the bottle of wine which Alison had left on the kitchen table and took it into the dining room.

"Supper's ready," he called through to the den "I'm just going to serve it up." He heard Alison saying she had to go and she'd call again later and surmised that it was Leanne she was talking to.

"What's the occasion?" asked Alison, as they both came into the dining room from different directions. "For eating in the dining room, I mean?"

"Celebration of your homecoming."

"Really! Wow, candles, too," she said, as he put down their plates and proceeded to light the candles in the centre of the table. "Oops, I left my wine in the den."

"Don't worry about it. I put fresh glasses on the table, anyway. Sit down."

"It looks really good."

"Uh-uh, wine first."

Ian poured them a fresh glass of wine each and held up his glass.

"To a lovely lady who went out of her way to help a young girl feel better." he said.

"To a wonderful man who spent five days worrying about her."

"Am I so obvious?" Ian laughed.

"No, of course not. I just know you thought I was taking on too much and you were right, but I'm glad I made myself stay with people I didn't really know very well and make the journey home alone. It's sort of like creating a benchmark. I know that I can do it and won't be letting anybody down by being too afraid to do such things if I have to." She broke off to try some of the stir fry. "Mm, this is good. You always did make a better stir fry than me."

"Rice went a bit sticky but we didn't have any of the quick stuff and I wanted to be able to have everything ready to go, so I cooked it before I left so that I could just heat it up."

"Never mind. I wouldn't even have noticed if you hadn't mentioned it. I told your mother that you were making your speciality and she said it's amazing how things have changed. Your father would never have dreamed of making supper. I said she was to be congratulated on bringing you up to be a liberated man when it couldn't have been a very easy thing to do, under the circumstances."

"And she said 'Ralph meant well. He just had old-fashioned ideas'?"

"Right."

"Well, let's not get into all my old guilt complexes about that.

Was she happy to hear that Leanne should have no problem with going back to school when it starts? Except for the cast, of course."

"Actually, those new kind of casts aren't nearly so awkward to get around with as the plaster ones. Anyway, Janet's glad to hear that Leanne's happy with her progress, although it wasn't as if I had anything to tell her that Leanne, herself, or Susan hadn't told her already."

"Well, you know... you were just there. It's more real than long distance, maybe."

"Maybe. Anyway, then Fluffie batted the phone out of her hands, you know, the way he does when he thinks she's paying more attention to the phone than to him..."

"Yes, I know. And, talking of Fluff, I hear the back door getting scratched again. I'll go and let them in. Finish up the wine. I bought your favourite liqueur to have with coffee."

Ian took their dishes out to the kitchen, let the dogs in and poured two cups of coffee.

"Terri phoned me," Alison said as he came back into the dining room. "Well, you know that already. That day when we went to Ruskin's house, we were talking about how you never get around to going to the tourist attractions in your own area. It made her realize that the children know next to nothing about Canadian history, so she's planning on taking them to Fort York, Black Creek Pioneer Village, Dundurn Castle and the Military Museum, then down to Fort George and the Brock Monument and all those kind of things next week. She's roping in her old neighbour, Crystal, and her kids for the Niagara-on-the-Lake/ Queenston expedition."

Ian sat down again, after getting the Kahlua and liqueur glasses.

"It's a pity you can't go with them."

"No way. I've done my exposure to strange places bit for a while. I'm settling for the safe and familiar for the foreseeable future. Anyway, it's a moms and kids trip and I'm not a mom... yet. Ah! Kahlua. You're really spoiling me."

"What did you just say?" asked Ian, putting down his coffee.

"Ah! Kahlua. You're really spoiling me," Alison repeated as she picked up her liqueur glass.

"You know that's not what I mean."

"I know. I said I'm not a mom, *yet*. I started thinking, when I was trying to distract myself and get my heartbeat back to normal – it's horrible when you can hear your own heartbeat – that if we didn't do something about it now, it would be too late."

"I thought you didn't want children," Ian said.

They had never really talked about it because, from his viewpoint; he wasn't about to put pressure on her by acting like some pre-women's lib man for whom a son and heir was a right and, from hers; because she didn't feel equipped to be a very effective mother.

"I think you know that it's not that I don't want them," she said, then smiled when he opened his mouth to protest. "It's okay, I know you were only thinking of me. I just didn't want to risk my children having to grow up with a mother who was too scared to leave the house, like my mother and her sister and brothers did. Mom once told me that the happiest part of her childhood was when she and my Uncle John were in foster care and that seems like such a terrible thing for somebody to think, doesn't it?"

"Of course. But I'm not a wife and child-beating drunkard, so there's no danger of that."

"That's not what I meant, silly. The reason for Mom feeling that way doesn't have any bearing on the reason they were in foster care, but the fact that, even before their father came home from the war and that happened, she remembers things like she and John getting the groceries and John taking her to kindergarten the first day. Goodness knows who took *him*. My grandmother had a sister who helped out a bit, as far as I can make out – you know how Mom doesn't talk about it much. I only know this stuff because we *did* talk about if a few times, back before you and I got married. It was Mom, actually, who finally convinced me that not wanting to have children wasn't a reason for not marrying you. That you'd understand."

"Well, of course..."

"But, unless something really awful happened and I had a major relapse, I can't see myself *not* making myself do the mother things that would be my responsibility, if you see what I mean. I'm not being very articulate, am I?"

"I know what you mean. But don't make the decision based on getting older, not being fair to me, wanting your parents to have grandchildren – all those kinds of things..."

"Well, I'm not about to pretend that I haven't been cognizant of all those things, but I learnt a long time ago that putting myself first was not being selfish because, in my case, if I let up on doing what's best for me, I mess things up for the people around me. So, the decision to try for a baby is the result of very serious thinking, definitely not unselfishness."

"I love you. Want another liqueur?"

She shook her head.

"Coffee?"

"No, let's just shove this lot in the dishwasher and go upstairs and start trying..."

"I thought we were taking my mother to the Lake District next Spring. That would work out to –"

"It's hardly likely to be a one-off, my love. It's probably going to take forever and we're going to have to start figuring out ovulation times and all those things. I just meant we'd celebrate dumping the birth control pills. Now, I know that, by waking up this morning in Edmonton, I have a couple of hours on you, but the journey was tiring and, with all the booze you've been feeding me since we got home, I can't promise I can stay awake much longer..."

Ian blew out the candles.

* * * * *

"She wanted to know if I needed her to bring anything this evening for the barbecue with Terri and Mark and the children. And, she says she wants to make us grandparents, after all," Moira said, taking the coffee pot out onto the patio with her. "I brought the rest of the coffee out."

Tim held up his mug without taking his eyes off the newspaper he was reading, then realized what she had said and jerked the paper aside.

"What did you say?"

Moira poured his coffee, then sat down and poured her own. It was Saturday and they were having a late breakfast outside in the sun.

"Alison wants to get pregnant. She says they've started trying. She also said she had a few bad moments on the journey home from Edmonton, but managed to relax and let the panic flow over her until it dissipated. Ian parked and went in to meet her, instead of picking her up outside as they planned, which she said saved her from having a panic attack when she got to the baggage reclaim and started to feel phobic about people looking at her, however much she worked at convincing herself that nobody had even noticed her. She thinks it was because she'd taken on too much in too short a time, and she was all right once she found that Ian was there. She was happy with her performance otherwise."

"Must have been to suddenly decide she was ready to take on motherhood after all these years."

"She's not that old," said Moira, "and lots of women wait until their late thirties nowadays. Anyway, you want to be a grandfather before you reach your dotage don't you? So that you can play with him or her before you get too old and rickety. Not to mention crotchety."

"When was I ever crotchety?" Tim drank some coffee. "Well, I know she's really come a long way from the time when she absolutely refused to face any person or place that was unfamiliar, and, especially during the last little while, but I didn't really think she was likely to ever feel in control enough to believe she could be an effective parent. You know Alison, she has to be able to do something well, or won't even consider doing it and that's just a character trait inherited from me, nothing to do with the anxiety disorder."

"Well, I suppose she feels confident enough in her ability not to let the anxiety faze her insofar as being pregnant and becoming a parent goes. The deciding factor, I think, has been the realization that she counts."

"What d'you mean? Of course she counts."

"I mean finding out that what she does and how she does it, her advice and guidance, just having her to discuss things with... how much it has meant to Ian's niece during the last few years. Then being out there and being able to be useful despite the anxiety of being in unfamiliar situations. It's made her realize that she can have children without her anxiety disorder impacting on them but, more importantly, she's actually *better* equipped to instil confidence in a child than somebody who hasn't had to work at applying it the way she's had to. That's what Leanne gets from her, so if she can be such a strong influence in Leanne's life, she can surely have the right impact on her own child."

"Her own child won't be a young teenager right away."

"Of course not," said Moira. "But the point is that it's made her realize that she wouldn't be doing a child a disservice in having a mother who might end up being – well, being a mother like mine was – which is what she used to think. Anyway, that's what the long conversation was all about. I wish she hadn't picked the middle of my breakfast to call. I think I'll make some more toast. This is too cold and soggy to eat. D'you want me to do you some more, too?"

"Sure, if you're making it. Maybe you could put on another pot of coffee while it's toasting, too."

"Yes, *sir*."

"I can come and do it, if you want."

"No, it's all right. I'll do it."

Moira went back into the house. She put fresh coffee on to brew and cut four slices of bread and put them in the toaster, then picked up the photograph, which Alison had given her just last week, of Alison and Terri with Daniel and Becky taken with the view from Terri's backyard behind them. She thought about how Terri used to call Tim and herself the children's third set of grandparents when they were little. Would they be good grand-parents? Most people became grandparents in their fifties or, even in their forties. They were both over sixty already and, never mind, Alison's joke about having 'started trying', it would prob-ably be a while before it actually happened. Would the child mind having old grandparents? But grandparents were meant to be old. She'd have to give Janet a call and see how she felt about it. She'd be starting all over again – Leanne, at sixteen, was her youngest grandchild now. Janet was a lot older than they were. For all Moira knew, the older daughter's boys could even make her a great-grandmother before Alison had a child.

The toast popped up and Moira came out of her reverie. She buttered it and poured coffee into two mugs which she could carry together without the risk of dropping them and, with them by the handles in one hand and the plate of toast in the other, went to go back outside.

"Can you open the screen, Tim? I have my hands full," she called to Tim, who was back into his newspaper. He jumped up and slid open the screen door, then took the mugs of coffee from her.

Once they were seated at the table again, he folded the news-paper and put it on an empty patio chair where he'd left the rest of the sections. He took a bite of toast and chewed it reflectively.

"You know," he said, "I find it difficult to believe that we're both sixty-one. I don't feel like sixty-one. I mean I don't feel like I always imagined sixty-one to feel like. D'you know what I mean?"

"Of course. I feel the same way myself. I think I've come to terms with the fact that I no longer have 'the rest of my life' left in which to get things done and the fact that I *do* look old to young people even though the mirror seems to see me as looking more or less the same as I've looked for the last twenty years or so, but I find myself often stopping and thinking 'Is this really me? Shouldn't I really be getting a presentation together to land us double page spreads for the new Vichy product in the next six issues?' 'Wasn't it last night we were at the awards dinner when Tim won the Obie for the TSO campaign?' Or, 'Aren't I supposed to pick Alison up from ballet?' Then I feel like I've been hit in the stomach because it's all over and this *is* the rest of my life and those things are never going to happen again."

"No, we only show younger generations how to sell advertising space and win awards now and Alison, with luck, will be picking *her* daughter up from ballet lessons someday soon," Tim said. "Yes, my love, that's what being sixty-one is. But, it's not the end of the world. I don't know what got into me. Well, I do. It was the possibility of becoming grandparents. All the time Alison didn't want to have a child, we didn't have to admit to becoming so – so senior."

"Well, we are and we can't afford to get maudlin. We have all the kids, big and little, coming this evening and there are all the Saturday chores to do yet." Moira stood up, as she spoke, and began collecting the dishes together. "I wouldn't have wanted any of it to have been different, though. Our life, I mean. Before we got to be sixty-one..."

Getting up from his chair, Tim took the dishes from her and put them back on the table. Then he put his arms around her and pulled her close.

"Me, neither," he said.

* * * * *

"Can we go for a walk when Auntie Anna gets here so's I can post my postcards?" asked Becky, just as the intercom buzzed in her grandmother's apartment where they were spending the second half of their holiday. She giggled. "Post my postcards, that's funny."

"Hello?" said Terri.

"It's me, Anna."

"Come on up."

Terri turned back to her daughter. "You have to write them first, don't you?"

"Yeah. But I'll do that while you two are talking about all the stuff you have to talk about that you don't want me to hear."

"Oh. I see. Okay. I was going to suggest going along the boardwalk to the park. I don't have any stamps, though."

"They have them in that *Mac's Milk*. I remember from when we've bought them there before."

"Oh yes. There's a mailbox just along from there, too."

"*Pillar* box."

"*Mail* box. We use the correct terms for the country we're in, right?"

There was a light tap at the door.

"There's Auntie Anna," said Becky, running out to the foyer. "I'll get it – I said that right! We 'open the door' in England, but we 'get it' here." She opened the door. "Hello Auntie Anna..."

"How are you doing, Becky?" Anna said, hugging her. She closed the door and followed Becky into the living room.

"You're here at last," said Terri as the sisters hugged each other.

"Sorry, it's been one of those days."

"Well, let's get a drink and sit out on the terrace. Becky has some postcards to write to her friends and then we're going for a walk to post them."

"*Mail* them," cried Becky.

"*Mail* them," Terri repeated. "We've been discussing semantics..."

"What's semantics?" asked Becky.

"The way language is used. Now you go and do your postcards. D'you want a drink to take with you?"

"Yes, please."

Terri took a can of Fruitopia from the small refrigerator hidden in her parents' drinks cabinet, opened and passed it to her daughter with a straw. Then she poured pina colada coolers over ice for herself and Anna.

"Heather sent you a note, Becky," Anna said, hunting for it in her oversized shoulder bag.

"For me? Oh, that's brilliant. Thank you Auntie Anna."

Anna retrieved the note and gave it to Becky, who took her drink and the note into Stella's sewing room which was serving as her bedroom.

"It's about getting you to take them to the McDonalds, where Heather works, sometime during the week," said Anna. "And I've found an evening when the other two will both be home so, perhaps, you can come over for supper on Thursday?"

"Yeah, we're okay for Thursday except I'll bring the kids and Mark can come from the office. You never know with him so there's no sense waiting for him and wrecking your supper. We got him a rented car – you saw it up at the cottage – so that I could have full use of Mom's car for taking the kids out while we're here. I don't know about McDonalds, though..."

"She's given Becky her whole schedule for the week so, even if it's just going in for a milkshake..."

"Okay. Let's go and sit out on the terrace. It's not too hot."

They went out onto the covered terrace which faced south-east over Lake Ontario so that it received the morning sun and was shady during the afternoon.

"Mark and Daniel have gone to Fort York, by the way," Terri explained, sitting on one of her mother's comfortable patio chairs. "We're having a few heritage education days. Tomorrow I'm taking them down to Niagara-on-the-Lake and Queenston, so they'll be experts on the War of 1812."

"We're going to Fort George," came Becky's voice from the other side of the screen door. "I don't think that sounds like too much fun for a girl, does it?"

"Oh, you'll like it," Anna told her.

"But it's all boys. Tristan and Ryan are coming."

"Our old neighbours, remember?" said Terri. "Becky, I thought you were writing your postcards."

"I am, but I need to know how to spell Beaverton."

"Just as it sounds – Beaver, as in 'beaver', and T-O-N."

"Oh. Okay. I just thought there might be a trick like in Etobicoke."

They heard her skip away.

"So, how is everything?" Terri asked Anna.

"You mean Colin and the kids? Well, now that Heather's decided she doesn't need to do as she's told anymore, none of them are seeing him. It's nothing to do with me. I've done my best to ensure that they maintain a relationship with him since he left, but they just find it embarrassing to have a stepmother who's only a few years older than they are and he doesn't have the brains see them somewhere other than his place and to leave her at home... Or, maybe she won't let him. Anyway, it's hands off as far as I'm concerned. Let them sort themselves out. I felt I had an obligation to keep working at it, but now that Heather's turned sixteen, I feel it's up to them, not me."

"Mom says you've been seeing somebody."

Anna rolled her eyes. "Mom still thinks everybody should be married, doesn't she? He's just a friend. I've known him for years. He's a music teacher."

"At your school?"

"Yes. His wife died last year. Cancer. I knew her quite well and she was a really nice person. Anyway, he just asked me to go out to dinner a few times, that's all. He's still adjusting to being on his own. It's harder for men, I think. But I'm really not interested in him. I'm used to being on my own now and don't want it any other way. Not that I'm exactly on my own with three grown kids. Well, two most of the time, with Jon being at Laurier and it being anyone's guess where he'll be for his co-op semesters.

"How is he doing?"

"Very well. Managed to get a couple of bursaries for this year."

"Good for him. You're saying 'this year' already. It's hard to believe that the summer's almost over. So, it'll be Kate's year to decide which universities to apply to?"

"Right on. Her best friend's looking at McGill and wants her to think about it, too. So, it could well be only Heather left at home next year. She says she's not university material and wants to take an Early Childhood Education course at Humber so she's not intending to stay for OACs. They're going to be phased out, by the way. Did you know that?"

"No, not that I ever figured out why we had them anyway. The gap year idea always seemed to me to be a better option than a formal year of so-called university preparation. Anyway, I would have thought being exposed to my kids as preschoolers would have put Heather off the idea of a career in early childhood education."

No," Anna shook her head. "She still wants to do it. Your kids weren't so bad, anyway. She's always been very attached to Becky. Remember that picture Mom loved so much of Heather holding Becky as a newborn?"

"It's on the wall in the den, still. Yes, she was always keen on looking after little kids, wasn't she? I suppose I can empathize, being the youngest, I never got to be a big sister either."

Becky slid open the screen door and came out onto the terrace waving her postcards.

"I'm all ready" she said. "Want to see them, Auntie Anna?"

"Well, I expect they're private, aren't they?"

"The picture side. There's Santa's Village for Billy, the little boy who lives next door to us. You saw him when you stayed with us. He's bigger now, though. Then, there's all the sand at Wasaga Beach for my friend Michelle, because she doesn't believe that you can have the seaside without the sea, the Big Chute for Gemma and, for my best friend, Emily, there's Ste-Marie Among the Hurons."

"More heritage education," Anna murmured to Terri.

"They enjoyed it," Terri said, defensively. "You liked it, didn't you, Becky?"

"The movie was a bit boring and that bit where you have to look at the displays, 'cept the interactive ones. But all the pioneer things are interesting and the chickens and things. And the dressed up people, cooking stuff and that... And the blacksmith, I liked him."

"D'you think you could have handled life in those times, Becky?" asked Anna.

"Well, it would be a bit hard for someone used to television and computers and everything like me, but it must have been easier for those Jesuits because they didn't know anything about technology. They didn't even know about electricity or gas, even. They only had fireplaces and candles."

"You know you're the same age as the kids in my class now?"

"I am? I'll be in year five in September."

"You'd be in grade four here. The difference is that kindergarten isn't counted as a grade. So, you're six in grade one but, over there, you're five in *year* one, that's right, isn't it?"

"Ah-ha. It would be funny if you were my teacher. I'd have to call you Mrs. Abbott. Are we ready to go out now, Mummy?"

"I suppose we are," said Terri. "Go and put your sandals on. You weren't thinking of going barefoot, were you?"

Becky giggled and ran back inside. Terri and Anna picked up their empty glasses and followed her.

2006

Chapter Twenty-Two

"*The Daffodil Princess*, Mommy, please, please."

Sylvie was three and a half and wasn't entirely happy about having a baby brother. Alison put the sleeping baby into the bassinette on the floor beside her and pulled her daughter onto her lap.

"We don't have time to read just now, Sylvie. Daddy's going to be home in a minute and it'll be time for supper."

Sylvie looked pointedly at the bassinette. "*He's* asleep," she said.

"You know that Ben's too little to have supper with us. We're going to leave him in the bassinette and you and I are going to set the table. We'll read *The Daffodil Princess* later when you're ready for bed."

"*The Bravest Boy*, too? *Then* I won't be cross anymore."

"We'll see. You'll maybe fall asleep."

"No I won't because *The Daffodil Princess* is my favourite story."

Alison decided not to point out that Sylvie quite often fell asleep when she was reading the book to her and hugged her instead. It was nice when your own child was your number one fan yet the fact that her mother had written the book she claimed to be her favourite had no significance at all. To Sylvie, it was just another book which she just happened to like best at the moment. To Alison, it was the highest commendation she could ever have expected. *The Daffodil Princess* was the first book in the series which she had, at first, self-published but which had since come to the attention of the country's premier publisher of children's books and was fast becoming a staple in young children's libraries.

The idea of writing a children's book had come to her the Easter she and Ian had taken his mother to England to visit the Lake District and stayed with the senior Havers in Coniston, fulfilling Janet's lifelong dream of seeing the wild daffodils she always referred to as 'Wordsworth's daffodils'. Alison's pregnancy had been confirmed the week before they embarked on the trip and, despite a bit of a growing problem with morning sickness, Alison had refused to let Ian cancel. One morning, she'd been up early, eating the crackers which she'd taken to carrying around with her, while sitting in the window seat in Mark's mother's kitchen which overlooked the town of Coniston and, more to the point, the patches of wild daffodils to be seen all over the fells. They'd taken Janet to Gowbarrow Park and to Rydal Mount, where Wordsworth planted his own daffodils, and were, in fact, beginning to feel a little overdosed in terms of daffodils. Looking down the fell in the early morning light, Alison thought about how different women of her mother-in-law's generation had been – the stereotypical mothers, with no lives of their own, that you saw in old 1950s movies and television shows. Yet, a scant ten years later, her own mother's contemporaries discovered that father didn't know best after all and had changed all that, pioneering the way for their daughters to have choices when it came to careers and motherhood.

She wondered what sort of life her own daughter would have – she had been quite sure Sylvie was a girl, even then – and, with a pang of misgiving thought about the possibility of her being predisposed to having an anxiety disorder. Annoyed with herself, because she'd thought this all through that day, the year before, on the plane coming home from Edmonton, when she was trying to keep distracted from the waves of panic washing over her, she determinedly pushed the thought aside. She was going to show the baby how to handle fear right from the beginning. If you consistently talked about not being afraid to feel fearful and how to think strategically when something scary happened, she reasoned, then surely a child would be conditioned to perceive normal fear and irrational fear as much the same thing and it wouldn't have any devastating consequences.

That's when the idea of writing a children's book came to her. By the time Ian had woken up and come downstairs to see if she was all right, she had borrowed a field of daffodils from Wordsworth, made *'daffodil dancing'* a simple metaphor for improving mood, had almost perfected the poetic prose style of the story in her head – more reminiscent of Dr. Seuss than Wordsworth, there – and was thinking about the illustrations which would complement both story and concept. Since then, she'd written and illustrated seven of the little books, not so little as the Beatrix Potter books, which she realized must also have influenced her thoughts as she sat not very far from where their creator had written them, but a comfortable size for a young child to hold, and had a contract to do five more.

"Mommy, you're squishing me," Sylvie shouted. "Why are you squeezing me so tight?"

"Because I love you," she kissed Sylvie's forehead and sprang up from the rocking chair, where they were sitting. She deposited the child on the floor and said, "Come on, we have to set the table, and it smells as if I should get the casserole out of the oven. Shush now, don't wake Ben." She lifted the bassinette and set it firmly on the coffee table. "I'll just put him up on the coffee table in case the dogs come in here and bother him."

The dogs were now twelve years old and spent most of their time in semi-somnolence on their pad in the corner of the kitchen. Felix raised his head and half-heartedly wagged his stubby tail when they came into the kitchen, then went back to sleep. Alison told Sylvie to stand back while she opened the oven, and took out the cheese and spinach casserole.

That done, they set the kitchen table for supper and Alison made a salad, letting Sylvie, stand on a kitchen stool beside her and arrange slices of cucumber around the outside of the bowl.

"Okay now. Jump down," she said, when it was finished. "I think I just heard the garage door go up. You know what that means."

"It means Daddy's home," shouted Sylvie, "and I need to get my picture to show him."

She ran to the door of the refrigerator where the painting she'd done at nursery school that morning was attached with a magnet. The magnet flipped onto the floor as Sylvie pulled the painting off to hold it in front of her, facing the door, waiting for her father to come through.

Alison put some dinner rolls into the still warm oven and put the salad, then the casserole on the table and filled the coffee maker and turned it on.

Ian finally came in.

"Well," he said, taking off his coat, "it looks as if some clever little girl has been doing some painting at school again today."

"Not some clever little girl, Daddy. Sylvie."

"You did this painting of your baby brother for us?"

Sylvie solemnly nodded her head. Alison looked at Ian, questioningly, wondering how he knew the painting was of Ben.

"The blue and green of the bassinette," he murmured, as he gave her a quick kiss on the cheek in passing. "Come along Sylvie. You come with me to put my coat away and we'll go and see the real Ben."

"We have to hurry though, Daddy, because supper's ready and I made the salad – the cucumber part..."

Alison listened to Sylvie's running commentary on how she had arranged the cucumber slices, followed by the low murmurs of the two of them as they progressed from hall closet to living room. She took the warmed dinner rolls from the oven and placed them on the table, breaking one and buttering it ready for Sylvie.

"So, you figure we'll keep him, then?" Ian was saying as they came back into the kitchen. He stooped to pick up the magnet which was still lying where it had fallen and, taking the painting from Sylvie, put it back on the door of the fridge.

"What?" asked Sylvie, scrunching up her face.

"You think we should keep Ben?" He lifted her into her chair, then sat down himself. "You've painted his picture, so you must have decided you like him. Right?"

"He's all right," Sylvie muttered. "'Cept he makes Mommy have a lot to do all the time." She either decided to change the subject or, perhaps, had just come to the end of her attention span. "Look, Daddy, see the salad – the cucumber, that's the bit I made. Can we eat some now?"

Alison smiled at Ian and shook her head to indicate that that was probably enough about Ben for now. She spooned salad into Sylvie's bowl and, then into her own, and passed the serving bowl to Ian.

"Heather dropped by this afternoon," she told Ian, breaking apart a warm bun and buttering it. "You remember? Terri's niece? The younger one."

"Heather? The one with the metalwork?"

"She grew out of that some time ago. She works in a day care centre now, off Dixie Road somewhere. Anyway, Terri called Anna and told her that Ben had arrived, so Heather brought a gift over for him during her lunch break, which is actually way after lunch when the children are having their naps. She brought Sylvie a nice colouring book, too, didn't she, Sylvie?" Sylvie made to get down from the table. "No, no, you can show it to Daddy after supper, honey. Finish your salad now."

"She's Jon's sister?" asked Ian.

"That's right. As a matter of fact, she said she was talking to Jon and he said to say hello and congratulations."

Jon had taken a co-op program to get his computer sciences degree at Waterloo, in preference to accepting help with tuition from his father, and Ian had helped him get his first co-op position. He worked for Microsoft now.

"Sorry, I get them mixed up. Scott has two boys and Anna has Jon and Heather...?"

"And Kate. You met her a few times back before Terri went to England. She used to baby-sit their children."

"Okay," Ian nodded, "I've got them sorted out now. Don't you want that, Sylvie? Here, are you ready for some casserole? If Mommy takes the salad bowls out of the way, Daddy can give everybody some casserole."

* * * * *

They read *The Bravest Boy* first and Sylvie was asleep before Alison came to the end of *The Daffodil Princess*. She finished reading the last page and a half out loud anyway because she liked the way it always made her feel strong and capable and able to tackle all her insecurities. Children liked the idea of 'daffodil dancing' changing sadness to happiness, crossness to contentment but she was never quite sure if they felt any sense of gaining control when they read the book or had it read to them, or whether it went over their heads and they simply heard the story. Of course she didn't really have many insecurities now. Not that anxiety was ever completely absent at the thought of facing places and people she didn't know, or even some that she did, but she no longer had so much difficulty in letting that first wave of panic ride over her until she was in control of herself again. The recent hospital stay had been harder than when Sylvie was born but it was probably because she was missing Sylvie as well as Ian and the safety of home. She'd spent a lot of time doing deep breathing exercises to stop the fear from building and had, consequently, had to explain her problem to her roommate who said she did t'ai chi to combat stress and understood. At the time of her first pregnancy, they had investigated the possibility of home birthing and finding a midwife but the doctor had said it wasn't really recommended in the case of an older first-time mother and Alison, who hadn't really considered it before, thought about how awful it would be if something went wrong and her baby died simply because she didn't have immediate access to hospital facilities. That was when she started putting the baby's welfare ahead of her own and the doctor, who had known her since childhood, arranged to take her through the obstetrics department at the hospital so that she wouldn't be going into a completely strange place.

This time, with Ben, it hadn't been panic as much as a constant uneasiness that prevented her from relaxing and getting her strength back. She had managed to get them to let her go a day before they wanted to because she knew she'd be better at home, even though her mother insisted on Sylvie staying with her for a few more days so that Alison could get into a routine with Ben. She wondered if it was coming home to find Ben firmly ensconced in her home, that had caused Sylvie's initial rejection of her baby brother. Perhaps it was better to bring the baby home to the child. She seemed to have missed that particular tip if, indeed it existed, when she was reading up on how best to get your older child used to the idea of having a baby in the house. Never mind, there had only been a couple of disparaging remarks about him today. She was starting to accept the inevitability of Ben being part of the family. A week ago her reply would have been firmly negative when Ian had asked whether she thought they should keep the baby. She put the books back on Sylvie's child-level bookshelf, adjusted the duvet around the sleeping child and kissed her goodnight, then went to check Ben in his bassinette which she had brought up to his room when she had come upstairs to put Sylvie to bed. She thought he would sleep for a bit longer before waking up for his next feeding. She went downstairs.

Ian was in the den, which was really a study or home office, on his computer so she told him she was going to get a bit of fresh air and take the dogs out and could he listen in case Ben woke.

"Don't go in the park in the dark," he said, without looking up.

He always said this when she walked the dogs alone at night. She actually did use a path, which was lit, to cut across a corner of the park because it made a convenient one-way route for her to take.

The dogs came running when they heard her getting her coat from the hall closet, almost knocking her over as she pulled a toque over her head and thrust her hands in her coat pockets to see if she'd left the matching gloves there.

"Okay, okay, guys. It's cold out there for us non-furry types. Let me get dressed properly."

They sat patiently waiting for her to put her boots on and zipper her coat. Finally ready, she snapped on their leashes and opened the door.

The early March evening was colder than she'd expected. Spring would surely soon be on the way, she thought, although March was as likely, she knew, to bring with it an Arctic deep freeze as it was to herald warmer weather. Some bulbs had pushed up in areas of the garden, close to the house, during week-long thaw just before Ben arrived and she hoped they'd survive. Transferring both leashes to one hand, she pulled the toque more firmly over her ears, looked up at the clear, starry night sky and walked briskly along the road with a tremendous sense of well-being.

"Hi there, Alison," somebody called. A neighbour was putting her garbage out for collection the next morning.

"Hi, Cathy. Isn't it a lovely evening?"

"It *is*? Too cold for me. You sure you're okay with taking the kids in the morning. I really don't mind doing it for the rest of the week to give you time to get back on your feet."

Cathy's son went to nursery school with Sylvie and they carpooled.

"No, I'm fine with it," Alison replied. "I need to get back into the routine to help Sylvie get used to Ben."

"Still doesn't like him, eh?"

"Oh, we're getting there. See you in the morning."

She carried on down the street towards the park. Children made it easier to get to know people, didn't they? They acted as icebreakers the same way that dogs did. She remembered Joanne with the Jack Russell who used to live over the other side of the park and how they'd come to know each other through walking their dogs. And there were other people who she'd come to know, over the years that they had lived here, from walking the dogs. You came to know people with young children the same way – just from being around. She did still get that jolt of fear the first few times she exchanged greetings with her neighbours, but not enough to make her actually avoid contact the way she once did.

She reached the park and walked briskly along the path. Although she thought Ian fussed, she didn't like to take longer than she had to. Once through, she slowed her pace and gave the dogs more time to sniff around.

By the time she arrived back home, Ben had woken and Ian

was waiting for her in the kitchen, holding him rather awkwardly.

"He smells awful," he said over the baby's crying.

"You should have changed him," she said, taking her coat off.

"I just can't, Alison. He's so small and I feel so clumsy. I will when he's bigger, I promise. I did with Sylvie."

"Here, I'll take him," Alison said, putting her coat over the back of one of the kitchen chairs and, takng the baby from him, started towards the hallway to go upstairs. "Can you look after the dogs? I let them through into the back yard. Their feet are wet and need to be wiped. Ooh, you really do smell awful, Ben."

Ten minutes later she brought the baby back downstairs. Ian had switched the television on and was watching the last part of *Fifth Estate* with the spaniels on the floor at his feet.

"Here he is all fresh and clean," Alison handed the baby to him. "And not hungry yet. He can watch the news with you. I'd like to put off feeding him as long as possible so that he sleeps for more of the night. Would you like some coffee?"

"Sure, if you're making it."

Alison went into the kitchen and put on the coffee maker. She emptied the dishwasher while she waited for it to drip through and thought about how nice it would be when she could drink coffee that *wasn't* decaffeinated again. She buttered a couple of bran muffins and put them with the coffee mugs and napkins on a small tray, then poured the coffee and carried the tray into the living room. She placed the tray on the coffee table and took the baby from Ian, spreading his blanket and laying him on the couch, then sitting down beside him.

"I think I got all the mud off," said Ian, referring to the dogs.

"The rug needs cleaning anyway, but let's not put it on the immediate agenda. There's enough to do with getting a new baby into a routine and getting his sister to like him..."

Alison sipped her coffee and took a bite of her muffin.

"She's coming round," Ian said. "It's quite normal. Mom says Susan was like it with me and she was a lot older, but she got over it."

"I probably have a problem with it because I never experienced sibling rivalry myself.

"You poor soul... that definitely made for a disadvantaged childhood."

"I just meant that I didn't experience having to share my parents' attention with another child. She must be talking about him at nursery school since she painted his picture. I still can't believe you recognized what it was."

"I guess I'm just more perceptive than you thought I was," he teased.

"I didn't think that you weren't perceptive – it's quite normal to have to ask what a three-year-old's painting is. Anyway, I'm going to start taking my turn in the carpool again tomorrow, so I'll see if I can find out how forthcoming about him she is there."

Alison finished her muffin and sipped coffee while they watched the rest of *The National*. Ben was still awake but seemed quite happy wriggling a bit and inspecting the ceiling. She put down her empty coffee mug and picked him up. He screwed his little face up in a grimace, then relaxed and opened his eyes.

"He looks so much like you, Ian. Come and look."

Ian got up from his chair and came to sit beside her, getting indignant looks from the two spaniels as he stepped around them. He put his arm around her and stroked the baby's cheek with his free hand and Ben stretched his hands towards him.

"He's just perfect, even if he does look like me..." he laughed. Ben, finding Ian's hand was not what he wanted, gave a sudden howl and screwed up his face again. "Perfectly hungry, too. Sorry, son. Only your mother can oblige in that department."

* * * * *

Later, after putting the satiated baby into his crib and tucking the blanket securely around him, Alison went in to check her daughter before going to bed herself. As she tucked the duvet more closely around the sleeping child, Sylvie awoke for an instant.

"Will Ben get big enough for daffodil dancing?" she asked sleepily.

"Oh yes," said Alison softly. "Every baby gets big enough for daffodil dancing sooner or later."

"Good," murmured Sylvie and fell asleep again.